THE IRISH BOY

THIS novel is the true story of a little Irish boy with a sweet singing voice who rose to international fame as an opera singer—a story of aspiration and success aptly termed by its author "a romantic biography". Michael Kelly was the son of a Dublin wine merchant. As a child he possessed a voice so pure that it delighted not only his father's friends but even the roughs of the city streets, and, more fortunate than many, Michael retained the gift of song after his voice had broken, deepening to a superb tenor. Miss Jacob re-creates in her inimitable manner the robust but endearing Dublin of Michael's childhood, and the reader experiences to the full Michael's enthusiasm for the singing lessons he receives from the flamboyant teacher, St. Georgio, and his excitement when he first meets the great operatic star Rauzzini. It was this which proved the turning-point in his career, for it took him to Italy and to world-wide acclamation. Thereafter Michael was privileged to mix with the great—he sang for Charles Edward, the Young Pretender, he met Casanova, and he became the close friend of Mozart, in whose operas he performed. Such is the author's skill that these characters come vividly to life as we read.

NAOMI JACOB

has also written

POWER
JACOB USSHER
ROCK AND SAND
THE BELOVED PHYSICIAN
THE MAN WHO FOUND HIMSELF
"SEEN UNKNOWN . . ."
THE PLOUGH
ROOTS
PROPS
POOR STRAWS
GROPING
THE LOADED STICK
"HONOUR COME BACK——"
BARREN METAL
TIMEPIECE
FADE OUT
THE MORNING WILL COME

THE LENIENT GOD
NO EASY WAY
STRAWS IN AMBER
THIS PORCELAIN CLAY
THEY LEFT THE LAND
SALLY SCARTH
UNDER NEW MANAGEMENT
THE CAP OF YOUTH
LEOPARDS AND SPOTS
WHITE WOOL
HONOUR'S A MISTRESS
A PASSAGE PERILOUS
MARY OF DELIGHT
EVERY OTHER GIFT
THE HEART OF THE HOUSE
A LATE LARK SINGING
SECOND HARVEST

ANTONIA

One-Act Plays:

THE DAWN

MARY OF DELIGHT

Autobiography and Biography:

ME: A CHRONICLE ABOUT OTHER PEOPLE
"OUR MARIE" (MARIE LLOYD)
ME AGAIN
MORE ABOUT ME
ME IN WARTIME

ME OVER THERE
ME IN THE MEDITERRANEAN
ME AND MINE
ME LOOKING BACK
ROBERT, NANA—AND ME

General:

ME IN THE KITCHEN

THE GOLLANTZ SAGA
Volume One
comprising

FOUNDER OF THE HOUSE   "THAT WILD LIE . . ."

YOUNG EMMANUEL

Volume Two
comprising

FOUR GENERATIONS   PRIVATE GOLLANTZ

GOLLANTZ
LONDON, PARIS, MILAN

THE IRISH BOY

A Romantic Biography

NAOMI JACOB

LONDON

HUTCHINSON

Hutchinson & Co. (Publishers) Ltd.

178–202 Great Portland Street, London, W.1.

London   Melbourne   Sydney
Auckland   Bombay   Cape Town
New York   Toronto

First published 1955

Printed in Great Britain by
WILLIAM BRENDON AND SON LTD
THE MAYFLOWER PRESS
(late of Plymouth)
WATFORD

To my dear friend,

Peter Holt, who has shown so much interest in this book of mine, given me so much help, and who is filled with the same love of opera as Michael Kelly. I thank him sincerely for all his help, and hope that he may be—at least moderately—satisfied with the result.

Mickie.

" Believe me if all those endearing
young charms." (Thomas Moore)

Air : My lodging is on the cold ground

Be - lieve me if all those en - dearing young charms which I
gaze on so fondly to - day   etc

AUTHOR'S NOTE

THIS is exactly what I have called it—a romantic
biography. The life of Michael Kelly has long fired my
imagination, and I have tried to bring out the character
of the man. Not only as he actually was, but as his
associates and friends saw him.

I admit that I have taken liberties, that I have used
certain "inventions", but I have tried so far as was possible—for the information regarding Michael Kelly
is not plentiful—to present a true picture of this little
Irishman who charmed audiences on the Continent and
also in England.

N. J.

CHAPTER ONE

THE curtains had not been drawn, and the light from many candles threw a broad fan of light through the open window on to the pavement. Several people stood there listening. The quiet, eminently respectable street seemed filled with sound; the sound of a very clear, very strong—though childish—soprano voice.

One man turned to his neighbour, "Be Jezus," he said, "it's that young Mike. Did ye iver hear such a voice, and him only t'ree years old?"

The other man answered, "To my moind 'tis a sin and a shame to keep a baby out o' bed at this time o' night, just to roar his little lungs out fer a lot o' guzzling old fellers."

"Ah, Oi take my oath the young chiselur likes it!"

The song had ended, and they passed on down the street. Inside the house elderly gentlemen were praising a very small boy, who stood on the polished mahogany table, from which the damask cloth had been withdrawn. The candlelight shone on his bright curls, his eyes were shining with excitement. He looked like some Italian painting of a listening cherub.

He was small even for his bare three years, his white embroidered dress was elaborate, he wore a wide pale blue silk sash round his waist, and long narrow pantaloons descended to his ankles. His feet were encased in small pale blue kid shoes and white silk socks.

"Now, Mike," his father enjoined, "show these

9

gentlemen how you can bow to thank them for liking your song."

The tiny boy, placing one hand over where he believed his heart to be situated, bowed gravely and with complete self control to the men seated round the table.

"Nicely done," one of them cried, "'tis easy to see you've not got a father who's Master of Ceremonies for nothing."

"Not a better bow was ever seen, not even in the Castle!" Whether the child understood them or not may be doubtful, but he sent his enchanting smile to them all; then stood there as if waiting to sing his solo again. He loved singing, and could sing "There was a Jolly Miller" with great effect. His voice was very powerful for his years, and came as sweet and true as the song of a blackbird.

The door opened and his mother entered; she was a pretty woman, more—she was a woman of considerable sense and character. The mother of four sons, the child on the table being the youngest; she was proud of them all, but this small, curly-headed boy, with his fair skin, dancing eyes and wonderful smile was, though she would never have admitted it, the nearest to her heart.

"Ah now, gentlemen," she said in her soft, clear voice, "it is time the baby was in bed and asleep; never mind standing there on the table, singing in a room filled with the smell of spirits and the fumes of tobacco. Mike asthore, come away to your bed."

The little boy held out his arms and she lifted him from the table, holding him to her. His curly head drooped on her shoulder, he was almost asleep. She smiled at him fondly.

"Thomas Kelly," she said to her husband, " 'tis

ashamed of yourself you should be. The poor little creature is half dead with sleep."

She said it without rancour, with a smile hovering round her lips, and her eyes gentle. She might have been reproving one of her sons for some small misdemeanour. A stout man, with a red face and very small, bright eyes nodded.

" 'Tis ashamed we all are, Mrs. Kelly. Not only Thomas but the whole boiling of us. Put it down to the attraction of your son, ma'am. He takes after his mother! Sure, he'd charm the birds off the trees—a gift that is, I make no doubt—inherited." His small eyes twinkled, he smiled at his host, "And not inherited from you, Thomas. Ma'am, we're going. May I wish you a good-night, and quiet sleep."

They all rose and as Mrs. Kelly mounted the stairs, the sleeping child in her arms, she could hear their voices dying away as they walked down the quiet street. She sighed. She loved her Thomas, found him the most delightful of men, their tastes were identical. Both had a passionate love of music, vocal and instrumental. Thomas Kelly stated that he would prefer to do without his dinner twice a week than not have his own box at the theatre. He was never obliged to do without either.

His business as a wine and spirit merchant was successful, for he had a fine taste in wine, and the nobility and gentry often consulted him with regard to the contents of their cellars. He was personable, moved with considerable grace and dignity, and the debutantes about to be presented at the Castle, sought tuition with Thomas Kelly on the proper mode to make their curtsies.

He was a kind husband, deeply in love with his wife,

and devoted to his children. Mark already showed promise as an actor, Patrick was to become a soldier in the service of the East India Company, and Joseph shared his parents' love of music. His great friend was a handsome lad called Tom Moore, and young Joseph was always welcome at the musical and artistic parties given by his friend's mother.

As Mrs. Kelly undressed the sleeping boy, who was so soundly dreaming that he never moved as she took off his clothes, sponged his face and hands, and finally laid him in bed, she sighed.

Thomas was all that any woman could ask—again that small sigh—he had one fault and that sprang from the fact that he was over generous. Never did the Kellys have a quiet evening together. Either they went hurrying out to the theatre or the opera, returning to sit up late discussing what they had seen or heard, or Thomas sent word from his place of business that he was bringing home four, five, six friends.

"T'measther tould me to say he knowed you'd be able to rustle up somet'ing for thim all to ate," the messenger would assure her.

How often did Mrs. Kelly exclaim to her cook, "Brigit, think of it. I'd a pair of ducks. How far will a pair of ducks go among half a dozen men—and all hungry!"

Something always was "rustled up" and Thomas Kelly won a name for generous hospitality in consequence. Only his wife knew what havoc that openhanded entertainment played with the household bills and how often she had to knit her brows to discover some way to make ends meet—or almost meet. There had been times when she told Thomas that the bills were too large

for the amount of money at her disposal. She had regretted
the shocked expression on his good-looking face.

"But, darlin', surely I give you all you ask for!"
She mentally amended his words to, "All that I *dare* to
ask for," but said:

"Thomas, you're completely generous, my dear.
But—" she smiled, "your robust friends have large
appetites and—" she laughed, "thirsts to match them."

"Ah, now, m' dear, the drink costs nothing. I get it
from the store. What's the odd bottle among friends?"

"It may come from the store, but you've had to buy it
first."

"Ah, but I make profits on what I sell. Only to-day, the
Hon. Patrick M'Bean came in, he accepted a glass of
port—did he smack his aristocratic lips over it! He did!
'Kelly,' says he, 'I'll be damned if that's not the best
port I've tasted—'" and so the story would go on,
developing into what almost amounted to a saga.

So Mrs. Kelly spent long hours with little Miss
O'Reilly, the dressmaker, planning how last year's
dress might be brought up to date with no greater
expense than the purchase of some yards of braid,
or ribbon. She always looked well dressed and when she
appeared in one of her re-fashioned dresses, Thomas
would stare at her, his eyes wide, and say that she was
the best dressed woman in Dublin, and the best looking
in Christendom.

"But, I fear you'll ruin me, with your fine new
dresses!" he'd add.

"Three years old, my dear."

"Glory be to God, the woman's a miracle worker,
nothing less!"

The box at the theatre meant additional expense

too. Thomas might pay for the box, though his wife suspected that he was allowed to rent it at a specially low figure on account of his services in coaching the debutantes, and the fact that he supplied most of the wine to the Castle and theatre. Then added to the cost of the box, was the price of the refreshments, for during the intervals Thomas Kelly liked to resort to the buffet, and parade his handsome wife and good-looking sons before the élite of Dublin society. Mark, growing to be a fine, upstanding fellow, with theatrical aspirations, already had a manner which caused ladies to look at him kindly; Patrick was less decorative, and his mother thought sometimes that a hint of melancholy lurked in his fine eyes. Patrick cared nothing for fine clothes; so long as his linen was immaculate, his shoes brightly polished, and his coat well brushed, he was content. Joseph, whose smile broke out on the slightest provocation, was like his good looking friend young Tom Moore, addicted to fine clothes, to cloth of rich hues, and as for little Michael, he loved bright clothes, and was as vain as a peacock of his bright curls and of the attention which was paid to him.

It gave Thomas Kelly a pleasure which he did not attempt to conceal, to walk through the brilliantly lighted rooms and know that eyes—and whispers—followed him, his wife and his four sons.

He loved to find himself addressed by some aristocrat in a wonderfully curled and powdered wig, a spy glass held to his—usually—slightly bloodshot eye.

"Ah, Kelly! Brought your family, eh? Patrons of the opera, eh?"

"M'lord, we're devoted to music. The lot of 'em."

"Umph, fine looking lads, Kelly. All yours?"

"My own unaided effort, m'lord."

"Unaided! Gad, give credit where credit's due! Unaided, not quite!" A slight unbending, a leer, even a dig in the ribs. "A handsome woman, Kelly, eh?"

"We're regarded as a handsome family, m'lord."

Thomas Kelly was a very simple minded snob. He loved a lord, to him it was the breath of life to raise his hat to some notable and see a finger lifted to the exalted hat rim in return.

He was kindly, affectionate, and, in days when fidelity was not counted particularly among the virtues, he never wavered in giving the whole of his affection to his wife.

He confided to Morland, the teacher he had found for little Michael to instruct him in playing the pianoforte, "There's plenty of girls, aye, and pretty girls—some of them of the highest—I repeat, of the highest rank though, being a man of honour, I name no names, who'd be ready and willing to hop into bed with Tom Kelly. If I said 'Snip', they'd say, 'Snap'. Sure, if the merit of withstandin' temptation lies in the amount of temptation resisted, there's little credit coming to me. Damme, I'm as much in love with my wife as I was the day I married her."

Morland, a brilliant teacher, but a drunken old reprobate, would shake his head, and murmur that "anny physician will tell you, that a change of diet is beneficial for us all."

To which Kelly answered smartly, "Why not change yours? As long as I've known you your diet's been— spirits. How about trying—porter?"

Morland boasted that he turned night into day, that he never really woke until eleven at night. For this reason, little Michael was kept out of bed until Morland—never completely sober—came round to the Kelly's house at eleven at night to give the child his lesson. Not that the child resented it in the least, his one thought was music. When he was only six years old, he stood leaning against his mother's knees, assuring her that he did not only want to play the pianoforte, he wanted to "know how music is made, mama."

"Made, my darling?" she asked.

"How people write it," he insisted. "I could put notes on paper, but it wouldn't make music. There must be rules. Like in eating our food, playing games. I want to know that, mama!"

He was a queer little boy, very gay, very attractive, but there was a good deal of serious thinking went on in that head covered with curls. He was strikingly independent, his memory for the music which he listened to, so intently, at the opera was extraordinary. He would listen eagerly to an opera which was entirely new to him, and the following morning, his mother would hear him singing the arias in his powerful, childish voice.

He liked to walk about Dublin alone, making his way not only to the fashionable streets but penetrating the narrow alleys. The big bare-armed Irish women standing at the doors of their untidy houses would see the small figure with its crown of curly hair, and shout, "Mickie, me dote, stop for a minit an' let's hear the sound of your voice. Ah, do now."

The slums of Dublin were no place for a well-dressed small boy, particularly a small boy who was attractive and who could sing for the entertainment of his audience. Again and again his mother had warned him, "Now, Mike darlin', keep to the decent streets and don't go near those dreadful places." Little Kelly had an inquisitive mind, he wanted to see everything. He wanted to understand the technical side of music, of singing, he wanted to know how the scenery in the theatre was changed, how artistes painted their faces, how the rich lived—and conversely, how the poor existed.

So, well dressed, his hair shining with cleanliness and much brushing, the child wandered about Dublin. Walking along the fine streets, he would suddenly recognize some lady who had spoken to him during the interval of the opera, and would swing off his hat with an air that even his father—the elegant Thomas Kelly—could not have bettered. Then growing tired of the well paved streets—well paved for Dublin in 1773 that was—he would turn into the side streets, narrow and poorly paved, and wander on until he came to the lowest and roughest parts of the town.

There the gutters were choked with filth, the stench of dirt and decaying refuse rose sickeningly in the air. The streets were narrow, and the amount of breeze which circulated there was small. The houses were little better than ruins or, frankly, hovels. Doors and windows were conspicuous by their absence; verminous children scrambled and fought in the stinking gutters their playthings the decomposed body of a cat, or the mutilated corpse of a sewer rat. Men lounged against the walls, sucking short clay pipes—usually cold and empty for they had no money to buy tobacco or even a substitute. Their eyes were heavy, their mouths folded into bitter or sullen lines, their clothes hung in tatters. Their wives, usually well-built women, were often naked to the waist, their breasts sagging and heavy from the feeding of many children. Their hair hung in greasy wisps, and they—like their husbands—lounged. The courage had been beaten out of them by fate; many of them had migrated from the country to the town in the hopes of finding work and evading the starvation which so often faced them in the less populated districts.

Deep in their hearts burnt a fierce love for their country, and a sense of profound resentment against the—invaders. They had a great history, these people, a history which many of them could relate with fluency and colourful phrases. They had been a proud people, they had practised the arts, evolved a literature, bred kings, princes and great leaders while the English were still content to live in ignorance.

"An' wasn't there gold—the purest gold—to be found in the Shannon?" and "Didn't the Blessed Saint Patrick himself come among us, choosing us out from other nations?" "Take a luke, if you get the chance— of seeing the golden ornaments they made in the old times, the Mass books they had, wid real gold to illu- minate the big letters at the starts of the prayers!" "They talk of the Conquest of Oireland, b' God, it's never been conquered, an' never will be. Then that old devil Cromwell—may his soul be rottin' in hell at this moment —luke what he did to uz."

But the heart had been beaten out of them, or so it seemed then, they were dirty because they had no means to keep clean, they were lazy because there was no work for them to do, and they lacked the energy to fight for themselves. Because of the lack of this energy it was easier to become beggars, petty thieves, wasters. They some- times contrived to obtain drink, and then all their pent up fury and resentment flared and blazed. Crimes of violence followed, throats were slit, corpses were robbed of their purses, their watches and rings, and for a few days these denizens of the Irish underworld overate, over-drank, and indulged in the wildest orgies.

Yet, when this small boy, with the curls and the enchanting smile, walked down their filthy streets, no-one ever thought for a moment of stripping him of his good clothes, of capturing him and holding him to ransom. All they asked of him was—a song.

"Ah, now, Mickie, c' way wid a song. Let's have a stave, me boyo, let's see if the ould voice is houldin' out!"

He'd stop, disregarding the dirty children who swarmed round him and with his hands in his breeches' pockets, his small feet set well apart, he would speak to them.

"Is it a song yer wantin'?" the clear rather shrill voice rose. "Faith, I don't mind givin' you a song—for it's all I have to give you. Me pockets are empty as a drum."

He would stand there, while the scruffy children drew back a little, and throwing back his head, would begin to sing. Morland had taught him the music of the old songs and with its old fashioned harmonies, he rendered those songs to them. Songs of the country-side, of the rivers, of good Saint Patrick himself. Once, when it was near Christmas, and Michael was muffled in his warm overcoat, he sang, "Come all ye faithful," in the Latin which they all knew.

The young, powerful voice soared up, reaching the higher windows of the dirty houses, where men and women in various stages of undress and raggedness, hung out to listen. The men sucking their cold pipes, the blowzy women, their arms folded over their un-washed breasts and bodies listened intently.

"Venite adoremus,
    Venite adoremus Dominum."

While the singing lasted—life seemed to have changed. There was hope, they were able to break loose from the chains of misery that bound them. The age-old message, "Come all ye faithful". Not only bidding the Kings from the East or the great ones of the world but crying to the humble peasants watching over their flocks by night.

A filthy alley in the lowest part of Dublin, where not a single person had a decent suit of clothes to wear, not a sound pair of shoes, or a stomach which was adequately filled; and there a little boy, swinging his hat in his hand, his head held high, singing a message. The last note died away, and a brawny man, who had been more often in gaol than out of it, sniffed.

"Glory be to God, 'tis an angel no less. Oi'll be away to Mass on Christmas Day t'ough me backside is hanging out o' me breeches."

Mollie Mcguire, a not too highly paid prostitute, wiped her eyes on the offensively dirty Hessian apron she wore.

"If he could sing ivery day, some av uz 'ud be better'n we are." The boy put on his hat, bowed, for already he had acquired the small mannerisms of operatic singers, and liked to display them, and walked off. The men, women and dirty children watched him as they might have watched the departure of a being from another world.

"Faith, 't'was wonderful to hear him!"

"Made you feel t'ere was somet'ing in religion, so it did."

"That's the truth you're speaking."

For several days the inhabitants of the alley might have been heard humming the melody of that great

Christmas hymn, then the songs faded from their memory —as did the determination to attend Mass.

Little Kelly walked back, a smile on his lips. He had realized even at that early age, that he could hold the attention of an audience. He continued to work with Morland, in fact he demanded so much instruction from that gentleman that he admitted to his crony Tommy Reddy, that he was getting tired of the job.

"Glory be, the child's a glutton. He has his questions ready, written out, if you'll believe it, on a piece of paper. There's myself, with my head aching, my tongue like a piece of flannel, and my stomach as queasy as it can well be, and him—piping up—'Now, sir, will you kindly explain to me the position of the rondo in form.' That at eleven at night, mind you! The child's a devil so he is!"

Michael was nearly eleven when he decided—for he had a clear and decided mind of his own—on his future profession. It was mid June, Michael was walking through the streets of Dublin, his head filled with the melodies he had heard the previous night at the opera, when he saw one of the singers. A tall, handsome man of the name of St. Georgio. Michael admired everything about him. He had admired his voice and bearing on the stage, now he was struck with his air of distinction, his fine clothes, and his hint of swaggering self-sufficiency. The small boy followed the singer, and stood at the door of a fruit shop which he entered.

The singer inspected the fruit which was for sale. Then he selected two choice peaches, three nectarines and proceeded to eat them with obvious enjoyment. These consumed, he wiped his fingers delicately on a very large, very fine cambric handkerchief, and turned his attention to some pineapples. With tremendous care he selected one, the largest and most completely ripe, and handed it to the shop man.

"Send that round to my lodgings at once. How much?"

With ease which betokened indifference as to the price asked, the singer drew out a silk, netted purse, extracted the necessary coins, and when the assistant turned away to obtain the change which was owing to St. Georgio, that gentleman with a magnificent wave of his hand, said, "Keep the change, my man, that's for your pains."

Michael flattened himself against the wall as the singer passed. He watched him walking down the crowded street, reverence in his eyes. That was an opera singer, this was how they lived. Walking into shops selecting what they wanted, with no thought of the price. More, there went a man who dressed well, who carried himself splendidly, and at whom passers-by gazed with admiration and respect.

Michael walked home slowly, thinking hard. He would be an operatic singer. Music, yes, he would study that too, he would work hard, he would come to understand all the mysteries of the composition of music, of harmony and counterpoint—but singing was the primary thing.

That night he spoke to his father.

"Father, I'm going to be an operatic singer."

"Now, and your voice not even broken yet!"

"I want it trained, so that after it has broken I shall know how to use it. And, father, do you know Signor St. Georgio?"

Thomas Kelly laid down the news-sheet which he was reading. "What's in your head about St. Georgio,

Mickie? Indeed I know him. Why, you heard him yourself the other night, a fine voice, and comports himself
well. A bit of a swaggerer is my own opinion—but,
what's interesting you in St. Georgio?"

"I want to have singing lessons with him, father.
Father, will you ask him?" The child's voice was very
eager.

"You'll have me all beggared with the lot of you!
Mark wanting to study elocution, Patrick with extra
studies to fit him for the East India Company, with his
uniforms, his boots, his God-only-knows what, an' now
you wanting not only music lessons from that old potheen
punisher Morland, but singing lessons with St. Georgio.
It's clear that I'll be ruined."

But his eyes twinkled, and two days later he told
Michael to meet him at his business premises in Mary
Street, adding, "I'm taking you to visit a gentleman, so
see an' behave yourself."

Michael wearing his best plum coloured coat, with his
long narrow pantaloons strapped tightly under his
highly polished shoes, his cravat spotlessly white and
beautifully laundered, went to the lodgings of Signor St.
Georgio.

The room into which they were shown was, to
Michael's eyes at least, impressive. The curtains were
heavy, if dusty, the carpet was covered with bright
flowers—roses, cornflowers and the like—true, it was
spotted as his mother's carpets were never allowed to
be at home, but the wealth of colour, if somewhat faded,
was enchanting. Signor St. Georgio, attired in a long
dressing gown of violet coloured velvet, tied round the
waist with a thick silk cord, greeted them warmly.

"Ah, this is the *piccolo* singer. *Bello!* Dear little boy

'Ow nice 'e looks, wiz curly 'air. 'Is name—Michael—
Michele. We shall 'ear 'ow 'e seeng, no?"

He went to the pianoforte and opened it, it seemed to
Michael that he immediately attained an added dignity, a
mastery.

"Seeng a scale—listen! Now!"

The clear childish voice sent a cascade of notes into
the somewhat stuffy atmosphere, they came clear as
crystal drops, filling the room with lovely sound.

St. Georgio struck a chord, "G," he said, and Michael
opened his mouth, "wide at the corners" as Morland
had told him, and again the notes soared. So it went on,
each scale rising higher and higher, until St. Georgio
said, "Ah!" and there was a sound of satisfaction in his
voice, "we shall try a scale in the minor. A—" he
announced, "nice modulation, eff you pleaze." More
scales, then he nodded, "Now for being good boy,
a leetle jam, eh? Not all scale, seeng for me a leetle
song."

Michael thought, then said, "Sir, it is written by a
friend of my brother's, his name is Moore. It is not really
finished, but he played it to us and I kept the music in my
mind."

"Seeng then this song of your friend."

"‘ ‘'Tis the last rose of summer
    Left blooming alone:
    All her lovely companions
    Are faded and gone.' "

He stopped and said anxiously, "Tom says he will
improve the melody, and—" the smile broke out, "it
may be, sir, that I have not kept it fully in my memory."

"*Dio mio*," St. Georgio said piously, "the boy's got a voice!"

Thomas Kelly said, "The child's mad about music. Nothing else matters a tinker's curse to him."

"And vhy, no need to 'ave only a voice, no?" He turned and laid his large, white hand on Michael's shoulder. "Togezzer we shall study the singing—the voice—the breathing, eh? Of necessity 'is voice veel break, but after—'e will know what to do wiz zee new voice, eh?"

Michael said breathlessly, "You will have me for a pupil, sir?"

" 'Ave I not said so? Leetle singing bird! I am 'appy."

"So am I, sir," Michael felt that at any moment his heart would burst with admiration and gratitude for this man who was willing to teach him.

That night after his lesson, at a quarter past eleven with Morland who breathed the fumes of stale spirits over him as he explained the mysteries of the augmented seventh, Michael lay in bed conscious that he was wildly happy. He would be a singer, he would entrance audiences —and oh, how much work he would do!

CHAPTER TWO

How he worked and how St. Georgio worked with him! Michael had additional lessons from his master's friends —Passerini and Peretti, he soaked up music as a dry sponge absorbed water. He was growing a little, but it was obvious that he would never be a very tall man. He was beautifully slim, with narrow flanks and well set shoulders, his skin was fair, and he never suffered from those distressing boils which attack boys approaching the age of puberty.

One day after a lesson, when Michael was about fourteen, St. Georgio, usually a hard and even stern teacher, spoke to him in a voice which held a softer note, a tone which was almost tender.

"One day, soon, I t'ink, your voice veel break. Ah, t'is is nature, eet veel indicate that you are now a man."

"Break, my voice break," Michael said, his face suddenly white, "Shan't I be able to sing any more?"

The big blue jowled Italian laid his heavy hand on the boy's shoulder. "Unteel it is—mended, no! But, alvays remember ve can vork. So much! To study the breath control, to study—vizzout singing, movements for the operas. Here—while I shall play on the pianoforte, you will learn to move here, to stretch out zee arms t'ere, to turn qvickly at a giffen moment. Ah, it veel be a great time for vork—zis time when your voice—takes a rest to decide 'ow it vill change itself. Shall it be tenor, shall it be baritone? If tenor—vat kind of a tenor, for t'ere are many. Ah, we shall have plenty employment!"

Michael walked home conscious that a load of depression lay on his shoulders. To be unable to sing! To be forced to wait until his voice returned—it was a terrible prospect. To be without a voice and to be told that—as a kind of reward—you had become a man! What did that mean? He lived in a robust age, an age which was sufficiently coarse and round his father's table he had heard bawdy stories of prostitutes and brothels. Was this the prize for losing that priceless treasure—a voice? Brothels had been pointed out to him, both high and low, and he had shivered. He knew plenty of the Dublin prostitutes, from the women who, shabby and unkempt, walked the streets, leering and smiling, to those who lived in well kept houses and drove abroad in a smart carriage drawn by a shining horse. He had been brought up a Catholic, as had all the family, no better and no worse than many other families at that time. He had been to a school where the teachers were priests, but the behaviour of many of them had not impressed him with the sanctity of a religious life. There had been Father Francis, with mild, kind eyes and a gentle voice, who could never keep his class in order, Father Ambrose who was not only clever but kindly, and who possessed a sense of humour —those and others, these were men who Michael felt lived holy lives, who knew that they had a duty to perform and carried it out to the very best of their ability. There were others—the heavy jowled Father Alban, Father Macarten with his narrow head and strange furtive eyes, Father Conleath who when he examined your exercise often breathed over you, what Eugene Cassidy said, "might be anything but never the odour of sanctity."

He had attended church regularly, but he had never absorbed the religion, the whole thing was a duty, a regular exercise, and an occasion for wearing your best clothes. He had spent much time in the company of men, and though they were fairly careful to keep their conversation moderately clean when ladies were present, when they were left alone the stories grew more and more salacious, the references more and more coarse.

Michael had at least one thing which might have been an attempt at rising about the loose and bawdy talk, the knowledge which was his of irregular lives, and promiscuous love affairs—he was essentially and completely fastidious. Dirt in any form revolted him, his linen must be crisp and white, his shoes shining, his clothes perfectly brushed and without spots. He spent a long time on his own personal toilet, washing with the greatest care, cleaning his nails and combing his hair.

He hated to see his father's friends eating carelessly, drinking noisily, and leaning back in their chairs replete, with their waistcoats undone, belching openly. Once when a great clumsy bluebottle had fallen into the glass of wine which Shameus Logan was about to drink, Michael had watched him remove it with his fingers, fling it to the ground, tread on it, and then gulp the wine. The boy had beaten a hasty retreat and been violently sick.

When he returned his father asked, "Been bringing up your dinner?"

"Yes, sir, I'm afraid so."

Logan shouted, "Tastes better going down than coming up, eh?"

Thomas Kelly patted the boy's arm, "Always been inclined to have a queasy stomach. Better take a taste of brandy, Mickie."

Another man added, "That's the thing, brandy either brings it up or carries it down."

He loved his father, but he hated these greedy, guzzling men who sat round the table stuffing themselves with food until they could eat no more. His mother, always so quiet, gentle, and yet with a smile ready to touch her eyes and her lips, he adored. At the opera he would slide his hand into hers, and feel the slight pressure which assured him that she was enjoying the music as he was.

To contemplate life without the ability to sing not only distressed little Kelly, it terrified him.

Weeks went on, nothing happened; true once or twice St. Georgio pulled down the corners of his moutn and said, "A leetle rusty, ch?" but he still sang. Then one day, at home, when he was alone and changing his clothes, he sang the scale of A minor, because he liked the augmented seventh. The slight melancholy pleased him.

His voice cracked suddenly. Panic seized him. He tried again. The first five notes came easily enough, the F was difficult, the rest—non-existent. His voice had broken. Michael Kelly sat down on the edge of his bed, buried his face in his hands and sobbed.

Slowly his sobs subsided, and he lifted his face, white and tear-stained and stared before him, miserable and hopeless. How was he to be sure that the voice would ever come back? How was he to know that for the rest of his life he would not be known as "the boy who—as a child—had a fine voice. Since it broke, there is nothing. He wanted to sing in opera, he is a clerk in his father's vintners business."

His lips twisted, for a moment he looked vicious and bitter. He rose and went to the drawer where he kept his handkerchiefs, there in a small wooden box made of

cedar wood—which he liked because it made his handkerchief smell pleasant, lay some money which he had
saved. He tipped it into the palm of his hand, counting
it. A guinea, more—nearly two guineas. He tipped the
coins into the pocket of his breeches.

Carefully he brushed his hair, his lips still twisted into
that strange, unfamiliar smile.

"I'm a man, eh?" he whispered. "That's it—a man,
a man without a voice and God knows if I'll ever have
one again. So, being a man, I'll learn what it all means.
Find out if it's so remarkable that—losing a voice is as
nothing!"

He knew that his heart was beating furiously, that his
breath came quickly, and that the palms of his hands were
damp. He put on his coat and walked out. On the
stairs he met one of his mother's servants, one Mollie
Reddy.

"Are you off now, Mickie?" she asked.

"I am, going to see a friend. We're—having some
singing. I may be a bit late. Tell my mother, Mollie.
I'll be back all right."

She looked at him, he didn't, she told herself, "look
himself". "It's some mischief yer're up to," she said.
"Sure, it's far over much freedom you get, wid yer music
an' yer singing' and——"

"Hold your tongue," Michael said, "leave me alone."

He ran down the stairs and out into the street. The
dusk was falling, and he made his way to that part of the
town where he knew the prostitutes paraded, ogling
and leering, smiling and flashing their eyes. He shivered.
One old woman, said, "Why, it's little Mickie Kelly.
Now darlin' what are you doin' out at this toime o'
night?"

He scowled at her, "Leave me alone, that's my business."

He walked on, trying to swagger in a manner which he copied from St. Georgio. He knew that he was shaking, that his mouth was dry, and that he wanted nothing so much as to rush home and find his mother. Instead he held his head high and tried to believe that he was on the brink of a great adventure.

As he drew near to the Smock Alley Theatre, a young woman spoke to him. She was dressed in clothes which aped the latest fashion, and as she moved she sent a wave of musk floating into the air. Her eyes lit on Michael, they were bright and hard, her smile was mechanical, and her voice when she spoke to him tinged with a heavy Dublin accent over which was laid a mincing affectation of overdone refinement.

"Is it all alone you are?" she asked.

Michael licked his dry lips, and tried to smile, he felt that the effort would crack his cheeks.

"I was—now I'm with you," he said.

"You're bould for a little boy!" she giggled.

"Little boy be damned! I'm eighteen."

She came a little closer, "Got anny money, darlin'?"

"Plenty. Don't let's stand here with all Dublin watching."

"Impatient divil ye are! Follow after me then."

She walked away fairly briskly, and Michael his heart, he felt, hammering in his throat, followed her. Where would she lead him? He had heard tales of such encounters culminating under one of the arches, in some doorway, on a piece of waste ground—he shuddered. They turned from the wider streets until he was following her down a narrow entry, with mean looking houses and a smell which made Michael's nostrils twitch with disgust, rising from the gutter. The woman stopped and turning beckoned to him to join her. A dimly burning lamp hung in the passage, he felt bare boards under his feet, and then the creak of worn wood as he climbed the stair. She opened a door on the first landing, and slipped into the room, Michael followed. She fumbled about and finally lit a candle which stood in a dull pewter holder.

She smiled her mechanical smile, "Want a kiss, darlin'?"

She began to fumble with the fastening of her dress, while Michael taking in the details of the room felt his horror getting the better of him. The sagging bed was unmade, the blankets—there were no sheets—looked filthy. Such furniture as there was looked dusty and unclean, clothes were strewn about, a pair of stockings hung on the back of a chair. The atmosphere was heavy, stale and held a strange odour which he had never smelt before.

Instinctively he wrinkled his nose, "What's that smell?"

She was struggling out of her clothes, and her voice came to him muffled. "That—what? Oh, bed bugs—not'in' at all. C'm me fine chiselur, it's a grand time I'll be givin' you."

He stood staring at her stupidly. She held out her arms, he could smell the odour of unwashed flesh mixed with the heavy scent of stale perfume. The bed, the room, the woman herself filled him with horror. So this was what you gained when you lost your voice, to come to filthy rooms, to lie on grimy beds, to allow your flesh to touch that of someone you had never seen before, someone who was unwashed, who stank. You were

supposed to be proud to do this—this—his mind
stumbled for a word—beastly thing.

She said more impatiently, "C'm on now, I don't
want to be waitin' here the whole night, toime's money
with me."

His hand went to his pocket, he felt the hard reassur-
ing guinea, the loose silver.

He shook his head, "I'm sorry, it's a mistake. I must
go."

She flung herself off the bed and stood before him
naked as she was born, all pretence of gentility in her
speech had gone.

"Yer dirty little basthard, you!" she screamed. "I'll
have me money, if yer have onny brass, you little runt
you. Ye'll be bloody lucky if Oi don't tear the guts out o'
you, if you *have* onny guts."

Hoarsely he said, "How much do you want? I'll
pay you."

"Not a far'den less nor a crown!"

He felt for the coins, dropping the guinea back into
his pocket, he extracted a crown and a shilling. He walked
to the table and flung the money down, he felt that he
could not have borne to feel the contact of her fingers
even for a second.

"There!" he said. "I'm going. Good-night."

"Good-night!" she mimicked him, "see you give
me a wide berth in future or I'll make your name stink,
all the girls 'ul know about you. Taking a girl's time,
making believe you wanted—" but Michael had gone and
closed the door behind him.

He stumbled down the rickety stair, and out into the
street. He felt physically sick. His own home was not
completely luxurious, but he had never been in a room

B

even remotely approaching that he had just left. He had never come into close contact with actual filth, and although he might have heard his father's friends—after the wine had begun to circulate—tell stories which were definitely bawdy, he had never heard a woman—except some screaming, drunken virago rolling home—speak as that woman had spoken. Slowly he made his way back to the respectable streets, where phaetons, carriages and gigs passed, spattering the foot passengers with mud. He began to breathe more easily, the foul air of the alley, the stench of the room had made him feel actually unable to draw an easy breath.

He reached home, and Mollie opened the door to him.

"Yer' singin' party's finished quick," she said. "I t'ought you said ye'd be late. Why, ye've only bin gone under the hour. Mickie, what's wrong with you, yer face is like a peeled turnip, so 'tis."

He bit his lip, for now the whole wretched encounter was over, he felt that he wanted to allow himself the relief of tears.

"That's why I'm home early," he said. "I wasn't feeling well, I felt sick and—and so I came home. I think I'll go to bed."

"To bed! Glory be, now an' have you forgotten it's an opera night? Yer ma an' pa are both gone an' Mark wid them. Now, I'll give you a sip of cordial, an' away afther them."

Resilient as he was then and always, Michael forgot his tragic loss of voice, forgot the affair of that very evening, and immediately, his face brightened. A trace of colour came back to his cheeks.

"It's *Comus*!" he almost shouted. "Yes, a little cordial, Mollie, and I'll follow them!"

St. Georgio was as good as his word, every moment which Michael could snatch from his studies at Doctor Burke's Academy, were spent in perfecting his knowledge of voice control, the various methods of singing, the extent or limitations of certain types of voices. Later St. Georgio taught him the rudiments of acting, he would sit at the piano playing the music while Michael went through the movements required on the stage. He had a real talent for acting, being graceful and utterly unself-conscious.

For a year he studied and worked, he was fifteen, and had celebrated his birthday by wearing a very handsome blue cloth coat, trimmed with silver braid, a pair of blue silk breeches, and white silk stockings, his feet encased in shoes with silver buckles. The whole costume was his birthday gift from his father and mother. He surveyed himself in the looking glass. There was no doubt that the clothes became him, his curly hair, his bright dancing eyes and his fresh, healthy colour all helped to set off the new clothes.

He thought, "One day I'll wear a suit like this on the stage, I'll sing in opera, I'll be the idol of the public wherever I go!" for the tragic loss of his voice had receded somewhat, his fears had been stilled by St. Georgio's good sense and reason, and Michael had come to realize that it was only a question of time before he would sing again, sing in a new, more mature and powerful voice.

He smiled happily at his reflexion, and struck an attitude, then still with his mind running on the opera house and the rôles he would sing, he threw back his head and sang the opening bars of a tenor aria which he had heard a few days previously.

He sang! His voice—a little rusty from disuse—still

held power, more it held also a new quality, a strength and *timbre* which were new. Michael stood silent, staring as if fascinated at the figure in the mirror.

"Dear God!" he whispered as if awestruck, "you can sing, you fellow in the blue coat with the silver lace, you can sing! You're a tenor, or will be once you get to know how to use your new voice. A tenor! Yes, and your name is Michael Kelly, no-one knows it now, but one day—ah, one day—London, Italy, everywhere they'll know it."

That night his spirits were at their highest, he told his father's friends that he felt like "someone who has been let out of prison". He even sang for them, and their applause was music in his ears. His mother watched him, her eyes filled with love and admiration. When she withdrew, young Kelly was given a glass of port, and probably with the excitement, the heat of the room, and the heavy fumes of tobacco smoke which filled it, he became a little above himself.

"Now that your voice has mended itself again," said old O'Rourke, "it's a man you'll be thinking yourself, eh?"

Cassidy, a well-known draper in Dublin, smiled slyly, "He'll be after the wenches without a doubt!"

"Thomas," old Connolly admonished, "see that you give the lad decent addresses now."

With some embarrassment Thomas Kelly muttered, "Och, time enough, time enough!"

Young Michael flushed with wine and excitement said, "I know where to find a whore if I want one! 'Faith, I've been home with one already." He leaned back in his chair waiting for the effect of his announcement to be apparent.

His father—with a face suddenly congested—spluttered, "Damme, what the devil are you talking about?

What's this? Now, sir, what does that infernal statement mean?"

Michael, half frightened at the reception of his boast, was determined to make the best of it. He had always possessed the ability to tell stories, whether for or against himself, and now he depicted himself as a complete simpleton. The older men listened intently, and when he ended his story their roars of laughter could have been heard at the end of the street.

Old Connolly shaking with mirth said, "Sure your Blessed Patron Saint had you in mind that evening. You came out minus a crown——"

"And a shilling," O'Rourke amended.

"And a shilling, God, you might have come out with a lot that you never went in with, mind that."

Later when they left, his father said, "Michael, I want a word with you. I can understand—what you did, thinking that you'd maybe lost your voice for ever, but—not again. Thank Heaven, you were protected, thanks to the manner in which your mother has brought you all up, you are fastidious, but—" he paused and poured himself out another glass of port-wine, "you little knew the dangers you faced. If—" the words came slowly, "if that kind o' thing is necessary to you, then—as I have told both your brothers—come to me." He suddenly cleared his throat, and drank his wine hurriedly. "Not that I have ever visited such places, naturally—devoted as I am to your sainted mother, but—well, a man *hears* things, hears names, and so forth. But don't run into danger, don't run the risk of ruining your chosen career. Mind now what I've said."

"Indeed I will, papa, and thank you."

He went daily to St. Georgio and one late afternoon

found him in a state of great excitement. He seized Michael's hands, shook them as if they were pump handles, and could scarcely articulate so greatly was he agitated.

" 'Oo comes to Dublin? I tell you. The great Rauzzini. 'Eem 'oo was so beautiful that 'e play the vimmen's parts—and to admiration. At zat time zee Pope didn't like vimmen—really vimmen on zee stage. Rauzzini play all parts. 'E go to Monaco—ah, Munich you call 'eet. Great success, but also an—what you say—entanglement. A lady, oh, so important admire 'eem too much. So for the sake of 'ees 'ealth—" he chucked, " 'e come to Italian opera in London. Not only great singer but great actor. Your fine actor Mr. Garrick often times tell Rauzzini, ' 'Ow good are you, Signor Rauzzini. Better'n me maybe'."

Michael said, "Shall we be able to hear him in the opera here?"

St. Georgio threw back his head and laughed, "Indeed—'ere is my leetle surprise—Rauzzini will 'ear *you*, if you vish you may go to 'ear 'eem, but to-day, 'e come to 'ear you, Mickee Kelly."

They were old friends it appeared, and St. Georgio meeting Rauzzini had spoken of Michael, and his belief that the boy had a fine voice, more, that he was a musician. Rauzzini had been interested, and stated that he would come to his friend's rooms to hear the boy sing.

Michael waited, terribly nervous, wondering what the great man would have to say. Rauzzini arrived, he swept in like a whirlwind. He was fairly tall, almost as slim as Michael himself, and he was, without doubt, the most handsome man Michael had ever seen. He spoke English rather slowly and carefully, but faultlessly.

"So this is the boy, the singing boy. Let us hear him. Thank you, St. Georgio, if you will play for him. I shall sit and listen, it is for you, Michele, to transport me to paradise. I am ready to be transported! I wait."

Michael sang several scales, he stood well, he opened his throat wide as St. Georgio had taught him to do, and the clear, liquid notes came out like gems falling through the air. Once or twice he heard Rauzzini make little noises, but whether of approbation or distaste he could not judge.

"Now," St. Georgio said, "zee leetle song by your young friend, Mickee. The one about a rose at the last of summer. Yes, zee song of Tomasino Moore."

When the song ended, Rauzzini was frankly wiping his eyes on a large exquisitely fine cambric handkerchief.

He began to speak rapidly in Italian to St. Georgio. Michael caught a word here and there, but not the full import of the conversation; when it ended, Rauzzini embraced St. Georgio fervently, and assured him that he had given a singer to the world. He turned to Michael.

"I have the permission of your wonderful *maestro* here to give you a few additional lessons, while I remain in Dublin. More important still is that I visit your father. I wish to interest myself in this matter. You will find yourself obliged to go to Italy. There you will have instruction in other methods of singing, it may be possible that you will obtain engagements. Please for a great favour inform your father that I shall call upon him this evening at seven o'clock. I shall beg that Signor St. Georgio will permit that you come to my lodgement (Michael thought, 'That's the only mistake he has made! I wonder if I'd ever learn to speak Italian as he speaks English?'). He will come with you, to-morrow at half past five. Now, we shall say—Good-bye for a short time."

Michael blushing to the roots of his hair said, "*Grazie, signor. A rivederla.*"

Rauzzini laughed, "Why, *Dio mio*, he's half an Italian already. *A rivederla, Michele.*"

That evening Thomas Kelly and his wife waited in the parlour to receive the two singers. Both Thomas and his wife were nervous, they knew very little of foreigners except when they were on the other side of the footlights, and to meet them in their own house was disturbing. True, they had often entertained St. Georgio, but Rauzzini was—a different kettle of fish. He was a really great singer, admired by London audiences which included the great Garrick himself.

"What shall I give them, Michael," his mother asked. "A nice dish of tea, think you?"

"They'd hate it, mama. Coffee is what they really like."

"Coffee," her tone was dubious, "with milk or——"

"Oh, black, mama. And perhaps a little brandy."

"In the coffee?"

"No, darling, served with it in little glasses."

She sighed, "I'll do my best."

The two Italians arrived, both were elegantly dressed, their manners were excellent. They kissed Mrs. Kelly's hand, and said flattering things about Mickie's voice. Much as she loved and admired Thomas she had to admit that in her own heart, she found them more polished and completely at their ease.

Coffee was served, and with it some of Thomas Kelly's oldest brandy, both were praised extravagantly. Thomas said, "Now don't be after giving me coffee, for I hate the stuff. Bad for the liver."

The coffee finished, the little brandy glasses emptied and refilled, Rauzzini began to talk about Michael.

"Mrs. Kelly, I believe that I am a judge of voices. I have heard your son sing. At this moment his voice is a very strong soprano with, shall we say, strong tenor tendencies. Given the right training as it develops it may well be a tenor of the first quality. My advice is—*send him to Italy*. Not that my good *amico* St. Georgio has not done very excellently well with your son, I am filled with admiration, but now he must—how do you say it—take the plunges, yes?"

Mrs. Kelly, listening intently, her hands clasped tightly, exclaimed, "Oh, sir, to Italy! He's only a child, just sixteen. Think of the dangers, the perils of the journey, the distance from his home and those who love him."

Rauzzini nodded his handsome head, "I understand these things, madam, but to become a great artist always means—sacrifices. If this boy is to make a great name, he must—like a little bird—try his wings. Time will repay you for your own sacrifices, madam. In years to come, when you shall hear him applauded in London, in Dublin, in Paris—though for myself I think poorly of the opera there!—you will say, 'Ah, it was well worth the separation'."

She sighed, "I wonder——"

Thomas Kelly said, "Well, we're greatly obliged to you, sir. In fact to both of you. Signor St. Georgio has been most kind. I'll think it over, discuss the matter with my wife here, give it my consideration. Another small glass of brandy, sirs?"

They accepted the brandy, and then took their leave. As they walked away from the house, Rauzzini, his cloak well muffled round his throat, said, "*Caro mio*, even if he had no voice, what a kindness we should be doing to that Michele in getting him to Italy."

St. Georgio answered, "Ah, indeed, avay from zees terrible climate, no?"

His friend laughed, "Away from that terrible coffee! Ugh!" he shuddered, "I have never tasted such dreadful stuff. I should prefer to take a purge, that at least serves some good purpose!"

CHAPTER THREE

THOMAS KELLY carried about with him for the days which followed the interview with Rauzzini an air which was at once conspiratorial and pontifical. The decision as to whether his son should go to Italy, after all, rested with him. Whether he had made up his mind or not, he consulted everyone he met; he alternated between being boastful concerning Michael's musical abilities, and heavily parental, in which moods he was apt to shake his head and express grave doubts as to whether the boy would ever make a singer. "Mind you," Thomas said —not once but very often—"I am against any idea of him singing in opera. 'Tis a medium which to my mind is unsatisfactory. To sing—to the accompaniment of instruments is a different matter."

"But, Signor Kelly," St. Georgio protested, "'eet is on opera 'is 'eart is set. For myself, I t'ink 'e veel do vell."

Thomas smiled, slightly superior; after all St. Georgio might make quite a good living but he was no international artist.

"Ah, now, Mickie's only sixteen. He fancies himself dashing about in fancy clothes, embracing wonderful sopranos! 'Tis the way of all young folk to have these fanciful ideas."

Michael himself, walked about in a dream. He was— he believed—going to Italy, he would have chances to learn, perhaps even to sing. He had heard of the beauty of the country, of the churches, pictures, and the music— ah, the music! It appeared that every Italian peasant knew the various operas by heart, that even in the cheapest cafés you could hear voices which were beyond the ordinary. He knew that his father was opposed to an operatic career. For all his open handed generosity, his carelessness concerning money, Thomas Kelly had a streak of caution about him. An operatic singer—yes, and for how long? Age took its toll, and while a man was still young he became too old to sing certain rôles, he became out-moded, he lost his favour with the public. Michael knowing all this, set his jaw, and clenched his hands and registered his vow, "I'll make my name on the operatic stage."

Both Thomas and Michael were excited, only poor Mrs. Kelly cried softly to herself, when unobserved. She had seen one son depart for India, she felt that she would never see him again, and now she was faced with the prospect of losing Michael, her darling, her best loved. She never spoke of her grief, of her firm belief that if Michael went to Italy she would never see him again; in those days women were brought up to keep silent, to restrain their emotions and to believe—or to appear to believe—that their husband's decisions were the wisest and best.

Then came Rauzzini again to the house. Mrs. Kelly had begun to regard him as a bird of ill omen. He was terribly excited, his sallow face was flushed, his eyes shining.

It appeared that there was a season of Italian opera at the Smock Alley Theatre, the company was distinguished, the singers of the first order—La Sestini, Pinnetti and Savoy. The orchestra had been reinforced from London, they would be meticulously dressed even to the extent of wearing swords! Savoy had been taken gravely ill, the doctors pronounced that it was quite impossible for him to sing.

The opera was Piccini's "La Buona Figliola" and the part was important, naturally for Savoy was well known and greatly admired. It was written for a powerful soprano voice.

Michael listened and clenched his hands. It was impossible! The very idea was fantastic. How could he—untried, untested possibly be asked to sing in the place of an artist like Savoy?

"Martini--the impressario," Rauzzini said, "will offer—anything, that is in reason, so that the opera shall not be postponed. Michael has studied this rôle with St. Georgio. If he is to go to Italy he must have money, no? Let him earn it! Martini will pay twenty pounds a night, imagine it!"

Thomas Kelly rubbed his chin, frowned, considered, then said: "Guineas."

Rauzzini nodded, "Yes, yes—guineas."

"Very well. Michael, my boy, you'll appear in this—what's its name—opera."

Michael prepared for his first appearance. His feelings were conflicting. He was excited, uplifted, yet he was filled with fears and apprehensions. He spent the day with St. Georgio, they went through his part, with the movements, and each time young Kelly felt that he was steadily growing worse and worse, more and more clumsy and inept. Finally, after St. Georgio had shouted, "*Porco! Imbecile!* 'Ave you t'en six 'ands, an' ten feet? 'Ave you no voice? God gave you one, w'at 'ave you done wiz eet?" he sank down in one of the big arm-chairs, put his face in his hands and burst into tears.

"I can't do it," he sobbed, "it's no use, I can't do it!"

St. Georgio stood there watching him, nodding his head. "So! An Irishman an' no courage. Ah, people veel say, 'So t'ey would 'ave little Kelly, but 'e 'ad not zee 'eart. Better to get Italian boy—a boy wit' a 'eart. Neffer mind, I shall spik wiz Rauzzini."

Michael's sobs ceased, or if they did not actually cease, they became subdued. He rubbed his eyes with his knuckles, as boys do, and then sprang to his feet. His face was scarlet, his eyes blazing. "I'll sing it, yes, I'll sing it! I'll make them applaud me. I can sing as well as any Italian boy. I'll show them!"

St. Georgio laughed, "*Bravo, piccolino!* Bravo. Now sing no more until it is time for you to walk on the stage, then—one scale, two scales—then arpeggio—La- la- la- la! The stage will be yours, go and take it. I shall be listening."

His mother, white to the lips with anxiety, gave him strong, clear soup, and pressed a bottle of honey and lemon into his hand, whispering, "Dearest Michael, we shall be there. Sing for me, darling. Let every note be for —mama. God bless you."

One of the other singers put on his make-up for him; a kindly old man whose breath smelt of porter helped him into his costume; Michael knew that he was shaking. Out there was—the audience. They had expected Savoy, instead they were being offered—little Mickie Kelly. It was a brilliant audience, the nobility and gentry were present, representatives from the Castle, even the Duke of Leinster was in his box. Michael waited in the wings. Suddenly his fears left him, he heard the orchestra, the voices, the applause. "That is going to come to me presently," he thought grimly. Then, whispering quickly and crossing himself he said, "Jesus, Mary and Joseph help me!" He heard the music which was his cue, licked his lips, straightened his back and walked on to the stage.

The audience saw a slim youth, with a beautiful figure, his head crowned with bright curls, his smile coming and going like sunshine between April showers. They took him to their hearts. His voice rose clear and true, there was no trace of *tremolo,* no hint, of "singing himself in". His performance at the end of the opera was as determined as exact and as melodious as it had been at his first entrance. His attack was admirable.

The opera ended, and the applause was deafening. There were shouts of "Kelly—Mickie Kelly—" and the good-natured artistes, smiling and showing their beautiful white teeth, pushed him forward. He bowed, his hand on his heart.

The artistes crowded round him, they shook his hands, many of them kissed his burning cheeks. They gave him praise without stint, and seemed to take a personal joy in his success. Then came St. Georgio and Rauzzini, and more congratulations. He felt overwhelmed. As he took off his make-up, he felt a sudden regret that this was the first and the last time. He would have loved to have been able to work again to-morrow with St. Georgio, to go over places where he had felt a little uncertain, and to have given—on that to-morrow night—a performance which the audience might have stigmatized as—polished.

So, in spite of his success, Michael Kelly—with twenty guineas in his pocket—walked home feeling a trifle sad. He had done well, he knew that—but he might have done better. His mother was waiting for him; as the front door swung open and the light streamed out, she caught him in her arms, whispering, "I have never heard anything so beautiful, darling. You were—wonderful."

In the hot, well-lighted dining room, his father sat at the table, the decanters circulating, men with florid faces watched Michael enter. His father cried, "Grand, boyo, grand! I'm proud of you, so I am!" The other men nodded, old Connolly said, "Now that was a grand performance you gave, Mickie. Not only for the singing, but for the acting!"

His father, his thumbs in the arm-holes of his elaborate waistcoat announced, "Help yourself to a glass o' port, boy. Gentlemen, I'll tell you all something, I've decided—after consulting with men who are no doubt wiser than myself, to allow my son to go to study in Italy!"

There was a chorus of, "Tommie, me boy, you're right," and "Now that's the decision of a wise man!" "Sure you couldn't do better for the lad, it 'ul be the making of him, so't'will."

Only Mrs. Kelly, standing at the door, her eyes fixed on the handsome, flushed face of her son, slipped away quietly closing the door behind her.

Michael said, "That's splendid news father, I shall do my best not to disappoint you."

"Now," said Thomas Kelly, "I have further news to impart. It appears that a very notable company, under the direction of the son of the great Doctor Arne—no less— arrives in Dublin in a short time. The Crow Street Theatre, aha! Now this Mr. Arne and Ryder, the manager—well known to me and to many present—have the idea, an' b' Gad it's not a bad one, that Michael here 'ud be a fine draw in an opera called—ah, me memory's going!—I have it—'Lionel and Clarissa'. It's the leading part they offer him, three performances and—on the fourth—a benefit!

Now, what d'you think of that? The lad will be sweeping the board!"

Connolly said, "We'll all be rustling round to make sure the benefit's packed out! I'll be there myself."

Cassidy said that not only would he be there but his wife and five daughters—everyone in Dublin knew Cassidy's five plain daughters! O'Reilly announced, "The lady who plays the female lead must be sent bouquets! It's—the thing to do."

Thomas Kelly spoke, "I'd the chance of a word with the Governor, and with His Grace the Duke, both intimate that they wish to be present at the benefit, though—" he smiled, "both added they'd not be able to keep away from the first night, for their impatience would get the better of them!"

Young Kelly stood listening to his father's voice. It seemed to roar in his ears. It could not be true—yes, some of it, but not all, it was fantastic, impossible. He had sung that night in opera, he had—he realized that—made a success, and now he was to have the opportunity to sing in that medium again. He was to go to Italy—*ah, lento, poco a poco crescendo!* Everything was rushing along too fast, the whole thing was becoming blurred, indistinct.

This success, signalized by the gathering of his father's friends, by the glass of port which he held, and dared do no more than sip, for he was drunk with the applause, the heat, the voices which seemed to batter on his tired brain; Italy, and before Italy an engagement, a benefit—this was a sudden, almost terrifying *prestissimo*. The full orchestra was playing *forte, sempre piu forte*. He felt dizzy and rather sick.

They were arguing now as to how much his father should allow him in Naples.

Cassidy said, "Tom, my boy, it 'ul cost you a divil of a lot!"

"Not of necessity," Connolly objected, "the lad must learn to live carefully, to count every penny."

"And when," demanded O'Reilly with a roar of laughter, "could you look for Tom Kelly's son to do that!"

Michael felt that they were not talking about him at all, they were discussing some other lad, and yet—he fought through the mists of his brain—yet, he was Tom Kelly's son! It was all very mysterious.

"Ninety pounds a year," Tom Kelly said, "my bank knows all about it. Over there they call the money *ounces*, a silly like thing, but it works out to ninety pounds a year. I'm having a great chest packed with stores—food 'ul not be too good or too plentiful on board a Swedish ship, I'm thinking. More, now, Mickie listen to this—"

Again Michael forced himself to listen intently, the clock in the hall struck three. Lovely mellow tones, bells, chiming softly and reaching you across water. Three o'clock, and already he thought that if he were in his small bedroom, he would be able to see the faint glimmer of the "false dawn" in the east. He sighed, the thought of cool sheets, of a soft pillow seemed the most attractive things on earth. With a great effort he said, and his voice sounded louder than he intended, "Yes, father."

Strange that he had said "Father", usually he said, "Papa". He was too tired to really wonder why, but said again, "Yes, father."

"Ah," Thomas Kelly drank deeply, and breathed hard, "Not only stores, not only plenty of good clothes, not only an allowance of ninety pounds a year—God bless the boy—but I'm sending him out with—you'll never guess —a grand pianoforte!"

Immediately there was a chorus of, "Glory be, Tom, that's a thing now," and "It's yourself, Tom, that has the grandest ideas." "Sure, he's a genius when it comes to thinking is Tom."

Thomas Kelly nodded his head—a head grown rather heavy with the amount of port which he had consumed, " 'Tis true. A good instrument will be a God's gift to him in his profession. What d'you think of the idea, Mickie?"

Michael stared at him. Grand pianofortes were rare, they were very costly, and here was his father ready to give him one to take to Italy. He blinked his eyes, and said, "Oh, papa!"

Through his mind ran the saying, "Those who the gods would destroy, they first make mad." That was what was happening to Michael Kelly. He was going mad, all the early part of the evening—the theatre, the music, the applause—was part of a hallucination. It had never really happened. This story of a pianoforte, that too, was part of this incredible dream. Michael Kelly was slowly going mad!

Connolly said, "Tom, it's all too much for the boy. He's as white as a sheet. Send him to his bed, sure, he's dropping on his feet."

His father stared at him, "Are you tired, Mickie?"

Uncertainly he answered, "Yes, papa, I think— perhaps—that I—am. Thank you for—for everything." He contrived a stiff strained smile to a circle of blurred faces, they seemed to swim like pale moons in a smoky sky. "Good-night, gentlemen."

It was a relief to find himself in the cool hall, dimly lit by a hanging lamp. It was an effort—though not an unpleasant one—to raise his hand and place it on the broad banister rail and then to mount—slowly—the shallow stairs. His own room was waiting, a room where there was no heavy atmosphere, no clash of voices, no recounting of events which seemed to have no semblance of reality.

The silence, the quiet of his room seemed to stabilize and tranquillize him. He undressed slowly, trying hard not to—*think*. He wanted to forget the theatre, the orchestra, he wanted to think only of quiet, simple things. He thought of the poetry of Tom Moore, that dark haired, bright-eyed fellow who seemed only to live to pour out lovely verses. Scraps came to him, some which Tom had recited to him, things which were as yet unpolished and unpublished.

" 'The light that lies in women's eyes'—not right yet, Mickie, but I'll make the whole world know it! and 'She is far from the land where her young hero sleeps—' that's goin' to be a lovely song, Mickie. A song to break your heart, so 'tis. 'Believe me, if all those endearing young charms—' That's not finished either, for sure they come crowding into my mind, I can't keep pace with them."

Yes, Tom Moore soothed you, it was as if he ironed out the creases, bless him.

Michael undressed slowly, the fresh air coming in through the window, the faint light in the east, had done their work. He folded his handsome clothes very carefully, and set his buckled shoes side by side. For a moment or two he stood naked, allowing the cool air to reach his skin, to wipe away, he felt, the smoke, the heavy smell of wines and spirits, the noise of voices. He raised his arms and threw back his head, drinking in great draughts of air, then reaching for his long, white night-shirt, he put it on and slipped into bed.

The smooth, cool sheets, the friendly pillow did their work, and Michael Kelly, after a long, childish sigh of relief and relaxation, fell asleep.

When he woke the sun was shining through the open window. He sat up and knuckled his eyes. Had last night been a fantastic dream? The theatre, his own voice filling it, the applause, the shouts of "Bravo. Kelly." Himself smiling, his face feeling stiff under its paint, his thanks—he could hear his own voice, very young and clear, "I thank you all! I am grateful. Thank you, thank you." His father's gay, confident voice, "Didn't I know that you had it in you! It's what I expected of you, Mickie!" His mother's eyes, suddenly sad, misted with tears. Dear mama. Then talk of Italy, Naples, a ship and —a grand pianoforte. He must have dreamed that.

Then he remembered the talk of "Lionel and Clarissa", a new opera, in which he, Michael Kelly was to sing the chief rôle of "Lionel". The venture—possibly the opera itself was his work—was in the hands of the son of the great Doctor Arne. Doctor Arne, the composer of "Rule, Britannia" of which the English had such a high opinion. Other compositions more acceptable to an Irish boy— "Blow, blow, thou winter wind" for one. Then his son— not possibly so famous as his father, but he had written at least one lovely tune which Michael loved, "The lass with a delicate air". He hummed it softly. And he was to sing in this opera. Three times, and then to be given a benefit!

He sprang out of bed, life was too exciting to stay in bed dreaming. He soused his body in cold water, enjoying the stinging freshness of the sudden shock, and the glow which he felt when he towelled himself with energy. He remembered his prayers—last night he had forgotten them—more shame to him! He knelt and tried to frame words of thanks to the Powers who had helped him. Then rising he dressed with his usual care, not in the magnificent clothes which he had worn the previous evening, but in his more sober, everyday suit of plum-coloured cloth.

He ran downstairs, the big clock which ticked so loudly, showed that it was already eight o'clock. His father was seated at breakfast, looking, Michael thought, a little bilious after his long session with his friends. He nodded to Michael as he entered.

"Hello, lazy-bones, remember you've to meet St. Georgio at twelve, he's taking you to see Mr. Arne."

Then it wasn't all a dream, he was actually going to discuss his engagement for "Lionel and Clarissa" with Mrs. Arne singing "Clarissa". He said, as he seated himself, "Yes, papa. Good morning, mama."

She smiled at him, that sweet, very tender smile which ever since he was a little boy had made him feel that the world was a warmer, kinder, safer place. It was the kind of smile, Michael thought, that seemed to linger in the air even after it had ceased; it was like notes of very sweet music, like the notes of a harp which did not die suddenly but remained with you for a long time.

"Have you slept away your tiredness, son?" his mother asked.

"Yes, thank you, mama. I've forgotten that I ever was tired."

Her smile came again, touching her lips and her eyes, "That's youth, my dear," she said, "Youth renews itself."

His father said loudly and assertively, "I could manage another chop. Thank 'e. And another tankard of ale. Michael, what are you eating?"

His mother answered for him. "He's drinking tea, Thomas. Small ale's not good for him so early in the morning. Now, Michael, can you manage some nice fried bacon? 'Tis a lovely piece. Ah, now, just try a bit."

He tried a slice, in fact he tried several slices of the good, mild bacon cooked to a turn, eaten with newly baked bread and fresh Irish butter. Thomas finished his second chop, drank his second tankard of ale, wiped his lips on the newly laundered napkin and rose.

"See you're not late for St. Georgio," he warned, then to his wife, "Mistress Kelly, I'll be away to my business."

His father gone, Michael was left alone with his mother. She watched him with loving eyes. He was so handsome this son of hers, with his fair curls, his clear skin and his dancing eyes. How proud she was of him, and how fearful for him in this new life which lay before him. Only sixteen, and to be sailing half way over the world, to face untold dangers, to be flung headlong into temptations, to be alone—without his mother to run to. Even though he was grown tall and had already made a name for himself as a singer, he still needed his mother, and—often—the shelter of her arms.

She slid her plump, well-kept hand across the expanse of shining damask, and touched his fingers. He looked up and met her eyes and smiled. She thought, "Glory be to God and all His Holy Saints, 'tis a smile that would charm the birds off the trees!"

He raised his eyebrows in a question, "Yes, mama—?"

"Michael, this going away to Italy——"

"Yes, mama."

"I shall miss you, my darlin'."

"Not more than I shall miss you, mama dear. It's a a chance for me, if I have it in me to be a good singer, well—I shall have to take advantage of it. It's sense, isn't it?"

She nodded, wishing fervently that she was wise, that she could give him advice that would help to guard him through the many pitfalls which were waiting for him. Thomas was kind, generous, more—he was good, but to Thomas it was the material things of life which mattered.

"It will be a different life, asthore. A life filled with temptations, and difficulties. You're young, and handsome—oh, yes you are, Michael, and I tremble for you. Never forget that you're a Catholic boy, don't neglect your prayers, go to confession, and never miss Mass. Never listen to people who speak badly of women. Never listen to jokes about them—" her usually pale face was scarlet with the effort she was making, "always remember that Our Lady was a woman, and because of her—because of her—all women have a right to respect." She paused and drew a deep breath.

Michael's eyes twinkled, "Even if they—forfeit that respect, mama?"

He saw the little beads of sweat gather above her eyebrows, she was in deep water and she knew it.

"Even then," she said, her voice shaking a little, "remember Saint Mary Magdalene, my son."

He stared at her in silence, then sprang to his feet, and coming to where she sat, he put his arms round her and kissed her with warmth and deep affection. She felt his kisses, smelt the youth and freshness of him, his smooth cool skin, the gentle strength of his arms round her— she thought, "At this moment I'm happy with my own darling son."

He let her go and raising her hands to his lips kissed them very tenderly.

"Darling mama," he said softly, "I shan't forget. All

women shall have my respect, because I shall remember—
my mother."

She wiped her eyes where the tears had overflowed,
Michael's were not altogether innocent of mistiness. They
felt very close, very dear to each other at that moment.

With a valiant effort she said, "There, we've had our
little talk. I wish that I were wiser, that I had more experience, could give you more help. I've done my best,
and it's a poor best I'm thinking. Now, where are you off
to? It's close on nine! I've a whole lot of things to do."

Michael nodded, "I'm taking a walk round the town
before I meet St. Georgio. Mama, how I love Dublin!
No matter where I go, I'll always be a real Irishman so I
shall! There, I'll be back soon, with all the news for you.
Sure, I'm better than the daily news-sheet."

She was smiling now, "Go on with you," she said,
"all Irishmen are chatter-boxes and you're one of them."

Michael walked out into the clear, warm morning,
warm with that hint of humidity which invariably hung
about Dublin. He set his hat at a jaunty angle, and walked
—imitating the swagger of St. Georgio through the
handsome residential districts—Grafton Street, Sackville
Street, Merrion Square which was already known to be a
centre for the best doctors in Dublin to show their
shining brass plates.

He hesitated as to whether he should walk down to
Pidgeon House Harbour, where there was always bustle
and stir as the packet boats left for England. He decided
against it, better to walk through the fine prosperous
streets, to admire the well-kept houses, and dream
dreams of the time when Michael Kelly, the celebrated
tenor, might live in one of them. Splendid houses, with
wrought iron holders for the torches. He loved to pass

when the torches were flaring, and the whole street lit with strange shadows and sudden spurts of light.

Dublin was a romantic city to young Kelly. He loved its dignity, he loved its old buildings, he even loved the slums which were in the shadow of St. Patrick's Cathedral. It was towards them he turned his steps, leaving the dignity and respectability behind him, and moving towards that part of the town where were gathered the lowest, the dirtiest and most forlorn of its inhabitants. Even the unspeakable stench did not affect him, he only paused to glance at the great Cathedral and wonder why the worst part of the town should have gathered practically under its walls. What did the respectable worshippers think as they passed by and caught glimpses of the squalor and degradation? There Dean Swift was buried along with "Stella". Michael knew very little about Dean Swift, except that he wrote *Gulliver's Travels*, which the boy had read in an unexpurgated edition and had been bored to extinction—even by the bawdy passages.

He passed on into the slums and stews of Dublin. There were the usual blowzy women, the listless prostitutes waiting for the evening to begin their work. There were the men who lived on their earnings and beat them when they seemed insufficient for the amount of money their men required to slake their thirst. There were other men, leaning against the doorposts which lacked doors, sucking black clay cutties and spitting into the foul gutters. Into these surroundings walked Michael Kelly, well dressed, well washed, his hair shining like gold. He might have run the risk of attack, even of murder for the sake of the decent clothes he wore, but long ago, these poor souls, the dregs of humanity, had taken him to their hearts.

" 'Tis Mickie Kelly!" "Now glory be to God, Mike, it's yerself has made a great t'ing singing in the theyater!" "It's a proud man Thomas Kelly must be to-day wid a son havin' all Dublin cheerin' him." "Sing us a song, Mickie boy!"

He stood and smiled at them, "I'm away to Italy—after I've sung again in a new opera. I'm to sing the lead."

"Italy? T'at's a divil of a place. It's a hell of a way off."

"I'm going in a ship, I'm going to sing to all kinds of people."

"I'd not doubt if the Pope himself sint fer ye to sing! No doubt at all."

"Might be," agreed young Kelly. "Now for a song! Perhaps my last to you, who knows?"

The familiar hush, the screaming children suddenly quiet, and the clear young voice rising above the filth, the stench and the squalor, singing a new song of Tom Moore's.

It ended, he smiled at them, waved his hand, and they shouted "God be wi' ye, Mickie lad," and "Good luck to ye, my bould boyo!" He walked away, treading lightly, his head held high, his lips smiling. Slowly he made his way to the lodgings of St. Georgio.

That gentleman was still in bed; Michael wondered when he was a real singer if he would lie abed until so late every morning, and then emerge—as St. Georgio did presently—looking somewhat yellow about the gills, and heavy under the eyes.

"Congratulations!" St. Georgio said, holding out his hand. "Eet is great 'appiness to shake zee 'and of good artist. Now we shall walk together to talk wiz Mistaire Arne. Come—my leetle artist."

CHAPTER FOUR

MR. ARNE was most affable, he was respectful to St. Georgio, and very pleasant to young Kelly. It appeared that they were to give Garrick's "Cymon" for three nights, and he proposed that for Michael's benefit—a "clear benefit" he was careful to explain—they would present "Lionel and Clarissa", with Mrs. Arne playing the woman's rôle.

Michael was enchanted. He was to have special billing, announcing that these appearances were his last before leaving for Italy to continue his musical studies.

"Remember," Arne said, "that in all probability you will go down to history as the youngest male singer to take the leading rôle in any opera. I'm taking a risk, I realize that but——"

St. Georgio interrupted, "W'en you 'ave 'eard Michael seeng, you veel know t'at t'ere is no reesks, none at all." With that he sat down at a piano which stood in the room, and striking a few chords nodded towards Michael, saying, "Michael, seeng!"

Michael Kelly was never troubled with shyness. Nerves might attack him, but shyness—never. He filled his lungs, and sang. Arne listened to the pure, unforced notes, they fell like balm on his always troublesome temperament. If this boy could sing like this in the theatre, the success of his venture was assured. He needed money, all his life a lack of that commodity was to complicate things for him and here—in the person of this good-looking lad—he saw in imagination crowds thronging to the box office, and the Crow Street Theatre packed to suffocation. Ryder, the manager who had entered while Michael was singing, stood by the door, smiling and nodding his approval.

The boy ended his song, and turned to them for approbation.

Ryder said, "B'gad, the feller can sing! Does he know anything about 'Cymon', think you?"

St. Georgio bowed, with dignity as befitted the *maestro* of a star artiste. "Wiz me 'e 'as studied zees rôle. The acting comes easy to 'eem, 'e is a born singer and," with due emphasis, "a born actor."

The whole matter was settled, twenty guineas a night and a "clear benefit". Michael went home treading on air.

Rehearsals began for "Cymon", and Michael found it sufficiently easy to play the part as well as sing it. He was, as St. Georgio had claimed a "born actor". He had no inhibitions, he had intelligence, and the ability to fling himself whole-heartedly into any rôle for which he was cast. Indeed, that was to be the key-note of his whole life—that ability to throw himself into whatever character came his way. Not only on the stage, but in life itself. He loved life, found it exciting and filled with interest. Many years later, he told one of his friends, who asked if, in his retirement, he never suffered from boredom, "Boredom! I've suffered from most things, including gout—which is a legacy from my forebears—but boredom and I have always been strangers. B' gad, I'll take particular care we remain so!"

While the rehearsals of "Cymon" were still in progress the management asked the artistes to begin working on Bickerstaffe's opera "Lionel and Clarissa". Michael was eager to begin, he was never tired, how could anyone become tired with singing? Rehearsals were a joy to him, and this new opera—the opera which was to be for his benefit, was most exciting to him. More than that, he met Mrs. Arne for the first time. She was to sing Clarissa. Michael saw her walk on to the stage. He felt that his heart missed a beat, he felt breathless, colour flooded his cheeks. Here was beauty!

She was a handsome woman, about twenty-eight, with fine shoulders and a good carriage. Her hair fell in ringlets, shining like polished jet. Her eyes were very bright, and her scarlet lips parted a little, as if in expectancy. Michael Kelly, who had never suffered from shyness, felt that emotion almost overwhelm him. This lovely creature was to be his "Clarissa"! He would sing to her tender love passages, towards the end of the opera he had to take her in his arms! His imagination boggled at the thought. He wished that he had worn a smarter suit, the plum-coloured cloth was growing a little shabby. To-morrow he would wear his dark blue with the fawn coloured waistcoat.

She was charming to him, "And you're the miracle boy?" she asked. "I heard you, of course, all Dublin's heard you. We're going to make this benefit of yours— the greatest success. What a cast we have too! And the orchestra—my husband at the pianoforte, the conductor no less than the great Pinto."

Michael, flushing like a girl said, "But most important of all, we have—Mrs. Arne."

She laughed, "Ah, you Irish! I believe you were paying compliments the minute you could talk!"

He went home that night, for they rehearsed late, that being one of the nights when they were not playing "Cymon", his head whirling. This was what being in love meant! The whole world was changed, he wondered how he could bear to leave Dublin for Italy—when Dublin held Mrs. Arne. What did anything matter but to be within sight and sound of her? During one of their scenes he had to hold her hand.

She had laughed at him, saying, "Hold it, Michael. It won't bite you or burn you!"

The thought of holding her hand made his heart beat faster. His mother met him, and said, "Darlin', you look tired to death. All this singing will be the death of you. There, something you like—cold roast duck and onion stuffing."

Michael shuddered. Cold roast duck and onion stuffing. He could not imagine Mrs. Arne eating a generous plateful of cold duck, with an equally generous helping of onion stuffing. Nectar and ambrosia, the most delicate chicken sandwiches, possibly a few oysters, for it was still April. Had he been able to watch Mrs. Arne and her husband indulging in a hearty meal of stewed tripe and mashed potatoes, he would have refused to believe his eyes. Still, the duck looked delicious, and he knew his mother's onion stuffing—beautifully flavoured and exquisitely prepared. He *was* tired, and even though he was experiencing the pangs and joys of being in love, he owed it to himself to eat well—for the sake of his voice and his strength.

He sighed, "Thank you, mama. Not very much. I don't think that I am very hungry."

She smiled at him, "Go along with you, Mickie boy! I've never known you not hungry. There, sit down and tell me how the rehearsals went."

He longed to tell her, "A goddess in human form descended to the earth, she is to sing 'Clarissa', and I have

to embrace her at the end of the opera!" Instead he talked
of other members of the cast. How good was Mr. O'Keefe,
how excellent Mrs. Heaphy as Lady Oldboy, and her
husband as Sir John. In short he spoke with enthusiasm
of all the cast, only when he wished to speak of Mrs.
Arne did the words seem to refuse to be uttered.

"And the lady who is to sing 'Clarissa'?" his mother
asked. "The wife of Mr. Arne, surely, isn't she?"

Michael, his mouth full of cold duck nodded, "Yes.
Oh, she's well enough."

"Young? Pretty?"

"Umph—young enough and pretty enough, I
suppose."

"I don't think she's impressed you, Mickie."

"I'm too busy to study the part, mama, to be unduly
impressed by anyone."

The next day he both waited for and dreaded her
entrance on to the stage. He felt that it was inevitable
that she should see the adoration in his eyes, hear a
tremulous note in his voice when he spoke to her.
Imagine if she went home to her husband and said:

"Michael, that young Kelly is in love with me! He
can't take his eyes off me."

Imagine if Arne, furious, rushed down to the theatre,
and accused him before the whole company of paying
unwelcome attentions to Mrs. Arne. He imagined his
reaction. He would be restrained, dignified, standing
silent with folded arms while Arne accused him.

Then, when the tirade was over, he would reply, "You
are right. This lady has my whole heart. I am not ashamed,
but believe me I would rather cut off my right hand than
hurt a hair of her head."

He could almost hear the murmur of approbation

which would run round the assembled company. "Spoken
like a man!" "Bravely said." "Any woman might be
proud to have such love bestowed on her."

Nothing happened however, she was charming to him,
but she was charming to everyone in the cast. True she
laughed at his attempts at love-making, saying, "Mickie,
you'll have to take lessons in making love. How old
are you? Sixteen! You must have been a very good boy
all your life to know so little about love-making."
Michael stood silent, his face flushed to the roots of his
bright hair. John O'Keefe laughed.

"It's the Dublin girls, ma'am, who are so good, that
they'll refuse even the advances of young Kelly."

Michael said nothing, but he resented O'Keefe's
remark, and resented still more the fact that Mrs. Arne
joined in the laughter which followed it. Later, when he
stood talking to some of the men, Wilder began to tease
him. Was he really such a good boy, had he had no experience with women, was he too shy?

Michael, scowling and furious, swaggered. "I'm not
given to boasting about my love affairs," he told them,
"I don't doubt that if I chose to open my mouth I could
surprise the lot of you."

Wilder stifled his laughter, the boy was amusing
when he put on that air of outraged dignity.

"Tell us about it, Mickie," he urged. "We're strangers
in Dublin, t'would be a charity to give us some advice."

"I recommend you to find out for yourself," Michael
said, "as I did. The finest women are on Sackville Street,
but if money has to be taken into consideration—try the
district round by Saint Patrick's Cathedral. Mind, it's a
rough part of the town, but—they know me there!"

Later Wilder confided to O'Keefe that young Kelly

c

knew his way about, he might not be able to make love on the stage, but—there were plenty of other things he knew all right.

"A devil of a fellow! And only sixteen."

O'Keefe shook his head, "Showing off, my boy. Show him a whore at close quarters and he'd run a mile."

The story grew, and lost nothing in the retelling. Michael gained the reputation of being a rake, the women eyed him from under lowered lashes, the men threw out dark hints in his hearing, and asked him pertinent questions as to how he spent his spare time. He was alternately flattered and a little disturbed. If these stories reached the ears of Mrs. Arne what would she think of him? Would she admire him for his gallantry, his recklessness, or feel a sense of disgust that he consorted with these women of the town? It might have been wiser to take up the attitude of a stainless paladin rather than that of a hell-rake.

Then one morning, while they were free for a few moments, she spoke to him. His devotion to her had grown beyond all bounds, he believed that he lay awake most of the night thinking of her. As a matter of fact he slept remarkably soundly.

She said, "Michael, I've been hearing some terrible things about you. Mr. Heaphy told Mrs. Heaphy. I was shocked. Are these dreadful things true, and you only sixteen?"

Michael drew a deep breath, "What—kind of things, ma'am?"

She shuddered, "I can scarcely bare to mention them —things about—women, low women and you, Michael. You remember when I twitted you for not knowing how to make love on the stage—after that you told some of the gentlemen—about these dreadful women."

She looked at him closely, he didn't look debauched, his skin was as clear as a child's, his eyes bright and his whole expression—if a little confused at the moment—was frank and open. She thought that one day Michael Kelly would make women's hearts beat faster.

He said, "Mrs. Arne, ma'am, I can swear to you that since I met you my whole life has been as innocent as a new born baby's."

She smiled, "But—before you met me, Michael?"

"Before I met you," he said, "I wasn't really alive."

"That's your Irish flattery," she told him. "But you can't like these horrid women, Michael!"

"Please believe me," he said gravely, "I look back— with horror."

"And you're a Catholic boy, too. Do you go to confession?"

"I do, ma'am."

"And confess—everything?" she queried.

He nodded, thinking, "And at my next confession I'll have to admit to telling a lot of damned lies—actually and by imputation!"

She laid her hand lightly on his arm, her voice was low, and very charming. Michael thought that this was the happiest moment of his life. "Listen, Michael," she said, "you're going to be a singer, and a fine singer. You've got everything necessary—looks, musical appreciation, and a beautiful voice. They're your—stock in trade. Abuse none of them if you wish them to serve you well. I won't talk about—sin, your priest can do that, I'm talking to you as a practical woman, a fellow artist."

Her sincerity was obvious, and Michael felt his eyes smart suddenly.

"You're an angel, ma'am," he said, his voice husky. "An angel."

He thought the whole thing over that night when—for once—he did not sleep immediately when he went to bed. What a vain, stupid fool he had been. Telling, and imputing lies, and about such a subject. Swaggering and bragging that he knew half the whores in Dublin! And then, what if he did? There was no particular merit in that, it was quite possible if you had sufficient money and—he remembered the woman he had gone home with, recalled vividly his horror of the surroundings, the smells and the dirt—were not particularly squeamish.

Mrs. Arne, he drew a deep breath at the very thought of her, had shown him what a crass fool he had been. Even then he had not possessed sufficient courage to make a clean breast of the whole silly business. She was an angel, that was what made him feel unbearably ashamed. No, Michael Kelly had not come out of that business with flying colours. He was no gallant fellow, merely a rather silly boy who thought it clever to pretend that he had slept with Dublin whores!

When next day Wilder said something to him about the gay life which he led, Michael—his fair skin flushing painfully, snapped out that he was "done with all that!" Even then he felt slightly ashamed, for he realized that he still lacked the courage to admit, frankly, that he had purposely misled them.

"If you ask me," Wilder said to O'Keefe later, "young Kelly's got more than he bargained for! He's got a bad fright, take my word for it. He told me this morning that he'd reformed."

O'Keefe smiled a trifle maliciously, "I doubt if any reformation was necessary. I always felt that the cockerel crowed too loud."

The three performances of "Cymon" were a great success, and Michael was happy to be back on the stage again. Now he had learnt how to paint his face, the wearing of stage clothes came easily to him, and he was confident as regards his voice. The theatre was packed, and the women watched him with unconcealed delight; the younger ones hoped that one day a slim fellow with bright curls and sparkling eyes might make love to them, the older ones sighed for their past youth, for the romance and the adoration which had once been directed to them.

Then—his "clear benefit", "Lionel and Clarissa". His father and his father's friends had been busy, and by this time young Kelly was an attraction. More, the Dubliners knew that this was their last chance of seeing and hearing this prodigy, he was leaving in a few days for Italy.

Michael's own feelings were mixed. He was excited at the prospect of singing "Lionel", but it was for one night only. Only once would he embrace Mrs. Arne— and this time he swore that she should find no fault with his lack of ardour. He sent flowers to all the women in the cast, "with the respectful greetings of Michael Kelly", but the flowers which he sent to Mrs. Arne, his "Clarissa", were far more exotic, expensive and beautiful than theirs. He wrote in his rather unformed handwriting, "To thank you for everything. This is the proudest night of my life; I shall still maintain this if I live to be a hundred, and I shall always be your obedient and grateful servant."

She spoke to him as they stood in the wings.

"Your flowers, they are superb!"

"My flowers?" he asked, "Did I send flowers?"

She smiled, "You didn't sign your name, but I knew——"

"They must look pale, trumpery things in your dressing room, where even the reflection of your face in the mirror is——"

She laid her finger on her lips, "Hush! More of your Irish flattery, Michael! Hush, listen—the band is playing. Are you nervous?"

"Only of not doing my best and possibly displeasing you."

The house was crowded, all Dublin society was present. There were splendid uniforms in the boxes, women wearing their choicest jewels, Michael's nerves left him. He felt gay and confident, he *was* "Lionel", and his voice came clear and sweet, soaring up to the topmost seats of the distant gallery. Somewhere, he knew, his mother was listening, straining her ears for every note, watching him with that tender smile which he loved. How excellent everyone was—how amusing was O'Keefe playing the fop to admiration, how brilliantly the great Pinto conducted the orchestra, and how divine "Clarissa" appeared!

Between the acts Michael Arne came round, radiating good humour and content. He had heard nothing but enthusiastic praise from everyone. The Governor, the Duke of Leinster, the aristocracy of Dublin including Lord Edward Fitzgerald could not praise the opera and the artistes more warmly.

He said to Michael, "You're the lucky lad, remember this is your benefit! You'll leave for Italy with your pockets heavy with guineas, my boy."

Michael, revelling in his sentiment, his eyes turned

towards Mrs. Arne, smiled, thinking, "And a heart to
match them. How can I leave you? My first—and my last
—love."

When they reached the scene when he had to take
her in his arms and embrace her, he allowed his emotion
to have full sway. This was his moment, whatever might
happen in his life this would remain a memory. Again he
felt that he *was* "Lionel". She was not the wife of Michael
Arne, she was his own, his very own "Clarissa". His arms
were round her, and he rejoiced at their young strength.
He kissed her cheek, tasting the make-up as he did so.
It seemed the most delicious taste and scent in the world.
Her eyes met his, they were startled, almost incredulous,
he heard her breathe—almost soundlessly, "Michael!"

The opera was over, the audience thundered their
applause, there were shouts for "Clarissa", for "Lionel".
Together they took their call, hand in hand, Michael
turning to her—as if disclaiming any right to the applause
which should all be hers. He bowed, his hand on his
heart, their eyes met and he felt, "She knows, she has
realized at last!"

His father had arranged a supper party for the whole
cast, and Michael had been warned to hurry home to
greet the guests. He would willingly have absented
himself—to meet her again was too much. She, who had
been his "Clarissa", would be Mrs. Michael Arne. The
transition was too abrupt, too sudden. How could he
comfort himself with even reasonable equanimity?

People crowded to his dressing room. There was Tom
Moore, dark-haired and bright-eyed, "Mickie, you were
grand, just grand. Ireland has a singer worthy of her."

"And a poet worthy of her, Tom."

St. Georgio, resplendent in slightly theatrical evening

clothes. "Leetle Mickee, you 'ave done ver' vell. I am proud of you."

His mother, leaning forward, and kissing his cheek, "Darlin', it was wonderful, how I enjoyed it." Then, "Oh, get that nasty paint off your face, me dote, it tastes horrid!"

His father, fussing a little. "Now, Michael, hurry, I want you to be there to greet the guests. Listening to music makes me hungry! There's not a woman in the world can make a raised pie as your mother can. Hurry along or you'll get none. Actors are always hungry."

The Duke himself, urbane and kindly. "Admirable, my boy, quite admirable. Sorry that we're to lose you to Italy. Could do with that voice of yours to sing young Tom Moore's songs. My congratulations."

Then when at last he was dressed—in his splendid blue suit with the silver lace—he found a rabble at the stage door. There they were, ragged and dirty, his friends from the slums. Tattered and torn were their clothes, sad looking men with their short black cutty pipes, blowzy women, painted women, even children all waiting for him.

"Glory be to God, we've not a blanket left, Mickie. Pawned the lot to get the money for a seat." "Boyo, you were grand! 'Twas like a bird singin' in spring time, so 'twas." "Mickie, ye're off to Italee. Give as a stave, boyo, for the last toime." "C'm now, Mickie Kelly. Give us a stave!"

He stood there on the step, watching them, his bright eyes dimmed a little. They'd pawned their blankets to come and hear him! He hesitated for a moment, then sang "Greensleeves", sang it very simply and sweetly with that unaffected charm which had made them his friends. The

last notes died away, and he waved his hat to them, then
ran swiftly to the carriage which was waiting for him.

He felt that the first act of his life was over. Would he
ever sing in Dublin again, ever stand on the stage of
the Smock Alley Theatre, ever bow to the applause of the
audience?

The future would be open to him, he would have the
direction of his own life, the possibilities of a career. His
mind seemed to whirl at the thought of Italy, Naples—
what would Naples be like? He had an introduction to
Sir William Hamilton, to Father Dolphin, the Prior of the
Convent of St. Dominic, surely that was a good start.
He had sufficient money to be able to pay for his passage
himself, money earned by his own efforts. His father was
sufficiently generous, but there was a thrifty strain in his
character which made him demand that the guineas which
Michael had earned should be spent—in part at all
events—on the cost of his passage on the Swedish ship,
which, sailing under a neutral flag, was considered
safer than a ship which might come under the unwelcome attentions of either the British or the American
vessels.

Michael leaned back against the cushions of the
carriage, they smelt of tobacco smoke, straw and dust.
He found the combination disgusting but exciting. He
was going to make his entrance at home in all the glory
of his blue and silver suit, and there he would find—
"Clarissa". "Clarissa" whose startled eyes had met his for
a moment after that first embrace. Michael smiled, that
had been a wonderful moment, and now—looking back—
he felt that it had been the culmination of his adoration
for her. The climax, the ultimate justification of himself
as a lover. Already he felt, and felt too sudden regret, that

something of the intense fire had burnt out in his ardour for her.

It had been the love of a romantic boy, a boy who had been sufficiently stupid to lie about his imaginary exploits to other singers, and who had felt ashamed when she had spoken to him, kindly, wisely, even regretfully. He had seen himself as a young devotee worshipping at her shrine. He had asked nothing, he had only taken that one fervent embrace. He wondered if he had ever actually wished for anything more? Not even in his wildest dreams had he allowed his imagination to run riot in wild dreams of physical satisfaction. That would have been sacrilege. He had imagined himself doing deeds of daring for her dear sake, had seen himself striding through fierce flames—if the theatre caught fire—walking into her dressing room, and carrying her out disregarding any possible danger to himself. He had seen himself in Grafton Street when two immense and unbelievably powerful dray-horses rushed along completely out of control. It had been Michael Kelly who dashed forward, seizing their head-stalls, and saving Mrs. Arne by a hair's breadth from their thundering hooves. He had dreamed of walking home at some distance from her as she went back to her lodgings. He saw two footpads leap out of the shadows, heard them demanding her purse. That was when Michael Kelly had rushed forward. Well delivered blows, blows which came straight and direct from the shoulder had disposed of the villains. Dusting his hands with a handkerchief, he had offered his arm, courteous and unperturbed "Allow me, ma'am, to escort you to your lodgings."

Those had been his dreams, and whereas once they had seemed almost more real than reality, they had taken on a strange, dim and misty quality. Those dreams had belonged to Michael Kelly the boy—this fellow, seated in a hackney coach was a man—or almost a man—who was going out into the world to carve out a career for himself.

He sighed, there was something romantically sad about a dream which was over. He still loved her, he would always love her, but he realized that the whole thing had been unreal and unsubstantial.

The coach stopped, from the house he could hear the sound of music, saw the bright lights shining out of the windows. They were waiting for him. She would be there, lovely, charming, and as their eyes met, he might see again that sudden, half-startled, half-questioning expression. If she made any reference to his embrace, he must be guarded in his replies. He felt old, and a trifle disillusioned. The sensation was not altogether unpleasant. It brought with it an agreeable feeling of gentle melancholy. Michael Kelly, he assured himself, had left his youth behind, he was a man, facing the dangers and difficulties of life.

He got out, and felt in his pocket for the money for the fare. The driver, a jovial looking man, with a scarlet face and twinkling eyes, said, "Ah, that's all roight, Mickie, yer Dad's paid."

He gave the man the price of a drink, and walked into the house, feeling younger and less certain of himself. His mother came to him, smiling.

"Here's my boy! We began to think you were never coming."

He laughed, "I stayed to sing to some friends of mine, mama."

"Some friends of yours, Michael?"

"Yes, from the slums. They wanted a—last stave, so I

gave them 'Greensleeves'. They'd pawned their blankets
to get the price of a ticket for the opera."

His father's great jovial laugh filled the room, "More
likely they picked a few pockets, my boy! If you're
talking about that rabble from the slums!"

"Perhaps—well, so long as they didn't pick mine,
papa." He made his way to the long buffet, and realized
that he was almost unbearably hungry. Trust his mother
to have provided the finest dishes! Pies, brawn, cold
tongues, cold brisket of beef, her own special pork pies—
"the like not to be found in Ireland!" There were jellies,
custards, special tartlets—no wonder that his fellow
artistes were taking full advantage of the generous supply
of food.

Young Tom Moore greeted him, "Mickie, you were
grand, me boy. I was nervous for you, I'd no need to have
been. You took it all like an old hand, so you did."

"Tom, when I've made my name, I'll sing your songs
before all others, bless you."

Then looking up suddenly, Michael found Mrs.Arne
watching him. He smiled at her, and tried to remember all
the conclusions to which he had come on the drive home.
He went towards her, and said complimentary things
about her performance. He thanked her for the confidence
she had given him. "You chased away my nerves,"
he assured her, "I felt that with you on the stage—I was
safe."

She met his glance squarely, "Did you? It never
occurred to me that you were—nervous, Michael."

"I was nevertheless."

"Even in the last scene we played together?"

"Ah, then the—play was almost over—wasn't it?"

"Yes, of course."

"Except to say—to you—thank you for everything."

She moved away, for a moment he longed to follow her, to beg for a few moment's conversation alone with her, then he remembered the part for which he had cast himself. No longer Mickie Kelly, the boy—he was Michael Kelly, the man who was going out to make a name for himself.

Later he said to his mother, "Have the Arnes gone, mama?"

"They left some time ago, my dear. They are catching the early packet boat for England."

"Really? I didn't know they were leaving so soon."

It was surprising how little it mattered.

CHAPTER FIVE

MAY the first of the year 1779, Michael Kelly accompanied by his father and several friends arrived at the quayside, where the Swedish ship, *Svornson,* was ready to sail. The day was sunny and warm, but there was a strange sense of chill lingering in Michael's stomach, which he swaggered a little in order to hide. On boarding the ship he saw the great bulk of his grand pianoforte, in its case bearing his name and the direction "Naples". There too were the sea stores which his father had ordered, in his pocket a gold watch—a parting present from his father, and ten guineas which his mother had given him.

She had refused to come down to the docks, and together she and Michael had taken a tearful farewell in her bedroom. He loved his mother dearly, true he had an admiration for his good-natured, open-handed father, but all his real tenderness was reserved for his mother. For his brothers he had affection, but none of them really shared his tastes and under all his affection for them he felt a slight sense of superiority.

He was not actually a conceited lad, but the wine of success is heady, and he had been able to drink of it in considerable quantities. At heart he was warm-hearted and generous, never throughout his life did he deny whole-hearted admiration to other artistes, never did he indulge in those petty jealousies which are only too common in the world of opera as they are on the legitimate stage.

The captain, a huge, fair-haired Swede, greeted him, shook hands with Thomas Kelly almost wringing off that gentleman's hand in the warmth of his greeting. In the captain's cabin, young Kelly and his father were offered glasses of some Swedish drink which, as Michael said later, "Almost blew off the tops of our heads."

The pilot came aboard, and Thomas bade his son an affectionate good-bye. Michael waved to the friends who stood on the quay, the anchor was raised, and slowly the ship moved from the shore. There swept over Michael a sense of sudden loneliness. He was leaving his home, he was embarking on a great adventure, and although the thought was exciting, there remained a little nagging feeling of doubt. He had learnt sufficient Italian from St. Georgio and Rauzzini, he could make himself understood, he knew that arrangements had been made for Father Dolphin of the Order of St. Dominic to meet him and make him welcome. He had a letter in his wallet which gave him an introduction and a very warm one to no less a person than Sir William Hamilton and his intensely musical and gifted wife.

Sir William was British Ambassador at Naples, popular if inclined to be slightly ponderous and pompous; his wife was considered one of the best pianists in Naples, for this was long before Emma met Sir William and won his heart.

Michael went to his cabin, and sitting on the edge of his bunk decided that the future was sufficiently bright for hope, expectancy and confidence. He decided that he must make the best of his opportunities, take advantage of the chances which were offered to him and, after all, he reflected, he had a voice which had been admitted by Dublin audiences—even the highest and most critical of Dublin society—to be out of the ordinary in its power and quality.

Michael was by nature mercurial, and having considered his position, knew that his spirits rose. He stared at his reflection in the small hanging mirror, and smiled; that charming, infectious smile which was to win him the hearts of people for the rest of his life.

He washed and made himself very neat, for neatness was habitual to him, and throwing his cloak round him, for the wind was freshening, went up on deck. The crew were a mixed lot, there were Swedes, one Britisher, and a couple of Dutchmen. The first mate was a red-haired and cadaverous Scot. He greeted Michael, asking if he felt the increasing pitching of the ship.

He added, "Ye're not the only Irishman we've on board. There's a seaman called O'Grady, he hails from Cork."

"That makes good hearing," Michael told him. "I felt that I might be a little lonely."

"Mon, no call for ye to be that! Sailors are aye friendly folk, an' it's been haired that you're a singer. Gie them a wee song now an' then an' there'll be naething they'll not dae for ye."

That evening he dined with the captain and the officers except the one who was taking the watch. They were kindness itself to him, and Michael insisted upon having one of the cases which held his stores opened and offering to them some of the choicest delicacies it contained.

The Scottish mate, speaking very slowly and loudly, said to the captain, "Mind, sir, this laddie's got a voice like a mavis."

The captain nodded his huge blonde head, "Zee's I

'ave 'eard. I 'ave ver' mooch loff for music. You seeng for us, leetle poy?"

The cabin was full of tobacco smoke, the smell of heavy spirits hung in the air, but Michael had sung often enough in his father's dining room under the same circumstances; he had sung in the stench in the slums near the Cathedral, and he nodded.

"Gladly, sir."

He stood up, looking very slim and young among the heavily built seamen, and throwing back his head, filled the cabin with golden notes.

"Believe me if all those endearing young charms . . ."

The big captain wiped his eyes with the back of a very large, very freckled hand. The Scotsman said, "That was bonnie, whiles ye might be willin' tae gie the crew a song. Eh, sir? They'd think a lot o't."

"A goot t'ought, mister. If the little feller will be so kind."

So each succeeding day, Michael went and gave the crew who were not on duty, a song or two. They liked the curly-headed boy, always so meticulously neat, always with such a ready smile.

The days went past, the sea was calm and the winds fair; not until they reached the Bay of Biscay did anything happen to disturb the peace and tranquillity of the voyage. A shot whizzed past their bows, and from a ship came the message "Stand to". They were sailing under a neutral flag, but the captain—possibly because his conscience was clear—obeyed the order. The privateer sent off her long boat and a gang of ruffians boarded the ship. Michael was not, and never pretended to be particularly courageous; he stood back and watched these fearsome looking men swarm on to the deck.

The captain, a tall thin fellow, with a long upper lip and small, but vivid blue eyes, demanded a table to be brought and the ship's books and articles. He bawled at the Swedish captain that he was sailing under false colours, that he was in the pay of the British, and sat down to examine all that the papers could tell him. His companions rushed about, breaking open any case they found, and one of them, a great fierce looking man with a hatchet began to attack the case which held Michael's precious pianoforte.

Michael shrank back, crying, "Oh, my dear piano-forte," while tears rolled down his cheeks. The Irish seaman, O'Grady, said consolingly, "Now for God's sake don't be afther crying, Master Kelly."

The man at the table looked up quickly, then pushing away the papers which lay before him, rose and came over to where Michael stood.

"Is your name Kelly?"

Michael did his best to keep back his tears, "Yes— that's my name."

The man turned and bawled at the fellow with the hatchet, "Leave that case alone, you dirty bastard. Whin I want onnyt'ing done, Oi'll give me orders, blast ye." He turned back to Michael.

"Do you know onnyt'ing of a Mr. Thomas Kelly of Mary Street, in Dublin?"

Michael had his tears under control by this time, "My father."

The change in the hard, rather sinister face was astonishing. The man rushed forward and flung his arms round Michael's neck, crying: "Now, glory be to God, d'you not remember me? Jack Cunningham! The same. Whin you were a little boy didn't I spend hours playin' with you? Yes, at the country house your father had at Drumcondra. It's me little playmate Mickie Kelly!"

Michael's ready smile broke out, "Jack, I remember you so well. I remember too the apples and plums you used to gather for me—and the stomach aches I used to have in consequence."

The crew, and the privateer's men stood round, their mouths agape. Here was this formidable fellow almost reduced to tears at the sight of young Michael Kelly who had been known to him years ago.

The captain came forward, "Mister, veel you kom to my cabin, now you know zat I am a 'onest man? You and Master Kelly ken 'ave a drink togezzer. Alles us 'ave small drink, no? Ole freens meet, a time for rejoicement koms as well! Mister Mate, give a tot 'o rum to alles crew an'—" he laughed, flinging back his head, "an' alles veesiters."

In the cabin, where from his store Michael produced a bottle of Irish whisky, Jack Cunningham told his story. He was the son of the gardener employed by Thomas Kelly at his country house at Drumcondra. "An' if iver a gintleman was good to a lad, it was the father o' Mickie here, and badly Oi repaid him, an' t'at's the tru'h."

He had loved the small Michael, he told them, but he had wandered into bad company, had taken to drink, been mixed up in some robbery and was finally deported to America. "Ye may not t'ink that to be the first mate— for t'at's phwat Oi am—of an American privateer is annyt'ing to boast av. Niver mind, war's war, an' peace is no man's war. Mickie, me darlin', here's all that's good to you. Now, we must be off. Sure, that drink has warmed me heart, an' brought back t'oughts of dear ould Dublin.

Take care av yerself, Mickie boy, an' t'ink some toimes av yer ould friend, Jack."

So they rowed away and rejoined their ship. Michael waved to their boat until he saw them safely aboard. He sighed. He remembered so well the summer days, the great leafy trees under which Jack had played with him, so kindly and so gently, and here he was, with no doubt a price on his head and the shadow of the gallows always touching him.

The next day the Swedish ship was overhauled by an English vessel. The captain gave particulars of the raid; the very correct British officer took all his remarks down in a remarkably small and very neat hand.

He bowed to the captain, "Our thanks, sir, we'll be on her tracks, and Heaven help the villains if we catch them!"

Michael sighed again. He thought, "Whether he's right or wrong, please God, don't let them catch Jack Cunningham."

They entered the Mediterranean, passing the great frowning Rock of Gibraltar, and were nearing Naples, passing the Island of Ischia, when one of those storms for which the Mediterranean is famous, sprang up. The ship rocked and rolled, and as the mate said, "Just wallowed through it like an old sow in a field full of mud, blast her." Michael who had stood the voyage without an hour's sea-sickness retired to his bunk and lay there in misery. He lay there, thinking of his home, his mother most of all, dreaming—but without sleeping—of the spotless lavender smelling sheets, and the loving attention which would have been given to him. At last he fell into an uneasy sleep, and woke to hear the cabin boy announcing, "Now ve arre een the Pay of Nables, ver' beautiful."

The storm was over, and Michael going to his port-hole saw the lovely bay for the first time. Like a great bracelet it lay on the blue and tranquil sea. All traces of the storm had gone, the sky was clear with fleecy white clouds, and the white, shining buildings of the town seemed to glimmer, as the sea seemed to dance.

Raising his eyes, he saw the great smoking mountain of Vesuvius, and shivered a little at the thought that there was a living, burning volcano capable of wiping out the whole of Naples should it indulge in an eruption.

He was sent for, he already had a visitor, Father Dolphin, who had brought with him a smiling, gay young man named Fleming, one of the Irish Brigade. Later, through Fleming, Michael was to meet Plunket and the three of them were inseparable.

The young Irish singer, the story of whose success had already filtered through to Naples, was immediately a person of some importance and interest. Naples offered many amusements to young men in those days, it was teaming with life, the people were gay and hospitable and to Kelly everything was new, strange and attractive. If all the amusements were not as completely innocent as might have been wished, the three young men—scarcely more than boys, indulged in them light-heartedly and with no serious consequences. The Italian girls were handsome, kindly, and ready to be amused. True they were not aristocrats, but they were gay and warm-hearted and —not avaricious.

Michael, having engaged a hairdresser, for he was more than a little vain of his curls, and his general appearance, presented his letter of introduction to Sir William Hamilton. Sir William, pompous but gracious, invited him to an evening party. There were famous artistes to be present, and the kindly Sir William told Kelly that they might be useful to him; he was also not averse from showing off this young Irishman who had created something of a stir in the musical world.

Michael had never been to such a party in his life. Sir William's villa was splendid, and the paintings, marble columns, polished floors, the cabinets containing cameos and collections in which the Ambassador delighted, made a deep impression on Michael. So did the colourful uniforms, the sparkling orders and decorations, while the women all gowned in the latest fashion displayed their arms, necks and more of their busts than—at first— seemed to Michael to be in accordance with proper modesty. He was presented to Lady Hamilton, to the young—and rather stupid—Duke of Bedford. Mellico the singer and harpist was among the guests, and later played and sang delightfully, the custom being then, as it frequently is still, that artistes should "sing for their supper".

Michael was asked to sing, and sat down at the piano-forte ready to accompany himself. He presented a delightful picture, young and colourful with his clear skin and bright eyes. He had chosen to wear a black velvet coat, trimmed with silver lace, and worn with black satin knee breeches. The costume was finished off with a full cravat of exquisite Limerick lace, which Michael's mother had given him among her many presents at his parting. He sang first in Italian, and as the song ended the applause was instantaneous and sincere. He glanced round the great salon, his face flushed with pleasure.

"Ah, Master Kelly," Lady Hamilton cried, "one more song, please."

For his second song Michael sang in English, and

when he rose, the guests crowded round him, praises
were showered upon him, and the great Mellico paid him
handsome compliments, assuring him that his Italian
accent was excellent.

He went back to his lodgings with his head buzzing
with excitement, and sat down at once to write a long
letter to his mother. The letter told her of his success
that evening, and if, perhaps he gave himself praise which
was rather more than sufficient, he was very young, and
the heady wine of success was very potent. He wrote
at great length, and when he ended he heard the clock in a
nearby church strike the hour of three. He yawned,
stretched his arms, conscious that he was very tired, and
also that he had to call on the Ambassador at eight the
following morning. He slept heavily, and woke to hear
the same church clock striking eight, and the bells ringing
for early Mass. He dressed as quickly as possible,
wearing a suit of a quiet colour, and rushed out to the
Embassy.

He arrived there at a quarter to nine, to receive a
kindly rebuke, which he felt certain Sir William had carefully rehearsed while waiting for him.

"Your appointment was for eight, not a quarter to
nine, my dear boy. Unless you can learn to keep time how
can you ever hope to become a good musician?"

"Again, my deep apologies, sir. I sat up writing to my
mother, when I got back last night, telling her of the
brilliance of your wonderful party."

"Ah, you enjoyed it. Good. Now let us discuss your
future."

Michael explained that while his father wished him to
study the theory of music and composition with the hope
that he might when he returned to England compose and

teach; his own wish was simply to learn to sing in the best possible way.

"Without conceit, sir, I have a voice—it's strong, and not unpleasing I think." He smiled. "I made some success in opera in Dublin, and it is to operatic work that my whole heart is set."

Sir William nodded approval. "I am glad that your ideas are so definite and clear cut. Now Finaroli, the finest teacher it is said in Italy, is a personal friend of mine. I shall send you to him and I promise you that to find a better teacher would be impossible."

The ambassador asked the boy about the allowance his father had promised, and gave it as his opinion that while it was just and sufficient, Michael would have to limit his expenses if he were to live within his income. Here the Ambassador pulled out a wallet, and handed Michael twenty "ounces of gold", which was the currency used in Naples at the time, the value of his gift being about eight pounds.

Michael left the Embassy carrying with him the letter of introduction to Finaroli, and his pleasant and un-expected present. He reported the interview to Father Dolphin. The priest smiled and nodded, he agreed that Finaroli was admirable, and when Michael told him of the gift which Sir William had made him, he unlocked a drawer in his desk and extracted from it six ounces of gold, saying, "A poor priest cannot emulate the Ambassa-dor, except in the warmth of his good wishes for your success, my son. See Naples before you really settle down to work, it will repay you."

In company with young Fleming Michael explored Naples. He was excited with the things he saw there, the crowded streets, the great carriages of the aristocracy

with their "running footmen", called *Volanti*. He learnt
that a singer he had met at Sir William's villa, Morelli,
had once been one of these *volanti*, until his master, Earl
Cowper heard him singing at his work and, attracted by
the pure quality of his voice, insisted on paying for his
training as a singer.

The food in Naples was novel, strange and remarkably
cheap, and Michael and his friend delighted to sample the
new dishes, though Michael admitted that, at first, it
shocked him to find that a wine was called *lacrima
Christi*. They visited the theatres and the San Carlos opera
house, which was later destroyed by fire. He grew to know
and love "the town that never sleeps", and when he went
to see his new singing master felt happier than ever.

Finaroli was small, not unlike Kelly himself in figure,
with a brisk pleasant manner. He admitted Michael to his
school at the Conservatorio of the Madonna of Loretto.

"You like working here?" he asked Michael at the
end of the first week.

Michael looked doubtful, for he found the huge room
filled with students writing, working out harmonies
playing various instruments even singing, most dis-
tracting.

The teacher looked at him sharply, "Not very much, I
think?"

"I find it difficult to concentrate, sir, with so many
different sounds all round me. I don't want to complain,
indeed I am very grateful to have the chance to——"

"Say no more!" Finaroli cried, "I understand. It shall
be rectified, I like you, I have watched how hard you
tried to become used to the noise, you have tried very
hard, poor boy. Now in my house there is a small apartment, modest—you understand, but quiet. You shall eat

at my own table, and I foresee that we shall make great progress. This pleases you, Michele?"

"I should not like, sir, while being more grateful than I can say, to offend the authorities at the Conservatorio, who have been very kind to me, and shown their good-will toward me."

"No, no, every day you shall go to the Conservatorio, for there is much for you to learn there, but you shall have private instruction from your professor," he laughed and prodded himself on the chest, "who is—Finaroli! Now, let me see you smile and be happy."

"I am, sir, and deeply grateful. I'll work very hard, and one day I hope that you'll be proud of your pupil and feel that you are rewarded in some small measure for your goodness."

He did work hard, although he played hard as well. He was popular everywhere, there was a charm about the boy which made an instant appeal. Men found him bright and amusing, women admired his looks, his charming manners and the deference which he paid them.

Both Finaroli and Sir William Hamilton introduced Michael to their influential friends, he was probably the first British born singer to appear professionally in Italy. Not only did he get engagements to sing at the houses of the Princess Belmonte, the Princess Ghigi, the Duchess of Castel Duoro but he met singers of note, and became their friend. Sir William took him to be presented to the King and Queen of Naples.

"Here, sir, is an Irish lad, come from Dublin to study in Naples."

The King blinking his short-sighted eyes, and peering at Michael asked, "Tell me, are you a Christian?"

"I hope that I am, sire."

"I should like to hear you sing something. I love music, love opera, anything connected with the theatre. One day you must come to Caserta and see my little theatre there. It is perfect. Now, let me have a song in English."

The King then asked for a song in Italian, and again Michael sang. So he was able to supplement his father's allowance, but he was extravagant, he loved good clothes, liked entertaining his friends and money seemed to melt. He was lucky, popular, and made much of. Sufficient to turn the head of any boy of sixteen, but he remained simple and warm-hearted, although he appreciated to the full, the various opportunities which were put in his way. Like many Irishmen while being over open-handed, he had an eye to the main chance, though he was never capable—until many years later—of "holding money".

A new master came into his life, the celebrated Aprile one of the greatest singers of his day, heard the boy, and told Finaroli that he was willing to take Michael with him to Sicily, where he had engagements and apparently was regarded with almost adoration by the Sicilians.

He would take him, teach him without payment, put what work offered in his way, and look after his interests in every possible manner. Finaroli told Michael of the offer. "I believe that you ought to go, my dear boy. To have for a master the great Aprile is something which does not come to everyone. He is superb, acclaimed everywhere. Take his offer. Indeed if you refused it, my disappointment in you would be such that I should—and I have a great affection for you—ask you to withdraw yourself from my house and also I should decline to be your teacher any longer."

Michael begged that he might have time to think the

offer over, but Finaroli would have none of it. He spoke impatiently.

"*Now*, decide *now*: Is an artist of the stature of Aprile to be kept waiting for a reply to such an offer? Listen, Michael, you are a singer, that is your chosen career, there must be sacrifices if you will reach the height of your ambition. You love Naples, you have friends, you have received many kindnesses, but these must be set aside if you are to attain your ambition."

"Never, never set aside in my heart," Michael said, his eyes filled with tears, "Always I shall remember Naples and the people who showered kindness upon me." Suddenly he smiled, "I have sufficient to pay all my debts—yes, including the pretty widow Mac Mahon."

Finaroli raised his eyebrows, "You've been there, you young dog, have you?"

"No doubt too often. She is so charming, so attractive, and concocts the best punch I have ever tasted. Also, when I have been short of cash, she has allowed me to run up a score. No, don't look stern, I have sufficient to pay her in full—and in addition to leave a little gift."

Finaroli laid his hand on the boy's shoulder, "Michael, some of us are born into the world with a natural aptitude for drinking—I believe that you are one of those people. Be careful, my boy. Not that I think that drinking in moderation will harm you, but always remember that you hold your voice *in trust*. A trust imposed upon you by the Almighty Himself. Do not betray it."

"I'll try to remember that, maestro."

So Michael took leave of his good friends in Naples, paid his ceremonial visits of farewell on all his aristocratic patrons, and with real affection took himself to the Embassy to thank Sir William who had been, with Father

Dolphin, his sponsor into the fashionable world of Naples.

He was seventeen, he was still very slight, still wore his own hair which hung down brightly golden and was most carefully dressed and tied. He had gained assurance, no longer became confused and flushed easily, but essentially he remained simple and unaffected. His voice under the tuition of Finaroli had gained power and range.

He left Naples for Palermo with Aprile. He stood on the deck of the ship and felt his eyes fill with tears. True he had worked very hard, he had studied and, he believed, profited by those studies, but his heart was heavy when he thought of all that he was leaving. The gay bustle of the streets, the crowds of people, the kindnesses he had received, and the success which had come to him. He vowed that never would he forget Father Dolphin, Sir William Hamilton, and his dear master Finaroli.

Aprile, his hand on Michael's shoulder, said "Don't be down-hearted. Naples is beautiful, but you will find beauty in my dear Sicily. You are a singer, and the life of a singer means constant change. You will find friends everywhere. Now, smile again, and remember that you are going to an island of blue seas, the best wine imaginable, and the kindest people in the world."

Aprile was as good as his word, he gave Michael teaching which was invaluable, he studied for six hours every day, but when his work was over he had letters of introduction to many members of the Sicilian aristocracy, given to him by Sir William Hamilton.

They liked him, liked his good looks, and loved above all his willingness to sing to them. His voice had developed amazingly, it had always been pure and he possessed exact pitch, but with the teaching he had been given by

Finaroli, to which Aprile added with all his knowledge, it had gained in power, and also in taste.

Several months passed, when Aprile sent for Michael.

"My dear Michael, it is now time that we part. You are ready to take engagements—anywhere. I have a letter here to introduce you to Campigli, the manager of the Pergola Theatre in Florence. He is not only manager but he is in close touch with all other managers. I have recommended you to him whole-heartedly."

Michael stared at him, then burst into tears. To go to Naples with Father Dolphin waiting for him, to begin his stay there under the auspices of the Ambassador was one thing; to be sent to some unknown manager in Florence, to "sink or swim" was another. He felt lonely, abandoned and apprehensive. Manfully he fought down his tears, and gained control of his emotion.

"Maestro, I am so grateful to you that words fail me. I have only one thing to offer you as a proof of my thanks —my pianoforte which my father gave me when I left Ireland. I only wish that it were made of gold, then it might be worthy of you. Please accept it."

Years later, at a house in Merton, Kelly—the celebrated Kelly—was dining with Emma, Lady Hamilton. With them was that little, modest sailor, Horatio Nelson. Speaking of Naples which they all knew very well and loved, the great sailor said, "I have often heard you spoken of by your master, Aprile. He told me that you gave him your pianoforte when you left. He said that nothing in the world would make him part with it, and that he was proud to think that he had been your master."

So Michael left Sicily, and Aprile gave him thirty gold ounces, about twelve pounds, and generously paid his passage to Leghorn. The voyage was terrible,

Stromboli was in eruption, the wind howled and the rain beat down. The Sicilian sailors wept and prayed to their saints for protection. Apparently their prayers were answered, for the storm abated and they sailed into Leghorn under a gentle breeze, and with the sun shining brightly.

Michael was wearing a Sicilian *capote,* a full cloak, and his fair hair hung down over its folds. Standing on the quay was a young man, thin, good-looking and tall, and beside him a young, vivacious and charming looking girl. Michael watched them and felt certain that they were not Italians; he judged by their dress and their manner that they were English. As he drew nearer to them, he heard the girl say, "Look at that girl dressed in boys' clothes." He realized that—as is common with English people travelling abroad, she believed that he was a—foreigner.

He turned to her and said, very clearly and distinctly. "No, you are mistaken. I can assure you that I am a real *he* animal, and completely at your service."

The girl threw back her head and laughed, the sound was so clear, musical and unaffected that Michael was entranced. As she laughed her whole charming face lit up. There was humour, warm-heartedness in her expression. The young man with her laughed too, but in a more restrained fashion. Michael came closer to them, and in a very short time they were all talking and laughing. From then the three were firm friends, they liked him, he liked the young man, and knew that he had fallen instantly in love with the girl.

They were Nancy and Stephen Storace; he a brilliant composer, who was already classed with Mozart and Purcell, she was—though not yet fifteen—the *prima donna* at the Comic Opera at Leghorn.

Not only was Stephen Storace a brilliant musician and composer, his brain was of the first class, years later Sheridan was to say of him that if he had taken to the law instead of to music, he might have been Chancellor of the Exchequer. So on the quay at Leghorn began a friendship which was to last for the remainder of the lives of these young people, and for Michael Kelly a new chapter of his life.

CHAPTER SIX

MICHAEL could not have found two friends who were more staunch and better fitted to help him in his career. They were the children of a Neapolitan, a double bass player of considerable standing who had married an Englishwoman. Both Anna—though she was always called Nancy—and her brother lived for music as well as living by it. Michael's quick and unexpected retort on the quay at Leghorn, had amused them, for they both possessed a great sense of humour. They asked him to come and dine with them, and their warm-hearted hospitality touched Michael deeply.

Stephen was about the same age as Michael, but more sophisticated and already well established in the world of music. His quiet, musical voice gave Michael real pleasure, he longed that this young man should go on talking— with frequent interruptions from his vivacious sister. While Michael listened to Stephen, his eyes wandered continually to Nancy. He thought that he had never met anyone who appeared to have so much zest, to enjoy everything so completely, to be so ready to laugh and in a flash, should the conversation change, her beautiful eyes grew soft and serious.

Michael's one thought which emerged clearly as the evening passed was:

"I want the brother to be my friend, I want the sister —ah, to love me."

He watched her beautiful movements, her expressive hands, and knew that the pictures of Neapolitan and

Sicilian beauties were fading rapidly from his mind. She was a few years younger than Michael, but she and her brother—his own age—had accomplished so much. They were firmly established, people to be considered, listened to, and sought after. The room where they dined was luxurious, richly furnished, and the table was laid with shining silver.

Michael sighed, and Stephen Storace looked at him sharply. Michael was to find out later that Stephen possessed an almost uncanny trick of sensing what went on in the minds of others. His heart was as soft as his intelligence was keen.

He smiled at Michael, "I know, my friend, it's a great career—singing—but the early stages are—hard going. I have heard of you, we have both heard of you, haven't we, Nancy?"

"Yes, indeed," she said eagerly, "we heard of what you did in Dublin, of your success, and of how when you set sail for Italy, the ship was attacked by pirates, and only through your courage and the fact that the captain of the pirates was an old servant——"

Michael blushing furiously expostulated, "No, no, Miss Storace, it was nothing in the least like that! I did nothing courageous, as a matter of fact I burst into tears when I saw a man attack the case of my pianoforte with a hatchet——"

"But you did make a great success in Dublin," Stephen said, "that we know to be true for Mrs. Arne told us when we were in London last."

Mrs. Arne—Michael's "Clarissa" to his "Lionel". How long ago it all seemed, as if it had all happened in another life. How deeply he had imagined himself to be in love with her, and how quickly all memory of her had faded—until this moment he had not thought of her again. Even now, he found it difficult to visualize her!

Stephen, whose keen eyes possibly sensed Michael's embarrassment, went on: "You've done well, stupendously well, but it is bound to be difficult until you are really firmly established. Once you have had a first class contract, become known in the big opera houses, everything will be plain sailing. You'll have security, and then even if for a short time you are without an engagement, you won't be oppressed with the idea of money running short. That's what I believe ruins so many careers—that lack of security, that's what drives artistes, yes, and first class artistes to accept engagements which are not good enough for them."

"Keeping the wolf from the door," Michael said.

"Exactly, and very unpleasantly that same wolf can howl! Oh, Nancy and I have known all that, only we've been lucky——"

His sister protested, "You've not been *lucky*, Stephen, you deserve and have worked for all the success that has come to you." She spoke so warmly and affectionately, that Stephen stretched out his hand and laid it on hers.

"Most generous of critics, Nancy." Then turning to Michael, he said, "Don't think that I am over curious, or intrusive, but—well, how is the financial situation at the moment?"

Michael cupped his hand round his ear, "I can hear the wolf howling in the distance! Not so very distant either."

Immediately the two Storaces began to make plans as to how money could be earned for Michael. The three young people, Stephen so much older than his years warranted, thin, earnest, and intent, the fine lines of his face lit by the candles which burnt in the branched candle-sticks, his sister—eager and ready to throw herself whole-heartedly into any project, and young Kelly listening to the plans which his two friends were making on his behalf. The light caught his bright hair, and made him look younger than he was.

It was an interesting picture, the big, well-furnished room, the gleaming white cloth on the table, the ruby depths of the wine throwing patches of colour on the cloth. The three young people, all so determined to carve out successful careers, two of them—in fact, well on the way to success, the third filled with hope and expectancy.

"What do light pockets matter," thought Michael, "when at every turn I seem to meet such good and generous friends?"

Stephen said, "Yes, that's the idea! A concert for a rising young singer. The people from the opera will be happy to give any help they can—and there are some fine artists. We must enlist the good offices of the British Consul, the Grants and the Frasers, those brothers of Perdita Robinson—" he snapped his fingers. "The name has escaped me."

Nancy, her eyes shining, her lips parted, said, "The Darby's."

"That's it, the Darby's. Oh, we'll do the thing in style! Now, Michael, it's time we broke up this happy party. Come round in the morning, yes, Nancy, I was going to say it, as I can see by your face so were you—come to breakfast at half past eight."

"I don't know why you should both be so kind to me," Michael stammered, "ever since I began to learn to sing, I seem to have met with the most astonishing kindness everywhere."

Nancy laughed, a sound which Michael thought was like silver bells chiming, "Even the captain of the pirates!"

Stephen patted his shoulder, "Thank your Irish charm, my boy."

Michael walked back to his modest room, his heart felt warmed and happy, his mind filled with thoughts of Nancy Storace. He laid awake for a long time—or what seemed to a boy of seventeen—a long time, his hands clasped under his head, thinking of her, trying to make a picture of her in his mind.

Was she as lovely as he imagined, or was it that her innate goodness of heart, her charm, her dancing eyes made one imagine her to be more strictly beautiful than she actually was? She seemed to radiate life and vitality, he had never heard her sing, but judging by her speaking voice it must be a joy to do so. She had told him that she had studied, as he had done, with Rauzzini, and Michael remembered how that master had insisted upon the importance of perfect enunciation.

"The music was written to sing," he had said, "but also the words were written to be heard, clearly and with distinctness. Never, never forget this. Artists who disregard the lyrics—rob the writer of his just due."

Sleep began to weigh his eyelids, his eyes closed as he murmured, "Leghorn, I shall always be grateful to you—for this—meeting."

Stephen and Nancy worked untiringly, and Michael felt proud to be introduced to many well known people through their auspices. The young people made an excellent impression everywhere—Stephen, serious and intelligent, Nancy so full of charm, and the slim Irish boy so attractive and modest, blushing like a girl when either of his companions praised his work and predicted his success.

The concert was wonderfully patronized, and Michael was given great applause. Nancy told her brother that he was a genius.

"You'll hear more of Master Michael Kelly, what a beautiful voice!" she said.

"Indeed, I agree. I only hope the women won't spoil him."

Nancy herself sang, she was adored by audiences in Leghorn, and whatever she sang delighted them. Michael listened entranced. Her movements were so graceful, and you felt that she enjoyed the pleasure which her audience showed. Stephen too, had a good and well-trained voice and this popular brother and sister did much to ensure the success of the concert. Michael left for Lucca with nearly forty pounds in his pocket.

He supped with the Storaces on his last evening in Leghorn. Stephen was called away on some business, and Michael was left alone with the girl who had grown to mean so much to him.

"I've been so happy here," he said.

"We shall meet again—quite soon. I go to Naples, then to Venice. Ah, how I long to sing in Venice! Oh, we shall meet, and—" she laughed "share our triumphs."

Michael leaned forward across the table. He longed to take her hand in his, to feel its softness and smoothness against his fingers.

"Nancy," he said, "dear Nancy. I wish that one day we might—share everything. Don't forget me, asthore, think of me sometimes, and the knowledge that you spare me a thought—at long intervals—will make me work harder. The future's ours darling—yours and dear

Stephen's and mine. You know that I love you, don't you?"

She smiled at him, a wide smile which carried no sting with it.

"Mickie, we're all very young, scarcely more than children. You're a fine artist at seventeen, so is Stephen, I'm a *prima donna* before I'm sixteen. We've all got to establish ourselves, to show that our voices, our musicianship are not just—flashes in the pan."

"Yes, but I shan't change, Nancy!"

"I don't think I shall. Whatever happens, you and I shall always be friends, great friends. If—later—that friendship should ripen—develop into something else— well, we'll talk about it then."

He protested, "I couldn't love you more than I do at this moment."

She looked at him wisely, "Mickie, love at seventeen is one thing, later it is a—yes, a different kind of love. Rosebuds are beautiful, but they haven't the scent of a full blown rose, my dear."

He left for Pisa the next day, with a letter of introduction to a well known tenor. He was kind and hospitable, but Michael felt lonely without Nancy and Stephen. He thought of her so often, wove fantastic stories in his imagination about their possible future together, of how they would sing Stephen's music and share triumphs everywhere.

He moved on to Florence where he presented his letter of introduction to Campigli who, impressed by Aprile's praise, offered Michael the engagement as leading comic tenor at the Teatro Nuova. For a season of ten weeks, he offered twenty-three pounds. It was not particularly generous, but living was cheap and Michael managed to find a rooming house for theatrical and operatic artists, where he could live in reasonable comfort, if not luxury, for one pound fifteen shillings a month!

Kelly loved Florence, the beauty of the place entranced him, he had introductions to all the English there, and in those days, it was the correct thing to make much of visiting artistes. In addition Michael's manners, appearance and above all his voice were passports to the English society in Florence.

He worked unceasingly, rising early—he was having his breakfast of coffee, rolls and fruit by six o'clock. If a rehearsal was ordered he was at the opera house by nine, having already done an hour's vocal exercises. The rehearsal over he wandered out to a cheap café with some of the company and took coffee. Then, going off alone, he would walk through the lovely squares, gaze with admiration at the statues, and so make his way to the Ponte Vecchio, where on each side of the bridge were the jewellers' and goldsmiths' shops. He would halt and stare into the windows, at the results of gold and silversmith's art, at the precious stones so exquisitely set, and imagine which things—were he rich—he would buy for Nancy Storace.

Apart from his own work she filled his thoughts. Michael was growing up! His sudden infatuation for Mrs. Arne, his dalliances with Neopolitan beauties were nothing. They had left no memories. His thoughts were forever turning to that vivacious and charming girl he had met at Leghorn.

He could imagine so many things which might happen. He had no illusions concerning his voice, it was growing better and stronger every day. He imagined himself standing outside some great opera house, listening to the comments of the people who read the notices of the forthcoming operas.

"Look, Nancy Storace and Michael Kelly! That's not to be missed." or "Nancy Storace—well she's Nancy Kelly really, for she and Kelly are married—and devoted."

It must happen! If work, application, and artistry could fit him to stand on the stage by her side, to entrance an audience with their voices, there were no sacrifices he was not willing to make.

So Michael Kelly wandered about Florence, another Dante meeting his Beatrice—in spirit—everywhere. In his dreams, they always met finally at the opera house, standing there listening to the plaudits of the audience.

Back to his theatrical lodging house, to eat the good if not elegant food, he would laugh and tell stories of his native Ireland, happy in the knowledge that he could not only please his listeners by his voice, but by his sense of humour and his ability to tell gay and laughter provoking stories.

A siesta, for the heat of the day was fierce, and he lay stretched on his bed, his shirt drenched in sweat, his eyes closed, longing for the cool, humid breezes which blew over Dublin. Then, a swill of cold water, delicious, refreshing and yet causing a slight shock as a sudden transition from the intense heat, a quick towelling, a cup of black coffee and it was almost time to go to the opera house.

He was, all his life, meticulous regarding his make-up, the dressing of his wigs, and the care of his clothes. He liked to be in the theatre at least an hour before the performance. More, he liked to wander into the green

room and to exchange the gossip of the day with his
fellow artistes.

At last, the performance ended, the applause still
ringing in his ears, he would return to his dressing room,
with the greatest care remove every sign of stage make-up,
don his elegant clothes and calling a *fiacre* drive to one of
the houses to which he was bidden. Lord Cowper, Sir
Horace Mann, a wealthy Polish prince who was a patron
of the arts, and always they clamoured that he should sing.

One evening Giuarduci, the famous male soprano,
came to him.

"You have a maestro in Florence, Master Kelly?"

"No, sir—I studied last with Maestro Aprile."

The Italian raised his hands, "Ah, that I should dare
to make an offer to someone who has been a pupil of
the great Aprile. But," he wagged his fingers, "if you wish
for lessons—come to me."

Michael bowed and smiled, "Maestro, I am working,
I can make a living, thanks to Signor Campigli, but—
lessons would stretch my purse too far. I am flattered that
you should have even thought of offering me such an
honour."

The plump white hands sawed the air again, the dark
eyes shone with protest. "Did I speak of payment? Ah,
Master Kelly, 'take the goods, the gods provide you'.
Come to me, together we shall add polish and knowledge
to that voice which God has given you. No?"

So Michael had more lessons from the stout Italian,
and knew that all this instruction from the best masters
procurable was doing good to his voice.

One evening when he was not singing, one of the
artists asked him, "Have you seen the King, Michele?"

"The King? Of Naples—yes."

"The King of England, Charles Edward Stuart."

Michael's naturally romantic spirit was fired. He had heard and read of The Young Pretender, the handsome young man who won the hearts of all the Scottish people, who met with success, and then disaster.

"He's here, in Florence?" he was almost breathless.

"Indeed, yes. He loves the theatre—the opera—though why I cannot imagine. In Florence there are ten theatres—yes, ten! He has a box permanently reserved for him at each one. To-night he is coming here. Be ready and see him."

Michael while passionate concerning his own country, was yet a complete romantic, and the thought that he was to see, and at close quarters, the Young Chevalier was almost too much for him. He was there in the vestibule, eager and waiting. A chariot drove up, with footmen standing behind, and another sitting beside the coachman, all wearing the royal blue and gold uniform.

The door of the chariot was opened, Michael held his breath. A tall man, magnificently dressed was assisted out by two of the footmen. It was evident that he had been astonishingly handsome, though now his face was heavy, the eyes dull and the fine mouth slack. He moved with great difficulty, the footmen almost propelling him forward, while he dragged his feet with difficulty.

Michael sweeping his hat to the ground bowed very low. The heavy eyelids lifted, for a moment the eyes seemed to light up.

"Who is this?" the voice was thick and blurred but Michael could realize that once it had been clear like a clarion call.

He answered, "Michael Kelly, sire, a poor singer from Dublin."

"Dublin, eh? God, the Irish can be unpredictable! But," a faint smile flickered about the lips of the well cut mouth, "they're gay."

"My dutiful respects, sire."

The Prince snarled at one of the footmen, "Hold me up, damn you! A singer, eh? What's your name?"

"Kelly, sire."

"Come and sing to me one evening. I adore music."

"At your command, sire."

"Gregson, take the address of this—this artist. I'll send a message."

Again, Michael bowed, "Might I suggest, sire, that you send—*commands*?"

"Very few people remember that in these days. I shan't forget." He held out a swollen, gouty hand towards Michael, who bending his knee kissed it respectfully. The husky voice went on, "Get on, you lazy hounds, get me to the box."

Michael watched his progress, heavy, ungainly, almost incapable, he was assisted to his box, where he collapsed into an arm-chair. The orchestra began to play the overture, before the curtain rose Prince Charles Edward Stuart sat there asleep, his chin sunk on his chest.

Two days later a message came. The Prince commanded Michael Kelly to present himself at the palace and both take wine with His Highness and sing to him. Michael had thought a great deal of Charles Edward, he had remembered his history—and not so very long ago after all, the gouty old man had been the idol of Scotland. The sight of him had roused people to a frenzy, he had received love, admiration, adulation. Now he lived obscurely in Florence, half forgotten except as a romantic figure who could never spell the word "sword"!

He finished his performance, hired a *carrozza* and drove to the palazzo. He was admitted, gave his name, and was ushered up the great marble staircase by a flunkey in the blue and gold livery. The place smelt of dust, Michael felt that if you shook the curtains the dust would fly in clouds, that if you trod too heavily on the thick carpets, or sat too heavily and suddenly on the magnificently upholstered chairs, you might be half suffocated.

He was announced. A great salon, magnificently furnished, and still that sense of decay and neglect. The Prince sat in a huge carved chair, dressed in a suit of purple velvet trimmed with gold. But the suit was improperly brushed, and the gold was tarnished.

The heavy eyelids lifted, the swollen hand was outstretched.

"Ah, our Irish nightingale!"

Michael kissed the outstretched hand—all his life he was to have a love for royalty—and said, "Here at your command, sire."

Charles Edward turned to one of the gentlemen present. Michael assessed them. A shabby lot, their elegant clothes worn almost threadbare. He summed them up immediately. "Hangers-on."

"Here's an Irishman," said the Young Chevalier, "who knows his manners. I'm glad to see you, Kelly."

With that engaging smile, Michael answered, "Sire, I am both honoured and entranced."

"Hey, you lazy dogs, bring some refreshment for Mister Kelly. He's been entertaining all Florence this evening. Gad, didn't I see him two—or was it three?— nights ago?" The lackeys brought dishes of heavy silver, but tarnished and unpolished, they brought decanters of wine, finely and beautifully cut, but lacking that gleam which belongs to well tended glass.

Michael was hungry; when he was singing he took nothing after his cup of coffee at four. It was now almost midnight.

The sandwiches were excellent, the wine superb, and he fancied that some of the rather seedy gentlemen eyed him enviously. As for the two ladies who were present, their clothes looked as did the carpets and hangings of the salon, as if they needed a good, and muscular beating. Neither of them interested him, his attention was fixed on the Young Chevalier.

He had drunk a considerable amount of wine, and his eyes had brightened, and his manner become more animated. He was talking in a voice which had suddenly lost much of its huskiness.

"Ah, I'd give something for an appetite like yours, Kelly. But you're young, you've your life before you! Ah, it's wonderful to be young, filled with hope. Years ago, before you were born, I knew hope, but since I've grown older she has waved her hand and—departed. There! Have you eaten enough? No, have more, these trifles were prepared particularly for you."

"Sire, if I am to sing to your Highness——"

Charles Edward nodded, and ordered a footman to refill his glass. The rest of the company were all drinking and when the dishes which were prepared for Michael were removed to a side table, Kelly watched how they all gravitated towards them.

"Do you require someone to play for you?"

"Sire, thank you, but I can accompany myself."

"Ah, splendid—these women play so badly. There! Music!"

He sat down at the magnificent pianoforte—the woodwork needed a polish and the keys were not too clean—and began to play. His young, clear voice filled the great splendid, dirty room. He chose his songs at random—Italian songs redolent of love, and sentiment, he sang two French songs, and then—greatly daring—two songs from his own country, one of which was his much loved "Believe me if all those endearing young charms".

He ended, the shabby gentlemen and the two dusty looking ladies were drinking wine with their backs to the pianoforte, Charles Edward Stuart was asleep.

The cessation of the music must have wakened him. He raised his head, the heavy lids lifted, and he smiled at Michael.

"Delicious. Quite delicious." The eyes lit up suddenly and Michael saw in a flash the fascination which this man must once have possessed. "I fancied that you might have sung, 'Wha i' the world hae we gotten for a king—'Ah, never mind—some other time." He bawled suddenly, "Gregson, bring that velvet bag, and the case. Michael Kelly, thank you for coming, another glass of wine? Yes, I shall ask you to join me."

There was a stir among the footmen, they rushed away with empty decanters, Charles Edward lay back in his chair, watching his "hangers-on", his eyes—suddenly steely—"You've finished the lot, eh? It's like you!"

Michael said, "Sire, there's a poet in your country, Scotland, and he writes some charming words, set to admirable music. Might I sing one more song for you, sire?"

"A Scottish song, Kelly?"

"It is, sire."

"No, no," the gouty hands signalled a negative. "Scotland belongs to the past for me. They may drink to me as 'The King over the water'—for the ultimate good of Scotland. Ah, the wine!"

They drank, the wine was wonderful and it was surprising to see how the Prince seemed to revive after it. "I wasn't asleep, Kelly. I was listening. Old men listen better with their eyes closed—" he grimaced, "I like to shut out—this. It's a beautiful voice, and I thank you. Ah, Gregson—that's right." He held out to Michael a red velvet bag, and a case which he flicked open. "It is nothing, a small watch made in France. Like most of you Northern people I suppose that you carry an enormous clock at the end of a thick chain. And the bag—ah, well, it may be useful. There, good-night, and it was exceedingly pleasant to listen to you. Another glass of wine? Yes?"

Michael drank his glass of wine, and with the knowledge that his head was reeling a little, bent his knee and kissed the puffy hand.

"The proudest hour of my life, sire," he said.

Charles Edward chuckled, "You're still very young! Good-night."

Out in the street it was good to breathe the cool air of the night—night! It was already after two o'clock. Michael walked back to his lodgings, his mind filled with impressions.

That man, old, bloated, infirm had been the spur to so many gallant deeds, the inspiration for so much self-sacrifice and acts of devotion. The last—but one—of the Stuarts, and his younger brother a cardinal. With them the line was ended, except for distant members who would never raise the Stuart banner in England. What a contrast, Henry, Cardinal York who had never fired the imagination of the people, who was known to be Godly, kind, and to possess a sense of humour, had always shunned intrigue, and abhorred politics. His brother, who had been gifted by nature with everything which the Cardinal lacked, and without the qualities which his brother had, was living in squalid splendour surrounded by "hangers-on", by people who were of no great importance. The flame which had burnt in him was dying low, flickering to extinction.

He carried away with him a recollection filled with great sadness. When he reached his lodgings he examined the watch, it was a beautiful enamelled toy, of exquisite workmanship. In the velvet bag were coins which represented twenty pounds.

In the morning, Michael sent a letter of thanks to the Prince, but Charles Edward must have lost interest, Michael was never bidden again to the big, splendid, shabby, dusty palace.

CHAPTER SEVEN

THE season at Florence ended, and little Kelly had to seek
another engagement. He went to Bologna, and had here
and there trifling engagements. He went to Venice,
where he was promised a contract and on arrival found
that the manager of the theatre had absconded because his
funds had run out.

The *prima donna,* Signora Palmini returned to Bologna
but Kelly was left in Venice. Luckily his allowance from
his father arrived in time to make life possible, for he was
down to his last pound. His mind still turned to Nancy
Storace, who was gaining fresh laurels everywhere. He
wrote to her constantly, telling her of all the trivial
things which went to make up his life when he was out
of an engagement. She was a bad correspondent, and
usually he received a long letter from Stephen, and a
message from Nancy would be added as a postcript.

How eagerly he read them, poor lad, trying to find in
their warm affectionate phrases something which would
show him that she returned—in a lesser degree—the love
which he felt for her.

He loved Venice, which seemed to him to be the
embodiment of all that was lovely. A veritable fairyland.
He wrote, later, "Venice! dear, beautiful Venice! Scene
of harmony and love."

Venice has always been in Italy *"La grande signora"*
and that was how Kelly found her. The people were kind
and hospitable, they were gay and had a passion for music
and pageantry. He lived carefully, even poorly, but found

114

happiness in the beauty of the wonderful town, which is more than a town—Venice is a world on its own.

Sitting one day in Saint Mark's Square, allowing himself a glass of wine at Florian's, the place was very crowded, and a gentleman—not very young—came to his table and asked with great courtesy if he might occupy a place there.

"Naturally, signor."

Michael noticed that several people who passed glanced, with obvious interest, at his table. The stranger did not speak. He was not old but he looked old. Michael thought, "He might have lived a hundred years, and lived every one of them to the full."

The face was that of a clever man, the forehead well and even nobly developed, the formation of the head was almost splendid, the mouth was both sensual and bitter. The chin jutted out like the prow of a ship. Michael looked at him and indulged in one of his favourite pastimes—speculation.

A man passing, stopped at their table, and spoke.

"Ah, Signor Casanova, I'm glad to see you back in Venice."

The man raised his eyes, they were cold and very hard, but Michael glimpsed in them a gleam of humour.

"Ah, Achille! Yes, they have kindly permitted me to return—but I must be careful never to speak a word against the laws of Venice, never to joke about matters which may appear to me to be archaic. In short, I must walk warily. Well, well, it will be a new occupation for Casanova to learn to hold his tongue."

Michael's eyes widened. So this was the fantastic, almost fabulous Casanova, who had escaped from the dreaded "Leads", who had been banished from Venice, and then permitted to return under promise of good behaviour. Here was the man who was reputed to have indulged in a thousand love affairs, who was said to be irresistible to women, and who possessed a brain which was sharp as a razor.

Presently Casanova said, "You are not an Italian, signor?"

"An Irishman, sir. A singer."

"You're very young?"

"Nineteen, sir."

"Are you clever?"

"No, sir. I have a good voice, I understand the principles of music, I have been taught well, but—otherwise, no, I am not clever."

Casanova considered him gravely, "You are clever," he pronounced, "clever in knowing that you are not—intellectual. To know one's limitations is a great thing. I have never known mine! I have always imagined that I knew everything, and to a certain extent I have been right but where did that belief lead me? Where did it lead me? To prison, banishment from my beloved Venice, and into more scrapes—" he laughed, emitting a sound which was, so Michael thought, like dried peas rattling in a leather mug— "than I can conveniently remember. Old men are apt to grow sententious, which is quite unforgivable to the young. How your Shakespeare's Polonius must have bored his son with his advice! Yet as advice goes it was good. Only no-one ever takes advice! They may listen, and say, 'Yes, yes, indeed,' but in their hearts they say, 'Silly old fool!'

"A singer, eh? 'If music be the food of love, play on'. You see I know your Shakespeare. But, remember 'How sour sweet music is, when time is broke, and no

proportion kept!' Remember that—'proportion kept'.
But who remembers to keep—proportion? We're
greedy, the majority of us. We don't wish to sip delicately,
we long to *gorge* ourselves in what is pleasurable. *Dio,* I
am talking like Polonius—and to a little Irish boy!"

"Signor, it is interesting."

The cadaverous faced man laughed, "Ah, so it should
be. You are talking to Casanova. To-day, imprisoned,
banished, neglected. But—" he paused impressively, "one
day, my name will be known all over the world." Again
that rattling laugh, "Known if only as a byword for
men who—loved life. There, I have finished my
wine——"

"Signor, allow me to offer you another glass,"
Michael was eager. He had not so many people to talk to,
and even though there might be a strange, rather sinister
atmosphere which clung round this man, he was attracted.

Casanova bowed, "I shall be happy." The wine was
brought, and for another fifteen minutes Michael listened
to the conversation of a man who was witty, well-
informed and—a complete rake.

"You know something about women, Irishman?"

Gravely Michael answered, "Signor, at this moment I
am deeply in love."

"You've slept with her?"

Kelly stiffened, "Signor, forgive me, but I cannot
allow——"

"Pooh! In love! Spend a night—or a day for that
matter—with a woman, and you know whether you love
her or whether you loathe the sight of her. Mind, the
love may not last for long, but—ah, these romantic
adorations! They are born in the mind, possibly the
heart, but they must be hammered into reality—they

must be tested, translated by the physical. Remember that, Signor Irishman."

Suddenly Michael experienced a revulsion. He met the eyes of Casanova and found them hungry, avaricious. To think in the company of this man of Nancy Storace made him shiver.

Casanova was smiling, a strange, twisted smile, and Michael felt that he was ready to embark on subjects which he knew would repulse him. He was innately decent, and if there had been times when he had indulged in small follies, he had never felt able to discuss them with broad humour or salacious relish. His face flushed, and calling the waiter he paid his score, bowed to Casanova and rose.

"Permit me, signor, I have an appointment."

"With a—signorina, eh? Be careful in Venice. There is jealousy everywhere."

"My appointment is with an impresario, signor."

"They're all rogues."

Michael bowed again and walked away through the great square, with the lovely mosaics of Saint Mark's shining like jewels, the figures standing ready to strike the hours on the great clock, and with the pigeons strutting and preening themselves almost under the very feet of the passers-by. It was a relief to turn his mind to the loveliness round him, to stand at the west end of the square, and contemplate the beauty which lay before him. The talk with Casanova had left a nasty taste in his mouth! The cold eyes, the hard but sensual mouth, the strange rattling laugh which held no mirth. He walked back to his very modest lodgings, feeling depressed and unhappy.

There his mood changed, for there was a letter from Manuel the owner of the beautiful opera house at Brescia.

He offered Michael an engagement to sing there during
the great Brescia fair. The beautiful Ortabella was to be
the *prima donna*. Michael had met this lovely woman, and
she had been kind and very gracious to him. The thought
of earning money again, of being able to sing in such an
opera house as that at Brescia, sent his spirits soaring.

He wrote his delighted acceptance, and also a letter to
Stephen and Nancy. He was overjoyed, here he was with a
contract—and a good one for the very peak period of
Brescia's opera season! He left Venice with a heart as light
as his pocket, and travelled by barge to Padua, enjoying
the beautiful scenery which he could see from the deck,
the splendid villas—the summer resorts of rich Venetian
merchants, and the slow moving river Brenta. From Padua
he went by coach to Verona, and on to Desenzano on the
Lake of Garda.

The next stage of his journey was to take him to
Brescia. Rooms had been taken for him at the Albergo
Gambero, and there to his delight he found that the
beautiful and kind-hearted Ortabella was also staying.

The night Michael arrived, Bertini, the manager of the
theatre invited him to dine. Bertini was a good manager
and a man of considerable good sense. He leaned back
in his chair at the end of the dinner and eyed Kelly, a
quizzical smile touching his lips.

"What makes you smile?" Michael asked. "If it's a
joke—share it with me."

Bertini shrugged his shoulders, "It might be a joke,
on the other hand it might be anything *but* amusing. Tell
me, how well do you know La Bella Ortabella?"

"I sang with her when I had my first Italian engagement in Florence. She is one of the most beautiful and also
one of the kindest women I know."

"Other people share your views about her beauty, they also wish that she might be 'kind'—in the sense of—shall we say—granting favours." Bertini told him.

Michael whistled, "I think I could put a name to the person in question, I've already heard of him and his gallantries. *Il Cavaliere Prepotente,* eh? I don't imagine that Ortabella will be granting many favours in that direction."

Bertini laid his hand on Michael's arm, and spoke gravely. "Be careful, don't make an enemy of him. He's dangerous, if anyone offends him in the slightest degree, then—he is out for vengeance. I assure you this is true, Kelly. He has a band of assassins—they call them *sicari* here—they wear his livery, and do his bidding without question. Murder is nothing to them, nothing!"

"But," Kelly's eyes were wide, "can the State do nothing?"

Bertini shook his head, "I believe they have tried by every means in their power. And without success. So, I beg you walk warily, and don't offend this man in any way."

"I'll remember, and thanks for the warning, but," he laughed, "we Irishmen are not particularly cautious!"

The season opened well, with Michael singing the painter's rôle in "Il Pittore Parigino". Brescia took to him, they loved his voice—stronger than ever, and possessing a clarity of tone which roused their admiration. In their beautiful opera house, they crowded to hear him and Ortabella, and in the streets he constantly heard his name whispered as he passed. "Look, the little Kelly." "There goes our tenor, Michele."

He remained on good terms with the dangerous Manuel, though he found his inquisitive questions annoying. Was Kelly comfortable at the "Gambero", or would he prefer that Manuel found him another hotel? No, Michael thanked him, he was perfectly satisfied with the "Gambero".

"What a charming woman Ortabella is!"

"Charming indeed and a splendid artist."

"You are old friends, I believe, Signor Kelly?"

"We have met before—in Florence."

"I suppose that you see quite a lot of her, staying in the same hotel, eh?" this said with something of a leer.

"Not a great deal, I have my friends and she has hers. Besides, she is the great La Bella Ortabella—I am only little Michael Kelly, from Dublin. Her name is made, I am in the process of attempting to make mine, signor."

That night when Michael reached the hotel, Ortabella sent for him. He found her in the greatest agitation, she was pacing up and down her sitting room, obviously deeply distressed.

"Dear Signora," Michael cried, "what is the matter? What has happened to distress you so. Sit down, be calm, and let me get you a glass of wine. Can I be of any help to you?"

She held up her hand in warning, "S-sh! Speak quietly. God only knows what spies that—that *beast* may have hanging about. Sit down, Michele, and I shall tell you. For several days I have known that this horror, this Manuel has wished to offer me his attentions—his most unwelcome attentions, let me say. This evening he came to my dressing room on some flimsy pretext, and said that he wished to talk business. Business! For that reason, he asked that my maid might leave us alone.

"He then," the indignation in her voice grew, Michael

could hear how it shook with anger, although she spoke quietly, "made certain proposals to me. Briefly that I should become his mistress! That I—Ortabella should accept the attentions of that assassin! You can imagine my reply—I allowed him to see how angry I was, how the very idea revolted me. He was furious! He said, 'You refuse the honour which I have offered you!' Michele, imagine it, the *honour*!

"He continued that I had refused this—*honour* because, I had too great a liking for you, 'that vulgar singer' he called you. He went on to say that if my refusal was due to any interference of yours, it would be the 'worst act' of your life.

"Michele, you're young and impetuous, this man has a hatred for you, and believe me—he sticks at nothing. I can protect myself, I am experienced in the world, you're young, without experience. I beg you to be wise, do nothing which can provoke him. I beg you," she laid her hand on his in her earnestness, "I beg you be prudent. Carry out your engagement, carry yourself with circumspection, and dignity. Oh, Michele, I do entreat you to be wise."

Michael nodded, "I promise, I won't provoke him though there is nothing I should like better than to take a horsewhip to him for his impertinence to you, dear Ortabella. How dared he! A *bestia* who rarely shaves, who thinks because he has money he can make such a suggestion to a woman—a famous, and gracious lady—like yourself. But I will be wise—dismiss your fears, and believe that I thank you from the bottom of my heart for your kindness in confiding this piece of villainy to me." He rose, lifted her hand to his lips and kissed it. "Beautiful Ortabella—"

At that moment he could easily have persuaded himself that he was desperately in love with her, then he met her eyes—kind, and very gentle, almost regretful. Perhaps she was saddened at the thought that this boy, with his bright colouring, his charm and his wonderful voice was so much her junior.

"Dear Michele," she said, and leaning towards him kissed him very gently and sweetly on the cheek. "There, remember that I have warned you. Good-night—Go with God."

Michael determined to profit by her warning, but he was only nineteen, and perhaps even a little flattered that Manuel should have believed that he might be having an *affair* with so famous and beautiful an artist as Ortabella. He swaggered a little—and when he met Manuel treated him with an excessive courtesy which was more insulting than coldness or rudeness could have been.

The owner met his smiles and bows with black scowls, and Michael, conscious that he had done nothing to which the man could put any ticket of impertinence, lack of discipline or obvious offensiveness went on his way, smiling happily to himself.

Then one day he went to the great Fair, in company with several other artistes who were appearing at the opera house. There they saw a Neapolitan fortune-teller, who was assuring the crowd that if they gave him a small piece of money, and asked him any question he would give the correct reply, or even foretell the future for his clients. The crowd was laughing, some of them jeering, others impressed by the assurance of the man; Michael turned laughing to his friends.

"Now I shall test him! I have a question to ask." He pushed his way forward to the booth, slipped a small piece of silver into the man's hand, and speaking in a grandiloquent voice, said:

"Most wise and potent astrologer I have a question to ask you. A question which may seriously affect the future of me and my companions. A most weighty question!"

The "astrologer" slipping the coin into his pocket answered, "Ask on, oh fair skinned youth!"

"Tell me, oh, wise man from the East, will the proprietor of the theatre pay me and my companions our salaries when they become due?"

The Neapolitan pressed the tip of a grimy finger against his forehead in an attitude of deep thought and concentration. Then he sighed, and stared at Michael.

The boy, quite conscious that he was indulging in a silly joke, a joke which might have serious results, grinned back at him.

"Not one farthing if he can avoid doing so!"

Michael shouting with laughter rejoined his friends. They enjoyed the joke tremendously, but someone repeated the story to Manuel, who was furious and in a rage told Bertini that—except for the fact that Kelly's absence would interfere with the performances and damage the takings, he would have Kelly assassinated immediately.

Bertini shrugged his shoulders, "What, for a silly joke?"

"A silly joke! Am I, the owner of the theatre to be made game of by this raw foreigner? Who would miss him?"

Bertini answered, "You have admitted that the audience might."

"I can find twenty other tenors if I need them! I'll have revenge on the impertinent scoundrel. I'll show him

if he can make a public mockery of me. I have other scores
against him too. When I set my heart on anything—yes,
anything, may Heaven have mercy on the man who pre-
vents me gaining what I desire. No, let this fair-haired
strutting, over-dressed puppy take care of himself."

Bertini recounted this to Michael that evening. At
first Michael laughed.

"The whole thing is a farce," he said, "I might have
been foolish, but it was nothing. It's well known that
Manuel never pays any debt that can possibly be avoided.
Pooh, my dear friend, what a lot of stir about nothing."

His friend shook his head, "You're wrong, Michele,
this man is bad, through and through. He imagines that
you have robbed him of the favours which Signora
Ortabella might have given to him——"

"Never!" Kelly exclaimed. "She would never have
——"

"I don't doubt that you're right, but remember
Manuel is as full of conceit as eggs are full of meat! He
imagines himself to be irresistible to any woman, and
because the Signora refused his proposals, he cannot
believe that it was because he lacked any attraction
whatever—he always stinks of garlic and stale cognac—
but must find someone—in this case yourself—to account
for her, to him, incredible refusal. I beg you, with all the
seriousness of which I am capable, go and take advice
from your good friend, Conte Momolo Lana. He is a
man of the world, more he is a Bresciano and he knows
the danger of incurring this dreadful man's fury. Go
to-morrow, Michele, and ask his advice. I am not an
alarmist, but I swear to you," he spoke slowly and with
great gravity, "that you are in grave danger."

Michael thought it over, and visited the Conte to

whom he had been given an introduction by some friends
in Venice. Lana was a wealthy and influential man, and
had shown Michael many kindnesses since he arrived in
Brescia. He received him warmly, took the singer into
his handsome library, and ordered wine to be brought in.

"And what brings Michael Kelly here so early?"

Michael plunged into his story, with a laugh, asserting
that he was ashamed to disturb the Conte, but that he was
acting on the advice, "given most seriously" of a good
friend.

"To me it all seems a terrible exaggeration," he explained, "and apart from the fact that I admit I am flattered
that anyone—even this ill-mannered fellow, could imagine
that such an artist as the beautiful Ortabella could show
the slightest interest in me, apart from mere friendship—
the whole thing smacks of fantasy."

The Conte had listened with grave attention, now he
nodded.

"It may seem fantastic. It is, unfortunately, stark
reality. Let me tell you that only a few days ago a friend
of mine was standing in a wine shop, when some of these
paid assassins entered. They pushed him aside, saying,
'Give way there!' and deliberately shot a man who was
sitting there quietly drinking his wine. They made off
leaving the corpse lying on the floor. This is the kind of
thing that can and does go on. My advice to you is that
the sooner you leave Brescia—the better for you. If
anything should occur before you can get away, tell this
Manuel that you are here under my express protection.
If anything should happen to you, tell him that I swear
on all I hold sacred to revenge you."

Michael stammered, "How can I go? I am engaged
for the season."

"Your engagement won't be worth much to you if you're cold clay," the Conte said drily. "Now, listen— here is my plan. The ballet follows the first act of your opera, yes? Then immediately after you make your exit, lock yourself in your dressing room, remove your paint, change into your own clothes. While the ballet is going on, slip out as quietly and swiftly as possible. At the end of the street my travelling carriage, with my valet, Stephano, will be waiting. Drive off immediately—go to Verona. I shall give you a letter to my relation, the Marquis Bevil Acqua. Stephano can return with the carriage once you are safely in Verona."

Michael looked terribly distressed. He had a great respect for his profession, the thought of "letting down" his fellow artists was repugnant to him.

"But my contract?"

"Break it—and break it quickly."

"The opera? To leave it after the first act! What will they do, what will they think of me? I shall be disgraced, no-one will ever wish to sing with me again."

The Conte patted his shoulder, "My dear young friend, I do understand and respect your feelings. But, remember, I beg you, that your life is in danger, and immediate danger. I know this man, I know his vile reputation, his violence and his love of revenge. I beg you to do what I suggest. You cannot fight him——"

"So I must—run away from him" Michael said miserably.

"Unless you want to be knifed in the back, yes."

"But, I have done nothing wrong!"

"You have done a good many things which are wrong in the eyes of Manuel. You are young, you have won popularity, you have gained the friendship of a very beautiful woman—after whom he lusted—and you have made a joke about him in public. Plenty of men have done less, and their bodies lie rotting, believe me."

So poor little Kelly, who was beginning to feel considerably frightened, agreed that the following night he would make his escape. He was to confide in no-one, he was to make his preparations with the utmost care. His trunks were to be left at the hotel and Conte Lana would have them collected later by the invaluable Stephano. Stephano would also call in the morning for a bag containing clothes which he would hide in the travelling carriage. Lana would see that Michael was vindicated.

The next evening when Michael was suffering from what to-day would be called "butterflies in the stomach" he went down to the theatre. As he passed down the corridor Ortabella called to him.

"Michele, is that you? Come in, I want you to share a present which has been made to me." He entered her dressing room, she was smiling, "Two people—old people from Bardolino came to see me. They brought me presents—they are rich but very simple and kindly folk. Look," she pointed to a large basket, "eggs, fresh butter, two fine ducks, and several bottles of wine. The wine of Bardolino is famed! We'll drink to our respective healths, eh?"

The bottle was opened and the wine poured out. Ortabella, raised her glass. She was in great spirits.

"To Michele O'Kelly," for that was what for some reason the Italians had begun to call him, and continued to do so until he appeared in Vienna, when he was billed as "Signor Occheley".

Michael watching this beautiful woman felt his eyes

fill. He was going to leave her and the rest of the company in the lurch, and he felt wretched and ashamed.

"Drink, Michele," she ordered, "I've given you a toast, now give me one."

"To beauty and artistry both wedded to the kindest heart in the world and all embodied in—La Bella Ortabella."

She laughed, "Ah, that clever Irish tongue of yours! There, go and paint your face, *caro*."

He seized her hand and kissed it, "*Carissima* Ortabella, never think ill of me. Believe that I shall always have an explanation which will satisfy you."

She smiled, "We shall meet on the stage presently. Work is waiting for you!"

He mumbled, "Thank you for the wine—thank you for everything."

In the corridor he met Manuel, and realized that the man would suspect that he was coming from Ortabella's dressing room.

Michael bowed, "Good evening, Signor."

"Ah, the Irish nightingale!"

Michael replied, "I don't aspire to be a nightingale, signor. That title belongs to the Signora Ortabella. Where do the nightingales sing as they do in Italy? I am only a humble—what shall I say—thrush or blackbird."

Manuel scowled at him, "They can all get their necks wrung—these birds, remember that!"

The first act went splendidly, Kelly said afterwards to Stephen Storace that he sang with despair in his heart at the thought of deserting his good friends and companions. The curtain fell, there was immediately the hustle and bustle of preparing for the ballet. He rushed to his dressing room, changed his clothes, removed every

E

trace of paint and make-up from his face, threw his cloak round him and opening the door carefully saw that the coast was clear. He walked very quickly down the corridor to the stage door, and without casting a glance at the custodian who sat there, walked into the street.

There, a dark form proved to be Stephano, he swung open the door of the coach, whispered urgently, "Quickly, Signor Kelly—quickly, we have no time to lose!" The door closed, Michael sank back against the cushions feeling exhausted. The coach began to move. They drove through the darkened streets, past Santa Eufemia, then through villages where no lights showed, where everyone was asleep hours ago. Michael knew that the road was infested with bandits, and peering from the window saw again and again small crosses by the side of the road, which indicated that someone had been murdered there. He shivered.

Then, because the moon had risen, he saw a wide path on the surface of Lake Garda. This was Desenzano, the foot of the lake. The calm, shimmering water, the serene light of the moon, the stars which twinkled above the great lake, all served to calm him.

It seemed impossible that in a world where such beauty existed, there should be also hatred, violence and the insane wish for revenge for trifling or even imagined slights.

Miserable as he was, his spirits rose a little. He was leaving it behind, he was going to safety, to meet with ready kindness, and he would follow the path of beauty all his life.

Revenge, hatred, violence should have no part in Michael Kelly's life.

The coach drove on, he caught a glimpse of the "slow

moving Mincio" at Peschiera as they rattled over the bridge; then the long road to Verona, and more sleeping villages. The dark forms of the trees stood like sentinels on each side of the road, the road itself lay before them a broad white ribbon—leading to safety.

At last—Verona, and the dim outline etched by the light of the moon of San Zeno with its tall, graceful campanile.

The coach stopped, Stephano came to the window asking where Michael wished to stay.

"The 'Due Torri'. We have made a good journey, Stephano. Now, I wish you and the coachman to have comfortable beds, and the best supper—" he laughed, "it is nearly breakfast time—that the albergo can provide. To-morrow I shall get horses so that you may return to your gallant master."

As he descended from the coach, Michael staggered. He was terribly tired, and since his cup of coffee, and the wine which Ortabella had given him, he had eaten nothing.

He ordered food for himself and the two servants, "And remember although it is so late, it must be the best that you can provide."

The meal came, it was ample and well cooked. Michael ate with a great appetite, but when they came bringing him cheese, he was sound asleep with his head on the table.

CHAPTER EIGHT

MICHAEL woke late the following morning, rubbed his eyes and for a few moments wondered where on earth he was. Then slowly the events of the previous night came clearly to his memory. He sprang out of bed, dressed—galvanized into immediate action. He hired a good pair of horses to take back Count Lana's coach, and Stephano. He gave the man a good present and also the coachman, these gifts left his pocket sadly depleted, but his heart was light and he wandered out into—what Ruskin was to call later—"the peach blossom city" feeling in some strange way that his fortunes were assured. How and why he did not know. He was without an engagement, he had very little money and yet this belief persisted.

Things were going to go well with Mickie Kelly, he was barely twenty and already he had contrived if not actually to keep himself, at least to obtain engagements and to make valuable friends.

Three days after his arrival he had a long letter from Conte Lana, and his precious baggage. Once again he was able to wear those elegant clothes which he loved, and to know that as he walked in the streets of Verona, people stared at the elegantly dressed young man, and whispered their speculations concerning him.

The Conte told him in the letter of the happenings after his escape from Brescia. When the ballet was over and the second act of the opera due to begin, there was a frantic search for Kelly. The manager sent to his lodgings but no information was forthcoming. The remainder of the opera was played, and the scenes in which Kelly should have appeared were cut.

The Conte had published the account of Michael's departure, and his reasons for leaving. He had this sheet posted all over Brescia, and told Michael in his letter that "the public agree that you did the best and wisest thing. The temper of Manuel is well known, he had boasted to both La Bella Ortabella and Bertini that he would have his revenge on you, and everyone is taking your side."

Michael wrote at great length to Ortabella, offered his apologies and regrets, and later received a letter from her completely exonerating him from any fault in breaking his engagement. Michael's heart rose, he felt happy and confident. He was treated with the greatest kindness by the Marquis of Bevil Acqua and his wife. The Marquis invited him to their beautiful house, and offered him warm hospitality.

Michael said, "What a beautiful place you have here, the gardens, the fountains—it is like some wonderful picture."

The Marquis, an elderly man with a kindly, whimsical smile said, "Yes, everything is beautiful except my name! A name which is hideous in the ears of all good Italians— Drink Water. What an admission! And now, Michele, to everyday matters! How is the purse?"

"Light, sir, as usual."

"We must do something to make it heavier, though at your age a light purse does not make happiness impossible. Let me think! A concert in Verona, eh? We shall begin arrangements immediately."

How kind they all were, these aristocrats with their immense palaces, their army of servants, and their openhearted hospitality. The concert was a great success, and at the end of it Michael knew that he had established himself as a favourite in Verona. The Marquis handed him a purse containing the "takings" which amounted to over thirty pounds. The next day an offer came from Treviso offering Michael an engagement there for six weeks.

Michael told the Marquis of this offer, he smiled and rubbed his thin, brown hands.

"So!" he said, "it is true that success begets success. Go on, little Irishman, from strength to strength. You shall go to Treviso with letters of introduction to people who have a real love for music. You will meet the Signora de Petris who lives for music—and her lover!"

"I wonder, sir, if you have no doubts as to sending me among your friends—and such magnificent friends? What if I proved to be completely boorish and uncouth?"

The Marquis laughed, "No, no, Michele, if I have any doubts concerning any of my friends—then I do not give letters of introduction."

So to Treviso Michael went, and there met the beautiful de Petris. She was not a professional singer, but music was her passion, and her lover Vidiman was a patron of the arts and particularly of the composer Anfossi.

De Petris listened to Michael singing and exclaimed, "This singer and no other must sing with me in the oratorio which Anfossi has composed for Venice. His voice is perfect, exactly what we want. I am sick to death of fat tenors who imagine themselves irresistible. They give themselves airs, and grow black in the face when they have to take a high note!" She turned to Michael, her charming face smiling and friendly, "Signor Kelly, this oratorio is to be given in a private but very beautiful theatre—it belongs to a good friend of ours, Count Pepoli.

I assure you that it is perfect in every way. Now, Signor Kelly, when the season is over in Treviso, will you be ready to accept this engagement for Venice?"

"Gladly, signora. When is the date?"

"Ah, there is the difficulty. It cannot be given until Lent. Will you wait until then?"

Michael thought, he had enough money—thanks to the Verona concert—to see him through. He longed for another sight of his beautiful Venice. He nodded. "Of course, signora. I should be ready to wait for much longer to enjoy the privilege of singing with you."

She clapped her hands, "Vidiman *caro,* let Signor Kelly have the exact date. I know that he will be there."

Michael left Treviso with his pockets well lined with money. He had enjoyed a tremendous success, and decided that he would go and visit Parma, where he had a letter of introduction to no less a person than the Archduchess of Parma, a daughter of the great Empress Maria Theresa.

Sometimes when he thought of these great people who received him, with such unaffected kindness and simplicity, he felt that his head reeled a little. Here he was, the son of a Dublin wine merchant, who however well respected was most certainly not—in society.

When he looked back on his father's dinners and wine parties, on the dining room reeking of tobacco smoke, on the worthy but admittedly rather dull friends, and compared them with the splendid gatherings he had attended —the great rooms, the dazzling lights, the armies of magnificently dressed servants, and the gorgeous jewels of the guests, he wondered if his friends in Ireland would believe that among the guests was Michael Kelly?

The Archduchess was staying at her villa outside the town, so Michael dressed in his most elegant suit of dark

purple silk which he had bought in Brescia, his hair
carefully washed and curled, his shoes shining like ebony
and his silk stockings without the slightest sign of a
wrinkle, hired a coach and drove out to Colorno.

The chamberlain received him; Michael explained
that he had come with an introduction from Treviso,
and was taken at once to the billiards room, where the
Archduchess was playing with one of the musicians of
her private orchestra.

She listened to what her chamberlain had to say, then
turned to Michael, smiling. She loved billiards and nothing
delighted her more than to win which she invariably
did for she played a magnificent game.

"Wait one moment, Signor Kelly," she said, "I am
winning! This man thinks that he can beat me! At playing
the piccolo—yes, I admit, but at billiards—never!
Watch!"

The game finished, she had won easily, and the piccolo
player paid his debt, for the Archduchess always played
for some very trifling sum—a few pence.

"It gives spice to the game," she said. "To play—for
love, is like eating eggs without salt—tasteless. Now tell
me, Signor Kelly, where have you sung in Italy?"

"I sang in Naples, Your Highness."

"Ah, before the King and Queen?"

"At Posilipo, Highness."

"Then to-night, you shall sing before the queen's
sister. Now, who was your teacher?"

Michael said that he had had several, among them
Aprile.

She raised her hands, "Then you had the finest teacher
in the world to-day. Where is that poor, defeated piccolo
player. Ah, Mario, take Signor Kelly with you, and see

that he dines well. Signor Kelly, to-night we shall have a feast of music."

They were very kind to him, those musicians, and the treatment which was given to him was of the most generous. He was taken round the estate, and marvelled at the beauties which he saw. The piccolo player talked to him of the Archduchess, for whom it was evident that he had an immense admiration.

"She is not so handsome as her sister, the Empress of France, nor as the Queen of Naples, but she has a brain which is quite exceptional. As you have seen, she can play billiards with her orchestra, and never for one moment lose her innate dignity. It is she who controls this vast estate, she has all the facts at her finger tips. Her husband—" he shrugged his shoulder, "is well enough. A dried up, pedantic kind of man. They say here that he had only water in his veins, and it would not surprise me. They are always courteous to each other, but they have different bedrooms, and I doubt if he ever strays beyond the four walls of his own room!

"I think that she is glad to be relieved of her—" he laughed, "wifely duties. They must have been exceedingly tiresome and excessively dull. Now she has taken a lover to whom she is devoted."

Michael stared, "The Archduchess——?"

His companion laughed, "Two—to be exact—music and billiards."

That night Michael wore his finest suit. Blue silk, with lighter blue lines running through it. The colour suited his fair hair, and when he surveyed himself in the looking glass, he felt very well satisfied. He would be able to cut a good figure among these great ones of the world.

He went down into the magnificent drawing room,

with the huge mirrors on the walls flinging back its reflexion and making it seem twenty items its real size. Many ladies and gentlemen were waiting there, having dined with the Archduchess previously. The Archduke, thin, desiccated and colourless remained there for a very short time, speaking with the various guests, then excused himself. It seemed to Kelly that no-one missed him.

He sang and the Archduchess played his accompaniment herself; as he wrote to Stephen Storace, "She has a masterly command of the pianoforte, and unlike so many of these people who make effusive offers to accompany you, really did know what she had to do. A very remarkable woman."

The next morning he met her, again in the billiards room. She smiled and that smile redeemed her plain, though strong face.

"You play billiards, Signor Kelly?"

Now, Michael did play the game, and had been assured that he played it very well. He bowed.

"I know the game, Your Highness. I believe that I am but an indifferent performer."

She laughed, a big, hearty laugh which swept away all social barriers.

"Come and try your luck," she said.

Michael records, "She beat me hands down."

When he left, she told him that she had been delighted to have him there. She praised his singing, more—she praised the manner in which he had comported himself.

"Signor Kelly, always keep that pleasant air of modesty which becomes you so well, and which—unfortunately— we find so seldom. Please accept this—" she handed him a purse, and when he tried to refuse it said, "No, no.

Last night you entertained my guests, I ordered the concert—the labourer is worthy of his hire." Again that fresh, kindly burst of laughter. "And," her eyes twinkled, "this morning you lost and had to pay me the amount of our bet on the game. Signor Kelly, leave billiards alone, stick to singing. At one you excel, at the other—well, don't believe what your friends tell you. You Irishmen are too impetuous for billiards. There, may good luck accompany you everywhere."

He drove back to Parma, his mind filled with thoughts of this remarkable woman. A woman so certain of her rank and position that she could afford to be affable without the slightest hint of condescension. A woman who could sum up the mentality of the people with whom she talked, and who knew exactly who might be trusted not to abuse her friendliness.

He stayed the night at Parma, and then took the coach for Venice. His beloved Venice, now more than ever to be desired, because there Stephen and Nancy Storace were waiting for him. His heart beat more quickly when he thought of her—Nancy. She had met with one success after another, she had been to England so Stephen wrote, had come back accompanied by her mother. How he longed to see Nancy again, to spend evenings with her and Stephen, to talk, laugh, and realize that he was— desperately in love.

There was the oratorio of Anfossi to be sung, and for that time he was invited to stay at the splendid villa of Conte Vidiman, where—of course—was the beautiful Teresa de Petris who was to sing with him. It would be complete luxury, she was lovely, but Michael fretted at the time which the rehearsals of the oratorio would take him from Nancy's side.

De Petris had shown him every kindness when they met, indeed without being filled with undue conceit, Michael knew that she was attracted to him. Glances, smiles, and eyes brimming with affection—or desire—had not gone unnoticed by him. No doubt she was deeply attached to Vidiman, but she made no attempt to conceal the fact that she was attracted by the young Irishman with his fresh skin, and his meticulously ordered curls.

He remained only in Venice for a few hours then drove out to the splendid villa. If the villa of the Archduchess had been luxury, this exceeded anything Michael had ever imagined. He was treated with the greatest kindness, his room was filled with beautiful things, the food offered to him would have satisfied Lucullus, and yet he fretted and fumed and longed to get back to—Venice and Nancy.

The oratorio was a great success, Anfossi wrote in special music for Michael and he was offered praise and adulation on every side.

Michael was leaving early the next morning, and Vidiman who paid him what seemed to Michael to be a tremendous fee, spoke to him very warmly, and excused himself because he had to leave immediately, he must be in Verona the next day.

"However, my dear Kelly, I hope that my servants will take good care of you, ask for anything you want, remember you are a very honoured guest in my house. I hope that we may meet again."

De Petris also bade him good-bye, "I may not see you to-morrow, Signor Kelly, I am not an early riser I'm afraid. We must sing together again, I have enjoyed working with you and listening to you."

Michael went to his luxurious room, he heard Vidiman ride away, heard de Petris call from her window bidding him return soon. Methodically Michael packed his bags, for he was particular over such things and very neat in everything he did. His heart felt light, to-morrow he would be back in Venice, to-morrow he would listen to Nancy's adorable laughter, to Stephen's dry comments on all they had seen and done since last they met. How they would talk!

The house was very quiet, the guests had all dispersed. He stood looking out of the window at the splendid park with its fine trees, where the shafts of moonlight lay like splashes of silver in the dark shadows. He was indulging in such dreams as fill the mind of a young man who is deeply in love, filled with hope and certainty that the future will be bright for him—that his hopes might become realities.

A very slight sound made him turn, the door had been closed very softly and he saw that de Petris had entered. She stood there, smiling at him, her eyes very dark and soft.

"Michele," she whispered, "Tell me that you're glad to see me. I had to see you again—and alone."

"But—but—" he stammered, "this is very unwise— I mean if——"

She interrupted him, "Is a woman in love ever wise? You must have seen, Michele, all that my eyes tried to tell you. You must have heard what I was trying to tell you when we sang together! What did the actual words matter? I was singing—other words—in my heart to you. Michele, come and take me in your arms."

"But, Signora, I am distressed beyond words if I have done anything to make you believe——"

She laughed softly, "You have done nothing that was not perfectly becoming! You have been your dear,

wonderful, amusing self, but—oh, Michele, the night is
ours, yours and mine. I am yours! I'll give you—everything!"

He knew that his heart was beating furiously, she was
beautiful, and her *négligée* did nothing to conceal the
loveliness of her figure. He stared at her fascinated and
yet unable to find words in which to speak to her.

She came nearer to him, and he caught her hand
and raising it courteously, but formally to his lips,
kissed it.

"Signora, I am conscious that you have paid me a
great honour, and that had you not trusted me you would
never have come to this room. You must have known
that I am a man of honour, for if I were not—if I were a
gossip, then your own honour would be in jeopardy.
I shall confide in you—to-morrow I return to Venice,
where I shall see again the lady who I hope will consent
to be my wife."

De Petris stared at him, blankly incredulous. "You're
—refusing what I offer you! Or don't you understand?
How could this night, spent with me, affect this—lady?
Michael Kelly, don't be a fool. Look at me!"

She drew her hand from his, and flung open the soft
white gown which she wore, standing before him in all
the beauty of her rounded nakedness. There still remained
in Michael Kelly something of the shyness of his extreme
youth, a good deal of his strictly Catholic upbringing.
Before, as she had stood there with her eyes shining
softly, almost tenderly, she had been beautiful. He knew
that he had—for some moments at least—been tempted.
Now, the sight of her scented flesh revolted him.

He licked his dry lips, "Signora, I may be a fool, but
I am not knave enough to abuse the hospitality of Signor

Vidiman. If you wish to remain here, I beg you to excuse me, I shall return to the salon."

She stared at him, her eyes wide; she was both astonished and angry. With a sudden, almost convulsive movement, she gathered her robe round her.

"You prating *cretin*! You posturing ignorant Irish booby."

Michael moved to the door, she rushed after him, tore the handle from his grasp, opened the door and disappeared down the wide, dark corridor.

Michael undressed and lay down in the cool sheets of his huge bed. He felt desperately tired and yet sleep refused to come. Did all women, then, high or low behave as—years ago—the whore in the Dublin stews had done? The thought revolted him, and he pushed it from him. He didn't believe it! He had a great admiration and affection for women, he had flirted outrageously with many of them, but such very fleeting affairs as those in which he had indulged had been conducted with sufficient decency to make them devoid—to Michael Kelly—of offensiveness and coarseness.

All his life he retained that touch of what might be called prudery, he loved life, already at twenty he knew that he enjoyed the good things which life held. Possibly on occasions he had drunk more wine than was strictly good for him, he spent more money than he should on the fine clothes which delighted him, he gambled too heavily, but the so-called gallantries of the age, which were based on nothing more exalted than sheer lust, disgusted him.

She was beautiful, more she had a voice of great clarity and she used it with considerable artistry. She might have proved a valuable patron with the immense wealth of

Vidiman behind her. A patron! Yes, so long as he had
pleased her in other ways than by singing!

"I can imagine it," Michael thought as he lay there,
"to be engaged to sing here, to go there, to come to heel
when she ordered me, when Vidiman was away." He
shivered with sudden disgust. "A kept man, kept by his
mistress on the money lavished upon her by her rich
lover. Pah!" He sighed, and closed his eyes. Already the
window showed the coming of the dawn. A new day, a
day which would hold Nancy. Nancy with her vivacity,
her bright curling hair, her smile and her innate friendly
dignity and essential decency.

The thought of her soothed him and he fell asleep.

He woke early, shaved and dressed with his usual
meticulous care, and carrying his bags made his way down
the wide stairs. A footman in Vidiman's livery rushed
forward to take his bags, and told him that coffee was
served in one of the smaller salons.

"No-one else is down as yet, signor. The master,
before he left last night gave orders that you are to be
driven into Venice at whatever time is convenient to you.
He said that whatever orders you gave were to receive
immediate attention."

Michael drank his coffee, and ate his fresh crisp rolls
and butter with appetite. All the disgust and even anger
that he had felt last night had vanished like the mists of
early morning. He asked for the coach in half an hour's
time, and was waiting on the steps of the villa when it
came round. He asked to be driven to Mestre, there he
would get a gondola and enjoy the slow, gentle movement as the gondola made its way down the Grand Canal.

He had asked Stephen to get a room for him in the
house where the Storaces were staying; he had written,

"Things are more prosperous with me in these days, fortune has been kind, and I can afford to live in pleasanter surroundings."

His gondola drew up at the quay of the Piazza S. Marco, Kelly called a *facchino,* and gave him the address. He was too excited to walk sufficiently slowly for the porter, burdened with two heavy bags to keep up with him.

"You have the address," Michael said, "I am in a hurry, follow me as quickly as you can."

How good it was to be back, how wonderful everything looked. Past Florian's, where he had once sat with Casanova, under the arch, casting quick glances at the attractive shop windows, and disregarding the importuning of the vendors who wished to show him lace, glass or jewellery. How well dressed the women all looked; even those who were obviously not able to afford elegant clothes, yet looked neat and attractive. The men—except such as were evidently manual workers, wore clothes which were expensive and brightly coloured. There were flowers on the stalls at the street corners, here and there a beggar whined a request for "*carita*"; dark jowled priests, monks, their tonsure just showing like a crescent moon beneath their skull caps, white coiffed nuns, their eyes downcast, their hands folded primly; two officers resplendent in uniform with their spurs and swords clinking and clattering passed laughing and chattering. At a fruit stall where the fruit shone in the sun was a girl buying fruit, and turning to speak to the servant who stood behind her holding a large marketing basket. Michael almost shouted her name, then contriving to subdue his excitement, he hurried forward.

"Signorina Storace!" he swept off his hat so that it

almost touched the ground. She turned at the sound of his voice, her charming face alight with surprise and pleasure.

"Michael! Oh, how delightful. I was just that moment buying fruit for our dinner. There, Maria, you must buy the other things alone, be sure and buy wisely. Signor Kelly will escort me to our lodgings."

She took his arm, and he felt the slight pressure of her fingers as she said in the ingenuous way he remembered so well, "Oh, Mickie, isn't this pleasant! How pleased Stephen will be. Poor boy, he hasn't been well, he is so thin. Mama and I get so anxious about him. He won't rest and when we beg him to do so, he quotes some old man who said, 'Have I not all eternity to rest in!' It makes me so cross!

"Not really cross, Mickie, I could never be really cross with Stephen. And what wonderful things you have been doing! Stephen reads me your letters, such good letters too! That terrible man at Brescia, what a villain. Mickie, tell me—" her face assumed an expression of gravity, but he saw that her eyes were dancing with merriment, "tell me truthfully, had he any reason to be jealous of you—and Ortabella?"

"Nancy, dear Nancy, don't tease! She was very kind to me, and I was and am grateful. But, Nancy asthore, there's only one woman who matters to me. Shall I tell you her name?" he asked.

He saw the colour rise in her cheeks, "No, not now. Here we are at the lodgings. Now to give Stephen and mama a surprise. Ah, here is the *facchino* with your bags."

The man, speaking in the broad Venetian dialect said, "Signor, you went like the wind. I only caught up with you when you met Signorina Storace."

Nancy laughed, that gay sound which was music to Michael Kelly.

"You know who I am then?" she asked.

"Everyone recognizes the Signorina Storace, except the blind men and they recognize her voice when she speaks, or her laugh when she is amused. I thank you, signor," for Michael had given him far more than he would have dared to ask. "Signorina Storace, your dutiful servant." He pulled off his shabby hat and bowed.

Nancy smiled, "I believe every man in Venice is—well bred. Come, Mickie, let's go in."

The staircase was wide, and the handrail well polished. The house, Michael thought, smelt clean. The furniture shone, and the white cloth on the dining table was snowy white, the glasses bright, and the silver well cleaned.

Nancy cried, "Stephen—see who is here!"

Stephen rose from the desk where he was working, and came towards Michael with outstretched hands. How thin he looked! He had always been spare, but now his cheeks were hollow and he looked gaunt.

"Michael, it's splendid to see you again! What a time we shall have listening to your adventures, and recounting our own. Ah, here is mama. Mama, this is our dear friend, Michael Kelly."

The stately lady bowed and said in a slightly deep but very musical voice, "So this is the Mister Kelly of whom I have heard so much. Mister Kelly would like to remove the dust of his journey, I am sure. Your room is prepared, Mister Kelly. Stephen will show you where it is, and by the time you have washed—though—" she laughed, "you look as if you had just stepped out of a bandbox—dinner will be on the table. I hope you are hungry."

"Thank you, Madam. You're sure that I shall not be intruding? If so I can go to some eating house nearby, and perhaps join you for coffee later."

"And have both my children reproaching me all through the meal for being inhospitable to their dearest friend! There, away with you, Mister Kelly."

CHAPTER NINE

For Michael Kelly the days were never sufficiently long. He spent much time with the Storaces, though he had too much delicacy ever to allow himself to become a too frequent guest. They were so hospitable that they would gladly have entertained him at every meal, but often he excused himself on some pretext or other and took his meal at one of the eating houses.

His voice was in splendid shape, he was almost at the height of his career as a singer, Stephen Storace was writing excellent music, and Nancy was the adored of Venice.

At eighteen she was already an accepted *prima donna,* and when she sang at the opera house, the Venetians showered gifts upon her in a manner which was incredibly lavish. So prevalent did this habit become that whenever Nancy sang, her mother stood in the entrance hall of the theatre holding a silver salver. On to this the Venetians threw bracelets, necklaces, rings and purses of gold.

The earnest wish to ask Nancy to marry him was still the first thought in Michael's mind. To him she was everything!

One evening when he and Stephen were alone in the lodgings, he spoke of his hopes.

"Stephen, I want to ask Nancy to marry me," Michael said.

Storace looked up from his book, "Don't, Mickie. Nancy's very young, she's only turned eighteen. She's enjoying all the success which is hers—and rightly.

Wait, my friend. Give her time to grow accustomed to her success. I know that I'm right."

"But," Michael objected, "we're both young. Why shouldn't we enjoy the best years of our lives together?"

"Are you certain that they *are* the best years?" Storace asked. "May they not be the rather heedless years, the too impressionable years? You, like Nancy, have made a success, you're sought after, but—and forgive me for saying this—not to the extent that Nancy is. No, Mickie, try to be patient, give her time to grow up, to understand her real feelings."

Michael sighed, "But, I'm so desperately in love with her. I think of her—literally—all the hours of the day. You think that she likes me, don't you? She was glad to see me when I came back to Venice."

The grave young man, with the heavy, tired eyes smiled.

"She has a real and deep affection for you, Mickie, but whether it is the affection of a sister for her brother," the smile widened, "her successful and very attractive brother, I don't know. I'm certain that at the moment Nancy does not want a husband, she does not even wish to become engaged to anyone. She wants to enjoy her freedom, her success and her popularity. Because of the love I have for you, I say—wait."

Michael Kelly was not a patient young man. He rose and paced up and down the big room, while Stephen's eyes followed him.

"And while I wait, I may lose her!" Michael exclaimed.

"You should take that risk, my friend."

"No, no, Stephen, I can't. I shall ask her to marry me!"

Stephen turned back to his book, "Then you must do

what you think best. I still think that my advice is wise."

"Wisdom and love don't always go hand in hand, do they?"

"No, more's the pity."

The next morning, the sun shone and Michael felt that his spirits were rising. There was a tree in the garden outside the house, and the sight of its green leaves, two sparrows hopping about in the branches, made him feel happy and light-hearted. He asked Nancy to come and take coffee with him at Florian's. He had no rehearsal, neither had she.

"Yes, it will be fun. We shall have all Venice staring at us."

Sure enough all Venice—or a large proportion of the inhabitants—did stare, and speculate about the two good-looking young singers.

"Look, the Storace! With Michael O'Kelly— They say that they're in love—I heard that they were to be married— She's only eighteen, and he is barely twenty. Children! But remarkably successful children— See how he looks at her! Surely it's a romance."

Nancy sipped her coffee, "How I love being here. I feel that we're living in a time which is crowded with happiness and sunshine. There's colour everywhere. Everything in Venice seems to be just a little more beautiful than it is anywhere else."

He watched her, his eyes filled with love and admiration.

"To me," he said, "wherever you are is always a little more beautiful than anywhere else."

Nancy laughed, "Oh, you inveterate Irishman, always ready with a compliment, aren't you? Just a flatterer!"

"I swear that wasn't an empty compliment, Nancy,"

Michael assured her, "it was the sober truth. Darling, you must know how much I love you, how much I hate ever being parted from you. Marry me, Nancy dearest— marry me soon and let's be together for the rest of our lives. Ah, say that you will—please, please promise me."

Her smile faded, she looked at him, her eyes clouded and troubled.

"Michael, there's no man I love more than I love you —you and my dear Stephen. But I won't marry you, not yet anyway. You see we shouldn't always be together, we couldn't be. I might be engaged to sing here, you might be engaged to sing in—oh, London, or Paris. You'd wonder about me, perhaps grow miserable at the separation, I should wonder and speculate about you— we should rub all the brightness, the companionship away.

"Then, again, my dear, we're both—yes, we are— stars. We're going to shine even more brightly in the future. I've heard it said and I think there is a great deal of truth in it, that stars of equal magnitude can't live in complete accord. It's human nature perhaps; we might love each other, but at the same time we might be jealous of each other as artists. Do you see what I mean, my dear?

"I'm young, we're both young, but at eighteen I don't feel that I've seen enough of the world, that I have met sufficient people really to know my own mind as regards falling in love and marriage. Eighteen isn't very old, Michael, plenty of girls are still being taught lessons by a governess, living in the nursery and only allowed to come down to dinner on special occasions. Give me time, Mickie, give me time to understand myself."

He said rather heavily, "You don't tell me to give up all hope?"

"I don't—but I don't make any promises. I don't know if in another two years I may be the same Nancy Storace that I am now. I may have changed—so may you."

"I shall never change," Michael said stoutly, "I shall always feel exactly the same about you. I shall always think of you as everything that is most adorable, desirable and charming. I shall never change, Nancy asthore."

Slowly her smile returned, "If Stephen were here he'd say that statements like the one you have just made are only made—ever—by people who are very young. I've heard him say that so often."

"Yet Stephen is only my age, you'll accept what he says as the truth, but you'll doubt me—because I'm young! Don't I know as much of the world, of my own heart as Stephen can possibly know?" He was almost indignant at the idea.

"Stephen was born older than you, Mickie. I don't think that he has ever been really young, or immature. There, look at the sunlight on the mosaics, look at those strutting pigeons—I've seen some pompous singers walk exactly like they do! Let's have more coffee and be gay, enjoy the sunshine and remember how lucky we are to be young and in Venice—our dear, beautiful Venice."

So Michael vowed that he would be patient and wait, and together they extracted every ounce of pleasure out of their leisure hours in Venice. After the opera they would return home by gondola, instead of walking back through the strange, narrow streets, for the sheer delight of the gentle movement, the play of lights on the waters of the canals, and sit holding each other's hands like two children delighting in some unexpected treat.

Nancy was given a benefit, and the theatre was

crowded, the gifts which were showered upon her were fantastic in their value. Then came a rumour which was later proved to be founded on hard fact. A certain prostitute had come to Venice, and had begun to ply her profession in a house in the Calla di Carbone, the section of the town where "Ladies of easy virtue" were forced to reside. The Venetians had no particular objection to prostitutes, but they must—according to the laws of the state—remain in their own quarter.

The newcomer hung her portrait in the window, this being the customary manner for them to advertise their charms to possible clients. Under the portrait was written in Italian, "This is the portrait of the sister of Signora Storace."

The excitement was intense, the clients flocked to see the lady, money poured in, and the story was soon on everyone's lips. The sister of Nancy Storace, a whore in the Calla di Carbone! Michael heard it whispered in the theatre Benedetto in the green room. Two minor singers were discussing the tale.

Michael spun round, "Phwat's that you're saying?" for when he grew angry he dropped back into using his Irish accent and inflexions. "Phwat's that—repeat that and at wance!"

"It's a story that's going all round Venice, Signor O'Kelly."

"I asked you to repeat the story," he was making a great effort to keep his temper. "Please oblige me by doing so."

Almost unwillingly the men told the story; O'Kelly was known to have a fiery temper, more, he was known to be on intimate terms with the Storaces. Michael listened, his face white and grim.

"'Thank you," he said when the story was told, "I am, as you know, a friend of the Signora, of her mother and her brother. I can speak with authority. Signora Storace has no sister—the only children of her mother's marriage are Stephen, the composer, and the *prima donna* Storace. Make very certain that this business will be investigated, and let me advise you to go to great pains to contradict this vile *canard*. You have my full permission, indeed, I shall make it an earnest request, that should either of you hear this abominable lie again, you will refer the speaker to—Michael Kelly. I'll deal with him—with twenty of them if needs be. Thank you, gentlemen."

That evening when they were alone before Nancy and her mother returned, Michael recounted the story to Stephen.

"What is to be done? It's horrible, they told me that the woman is making money as fast as the mint!"

Stephen considered, "In the morning, we will go early to a lawyer and get his advice, I think, knowing how the Venetians regard Nancy, the authorities will have the wretched woman banished from the town."

They told Nancy when she returned, Mrs. Storace was horrified, Nancy was indignant but faintly amused.

"Mama, all these years you have concealed the fact that Stephen and I have a sister! For shame, mama!"

"Nancy, that levity is ill-timed, my dear. The whole matter is disgusting and disgraceful. Stephen and Michael will visit a good lawyer in the morning. The whole thing must be put a stop to. Imagine if our friends in London heard of this!"

"Yes, mama, I agree. Certainly a lawyer. Shall I come with you to see him?"

"No, certainly not," Mrs. Storace declared, "it would

be most unseemly for you to discuss this matter with
three gentlemen, even if one is your brother. There, let us
dismiss the matter from our minds, and try to forget to
what terrible lengths these vile creatures will go. Thank
you, Michael, I will take some wine—this affair has upset
me."

Very early the following morning the door of the
lodgings opened and closed very softly behind a slim
figure heavily cloaked. There were few gondolas plying
for hire, but as one passed the cloaked figure hailed it
and gave the order: "To the Calla di Carbone, or the
nearest point possible."

The man repeated in amazement, "The Calla di
Carbone! Dio, you know what the district is?"

"I know where I wish to go, I am quite well able to
look after myself."

The man peered at what he could see of the face which
was mostly covered by the folds of the heavy cloak.

"Santa Maria!" he gasped, "the Signorina Storace!"

"And if it is? Just do as I have bidden you. I shall
want you to wait for me, bring me back and I promise
that you shall be well paid. Now!"

The man said stubbornly, "I shall come with you,
Signorina."

What happened no-one ever really knew, Nancy was
seated at the table when her mother entered to take her
morning coffee. She looked at her daughter sharply,
"Your hair is very untidy, Nancy. And what have you
done to your hand?"

Nancy glanced down at her hand, "Oh, that's nothing,
mama. I scratched it. I've washed it, it's quite clean."

Stephen and Michael came in, both intent on the
business of visiting the best lawyer in Venice. As they were

leaving, Nancy said casually, "The picture is no longer in the window."

Stephen stared at her blankly, "Where is it, then?"

"At the bottom of the Grand Canal, my dear."

He walked over to where she sat and said sternly, "Nancy, what have you been doing? If something that is against the law—for even prostitutes have certain rights remember—you may have done yourself more harm than good."

She smiled up at her tall brother, there was mischief in her expression. Michael watching thought that she looked like an impudent child found out in some naughtiness.

"Dear, wise brother," she said, her bright eyes twinkling, "I wanted the picture, I got it, I have it no longer. Now go and see your lawyer. Discuss this business and be thankful that mama forbids my coming with you. You will be able to use all those coarse expressions and improper words which might have brought the blush of shame to my innocent cheeks. There, go along with you both. Come back and report to me—with modifications of course."

As they walked briskly to the lawyer's, for the morning was very chilly, Stephen frowned.

"She's been up to something, Mickie! Where and how did she get hold of the damned picture?"

"God only knows," Michael said, "and He'll keep his own council. If I know anything of her, so will Nancy Storace."

Later Michael said, "Did you notice anything about Nancy?"

Stephen shook his head, "Nothing unusual."

"You're unobservant, my friend. Her hair was

disordered, and there was a long scratch on her left hand."

Storace stopped dead, "Mickie, you don't think——"

"I may think a devil of a lot," Michael returned quickly, "but I'm letting thinking do. If Nancy wants to tell us—she'll do so in her own good time. Be wise and let it go at that, Stephen."

The lawyer was indignant when they told their story, he admitted that he had heard it gossiped about and had wondered why the family of the Signora Storace did not take action. They need have no fear, he would apply to the necessary authorities, and the woman would be banished from the town.

When they reported the result of their interview to Nancy, she took it very calmly, merely saying, "So now that nasty incident is closed—for always."

They never mentioned it again, and where Nancy had been, what had happened remained her secret, shared possibly with the gondolier.

The season was drawing to its close, when Michael was sent for by the Austrian Ambassador to whom he had previously, on his arrival in Venice, presented a letter of introduction. He was received cordially by the Ambassador, one Conte Durazzo.

"How would you like to go to Vienna, Signor O'Kelly," the Ambassador asked.

Michael stared, "I understood that the Emperor had a company composed of French artistes, Excellency."

Durazzo smiled, "The Emperor *had*, but they chose to become impertinent and they are no longer in Vienna."

He told Michael the story. The Emperor treated his artists well, they were given £200 a year, their rooms— "and luxurious rooms"—food, wine and an allowance each day of wax candles—"of the finest quality." It appeared that one day when the artists were at dinner, in a room which looked out on to the palace gardens, they saw the Emperor pass. One of them, with a glass of wine in his hand, rushed out and dared to speak to the Emperor.

"Imagine the impertinence," said Durazzo, "he held out the glass of wine to the Emperor, and said, 'Sire, this is the rubbish which is given to your singers! We have complained, and are assured that it is—Burgundy. Sire, I beg of you to taste it, and I am certain that you will say—as we all do—that it is the worst possible trash!' Think of it, O'Kelly, imagine the abominable effrontery! The Emperor took the glass, sipped the wine with great coolness, then returned it to the expectant artist, saying, 'It seems to be excellent. I assure you that it would be quite good enough for *me*, but possibly not sufficiently good for *you*. Let me suggest that you might get wine more suited to your taste—in France.' With that he turned away, summoned his chamberlain and ordered the whole company to be sent back to France. The Emperor refused to listen to their apologies, and—he wishes to form a company which shall be known as the Italian Opera Company. More, he wishes you and the delightful Signorina Storace to be the chief stars. What have you to say?"

"To say, Excellency? Why that the idea is wonderful. But—an Italian Opera Company—I am Irish, and the Signorina Storace is English!"

The Ambassador laughed, "We can overlook that, I think. Will you put the matter to Signorina Storace, offering her my compliments and felicitations, and discuss the whole matter with her? Then come back and tell me of your decisions."

Michael sat up very late that night discussing the project with Nancy, Mrs. Storace and Stephen. Nancy was enchanted, it was well known that Vienna was the gayest, most brilliant capital in Europe. Venice without its sunshine had lost much of its attraction for her.

"I shall always love Venice, it will always enchant me —when the sun shines; its people are the kindest in Italy, the audiences generous and understanding; but, after all, we are nomads, we must move on—pack up and be on the move. Yes, let it be Vienna!"

Her mother and brother agreed, Stephen felt that with his great friend as the leading tenor and his sister as the star soprano it should not be difficult for him to have some of his work produced. Mrs. Storace agreed to come with them to Vienna, and then she would return to England.

"These places may be charming, the people delightful, but I like and know and understand my London," she said. "I know," she smiled at them all impartially, "that I can trust you all not to get into scrapes, not to commit follies which might be prejudicial to your careers, and to —remember that you are English people."

They left at the end of the season for Vienna, Michael —as usual well provided with letters of introduction to people who bore great names. He had a gift for friendship, people liked him immediately. He was gay, well-mannered, and good to look at. He on his side, appreciated the culture which he found among these aristocrats. He was never at any time a toady, but he loved luxury, good food and—above all, the real appreciation of music.

He thought Vienna the gayest place he had ever seen, he looked eagerly at the crowded streets, filled with elegant women and men in splendid uniforms.

"It is all so gay," he wrote to his mother, "everything is bright, shining, sparkling—except the Danube, that is gray!"

He called on Signor Salieri, one of the directors of the opera company. He took Michael to see the apartment which had been allotted to him. Two floors in a fine house, the rooms beautifully furnished, heating was provided, so were the necessary servants. Signor Salieri mentioned again, with pride, the allowance of four wax candles a day.

"The finest wax, Signor O'Kelly. The food is excellent. The Emperor regards the artists not as being in his employ, but as being his honoured guests."

Salieri talking excitedly and very quickly, told Michael that his own opera—*La Scuola dei Gelosi*—was to be put into production very shortly.

"The leading tenor rôle will be yours! It is a rôle which will offer opportunities which I am certain you will be able to use with great advantage. The fame of the Signorina Storace and yourself has reached Vienna, and the public are waiting to receive you with open arms."

The Viennese appeared determined to call Michael— Signor O'Kelly, and the name stuck to him, except later when he was actually announced on the play bills as "Signor Occheley". Life seemed to be particularly wonderful during these first days in Vienna. Nancy fell in love with the place, Michael and she were seen about everywhere together, they were fêted, made much of, and even shown considerable favour by the Emperor Joseph the Second himself.

Michael told Stephen that he had never been happier, that he really began to believe that Nancy loved him.

"She is always so happy when we are together, she loves it all. Even the cakes! She enjoys walking in the

F

Prater, she enjoys watching the people, looks forward to her visits—and God knows they are many—to her dressmaker. She calls on me to pass my opinion on what they offer her. Shall she have this or that? What do you think? Oh, Stephen, how happy I am!"

Stephen, immersed as usual in his music and compositions, would shake his head and say, "Mickie, curb that impetuosity of yours. Don't count your chickens while they are still in the egg."

There were constant invitations, Michael was invited by Prince Esterhazy to visit him and spend a few days in his splendid palace, so that he might meet Haydn. "Papa Haydn" as he was already called, was the organist and choir master in the Prince's private chapel. Michael found the musician urbane, dignified and affable.

"Not unlike his own work," he told Stephen.

"Some of his work is very fine, Mickie."

"Yes, I don't deny it—it has everything except—humour and I don't believe that Haydn can bring that to it, because he has none himself. No, the man I long to meet, who I must meet is—Mozart. Ah, there is a man I could worship. His genius, his gaiety and yet so easily he can slip into a sadness which is almost unbearable but never degenerates into mere sentimentalism."

"I believe that he is your life's hero," Stephen told him.

Michael rushed into Stephen's room one day, a card of invitation clutched in his hand, his eyes shining; Stephen glanced up from his work.

"You seem excited, Mickie!"

"I am, I can't tell you how excited. I am asked to a concert at Kozeluch's, and later to supper."

Stephen laughed, "That doesn't seem to me to be

anything very exciting! You can go to concerts almost any evening you wish when you're not singing."

"Ah, but listen!" Michael's eyes were shining like stars, he looked very young, very eager. "Listen! Mozart is to be there, he is to play some of his own compositions and—later join the supper party. I shall meet him, perhaps talk with him! How long I have waited and longed for this."

That night he listened, leaning forward so as not to miss one note of the compositions which Mozart played so brilliantly. Michael's eyes were fixed on the small, thin figure, the pale intelligent face and the hands which moved so firmly and yet so easily.

He was to tell Nancy later, "His left hand is a miracle, so strong and yet so capable to convey every shade of feeling. The modulations, the transitions, the facility with which he played—I cannot begin to tell you. It was a revelation. I have listened to many musicians—this man is *the* musician of the world!"

Later, to his great delight, Michael was seated at the supper table between Mozart and his wife, who it was quite obvious that he adored. He talked very quickly, and distinctly, asking many questions about Michael's work, and also about Nancy and Stephen Storace. Their mother had been a Miss Linley, and was the sister of the first Mrs. Sheridan. He had known Thomas Linley in Florence.

He spoke of him with generous admiration, his praise for Thomas Linley's musical ability was unstinted.

He told Michael how much he liked Vienna, how he loved dancing, and playing billiards. "I waste so much time dancing and playing billiards that my beloved wife has to be quite stern with me. We have taken a house

here, come and see us. When? Whenever you like, if I
am working I shall just shout over the banister, 'Go away,
come back later'!"

"You really mean that, Herr Mozart—that I may come
to your house informally?" Michael's face was flushed
with the added excitement.

Mozart laughed, "Why not! It's just like the house of
anyone else——"

"It can't be, it's roof shelters—Mozart," Michael said.

"How old are you, O'Kelly?"

"I have passed my twenty-first birthday."

"And I am seven years older. Keep your enthusiasms,
most people let them fade too early in life. They'll keep
you young. Ah, they are going to dance. I must join them
—I told you how much I love dancing. Remember, we
must meet again."

They met very often, and their friendship became a firm
one. Mozart was warm-hearted, and generous, he loved
to please people whenever it was possible, delighted in
doing them small services. Only when he was playing
did he become a martinet. At the slightest sound, the
least rustle or movement among his audience, he would
take his hands off the keys and wait, sitting motionless
until he was accorded perfect silence.

Life had not been easy for him, but he always retained
his gay outlook. He often said to Michael that he always
believed that fortune was only just waiting round the
corner for him.

His health was not good, and his liking for punch did
nothing to improve it. Not that he drank to excess, but
he drank knowing that it was bad for him.

He had just seen his opera *L'Enlèvement du Serail*
produced with great success, but he pointed to a pile

of manuscript lying on his desk one day and said to
Michael, "Yes, *'du Serail'* was not bad—my sister-in-law
sang it superbly, but—" he laughed his rather boyish
laugh which always delighted Michael, "I have something
there which is going to—make me! A new opera! I have
called it—*Le Nozze di Figaro*—and Michael Kelly and
Nancy Storace are going to make it the success I long for
it to have."

CHAPTER TEN

LIFE was splendid, Michael thought as he walked home that evening. Nancy was unfailingly kind, Stephen seemed better and said that his health had improved since he came to Vienna. Michael believed that the production of Stephen's opera had done much to improve his health. He had taken great interest in the production, and had glowed with pleasure when he heard the praises which were showered upon "*Gli Equivoci*" which was based on "The Comedy of Errors". Michael had played Antipholus, the Emperor and the Court attended the first performance, and Vienna had crowded to hear the new opera by the young English composer.

Stephen began to go out more, to enter society, to accompany Nancy and Michael when they were invited to the splendid houses of the rich Viennese.

"And now," Michael thought, as he walked homewards to those comfortable rooms where a deft servant would be waiting to take his cloak, to see that the wood fire burnt brightly, and to ask with real interest how the "performance had gone"; they were friendly folk, but their friendliness never degenerated into familiarity. "Now! The miracle of miracles—Nancy and I to sing in Mozart's new opera! We can't go any higher, we have reached the pinnacle. How excited he is over it, that dear Mozart! Good, excellent, it must be—he wrote it, that is the answer. It will be superb. I've always worked hard at any rôle, but I'll work at this with every ounce of voice and brain and heart that I possess."

Everything did not go smoothly with the production of "Figaro", three composers were commissioned to write operas—Mozart, Regini and Salieri. Mozart bitterly resentful that anything might endanger the production of his beloved opera, told Michael one day, "If there are any more discussions, arguments and the like, the world will never hear 'Figaro' for the whole score shall go on the fire! Yes, yes, I swear it!"

However the Emperor chose "Figaro" and all was well. From the first rehearsal, when Mozart stood on the stage wearing a crimson pelisse and a cocked hat trimmed with gold braid—for he was as fastidious about his appearance as Michael Kelly—the opera was destined for success.

"There are hundreds of indifferent artistes—and musicians," Mozart had said to Michael, "who believe that to have clothes which smell of dust and shine with grease, who are badly shaved, whose hair hangs like the tails of two dozen rats, acclaims them as a genius! Their mentality is as limited as their achievements."

Stephen, while he was always carefully and neatly dressed, never aspired to the brilliant colours which both Mozart and Michael loved. His good-looking, lean face lit up in a smile.

"Herr Mozart—the world knows that you are a genius, if clothes are to be a test, then they will have to acknowledge that Michael is one also."

Mozart laughed, for Stephen had the ability to make remarks which were dry, even sarcastic, but always they held the saving touch of humour.

The musician said, "Ah, it may be that you have spoken more wisely than you intended! Michael, my friend, did you not tell me that your new suit—

already in the tailor's hands—is to be cherry coloured velvet?"

"Cherry coloured? No, I told you that it was black, *maestro*."

Again Mozart laughed, "Ah, no genius, he does not even know that there are—black cherries!"

Mozart was delighted with the first rehearsal, so were the company. At the conclusion they burst into applause, shouting: "Bravo, bravo Mozart!" The little, thin man with the white face and charming smile stared at them, his eyes filling with tears.

"You—you are too generous," he stammered, "I—thank you all. Thank you for—for your kindness. I wish you good morning."

Nancy said, "Dear little Mozart, he is overcome. How modest he is!"

"I was standing near him," Michael told her, "when Bennuci sang 'alla vittoria'. He was murmuring all the time, 'Ah, bravo, bravissimo. A real artist, a fine artist!' He turned to me at the end of the song and whispered, 'How fortunate I am to have such artists to sing my music!'"

But he could be peppery and for that matter so could Michael Kelly. Michael was singing the part of the judge —"the stuttering judge"[1]—he had discussed how he would sing it with Stephen and Nancy.

"He stutters! Very well, he shall stutter!" Michael declared.

Stephen said, "Terribly difficult, Mickie."

"I know, I know," eagerly, "but I can do it. I've worked at it, and the effect will be splendid. I shan't

[1] A part now practically cut to nothing and in Kelly's time much more important.—N. J.

obscure the words, I can arrange not to do so. Nancy, I'm right, tell me that I'm right."

She nodded, "I'm sure that you're right, provided that it doesn't make the words unintelligible, it's the— the *artistic* way of playing and singing it. Try it, Mickie."

Kelly tried it, and although it was difficult, even the critical Stephen admitted that it was effective, and would certainly delight the audience. Michael had a great gift for mimicry, and his characterizations were perfect. More, his knowledge of music helped him to sing the part so that it lost nothing of the beauty of the music. His admiration for Mozart was far too great to allow him to do that, rather he would have sacrificed his idea of the character.

At the rehearsal Mozart listened, and it was obvious that while he was amused with the stuttering of the spoken word, he disliked the idea of that way of speech being used for the actual music.

He came over to Michael, "Admirable, admirable. A splendid study of character, but pray do not stutter in the *sestetto*." He smiled, "It will ruin my music."

Michael answered, "Herr Mozart, I know that it must appear to be great presumption on my part, but I would not—for my life—do anything that was prejudicial to your wonderful music. Just the same, it is illogical that I should stammer all through the act and then in the *sestetto* suddenly—be cured of my stutter."

The great little musician's pale face turned scarlet. "You'll sing it as I wish, Kelly! I wrote the music, surely I should know what can be done and what cannot be done. You'll ruin the *sestetto*! Understand, I will not permit it!"

Michael, his face suddenly very pale so that his hair shone more golden in contrast to his white face, his blue eyes blazing, and his full, good-tempered lips compressed, stared at the great composer. He bowed, "Herr Mozart, you are one of the great planets in the musical heavens for all time. I am only a small star, but I still give light, and have my own ideas. Either I sing this part as I have conceived it—as an actor—or with deep regret, I must resign my part. The decision lies with you, Herr Mozart."

Mozart frowned, pursed his lips, then said, "Try it—your way. I'll see what I think of it."

He turned on his red heels and walked away. Michael sang the part as he had wished to. Mozart sulked a little, scarcely spoke to him, and obviously resented Michael's stubborn determination to stammer.

The night of the first performance came, the opera house was packed. The Emperor was in his box, the court —in their dazzling uniforms and the women in their exquisite dresses made the scene one of colour and excitement. Mozart himself conducted, and the audience applauded the overture wildly. The opera was a foregone success.

Nancy was received with a great burst of applause, and when Michael entered playing the stupid old judge, stammering and stuttering, but acting beautifully, the bursts of laughter were continual.

Again and again the Emperor's laugh could be heard, again and again he called loudly, "Bravo!" Mozart's opera was a success.

When the curtain fell—after the applause had continued for many minutes—Michael went to Nancy and caught her hands.

"Darling, you were wonderful. This is the crown of your career. I am so proud to have shared a little in your wonderful success."

Mozart had hurried on to the stage, taking those short, rapid steps which were characteristic of him, he greeted the artistes, complimented them on their beautiful performance.

"The happiest night of my life—for any composer to have such artists is to transport him to Heaven. It was something I have dreamed of, but never expected to see and hear. For singing as you have done this evening, you will—undoubtedly—all go straight to Heaven, and there I shall conduct for you again. The choir there in Paradise will be green and yellow with envy! Mozart thanks you from the bottom of his heart. God bless you all."

He turned to where Michael stood and held out his hands.

"And you, rebel Irishman! You were right and I was wrong. The success of the opera belongs to you all, but—and I know that I shall give no offence in saying this—no, you are all too generous, too kindly—you Mickie Kelly—Signor Occheley were the great *individual* success. It was a risk, but you took it, and handled the whole part with artistry and brilliance." He swung off his three-cornered hat trimmed with silver lace, and swinging it so that it almost touched the ground bowed, "Signor Occheley, I offer you my sincere congratulations and my grateful thanks!"

Michael, his face crimson, his eyes smarting, murmured, "Ah, Herr Mozart, now don't." He laughed, a little shakily, "I want to go home and—burst into tears!"

"What did the Emperor say, Herr Mozart?" Nancy asked.

Mozart's eyes twinkled, "His only criticism was that owing to the number of encores, the opera ran nearly as long as—two operas! 'So, Herr Mozart,' he said, 'no encores in future. Otherwise, I have enjoyed every moment.' Then he laughed and added, 'Yes, even the encores.' "

Michael walked back to his lodgings as if he trod on air. Mozart was friendly again, he was satisfied, his hand-clasp had been warm and sincere. He slept that night the untroubled sleep of a child.

It was some days later when he was drinking coffee with Stephen in one of the pretty cafés in the Prater, that a man entered and coming to their table spoke to Stephen. His voice was harsh, and his face heavy and bloated, with a heavy jaw and eyes which seemed to Michael to be over small and fierce. He talked, the words poured out like a torrent, both Stephen and Michael—the latter who certainly was never silent in conversation—were not allowed to speak a word. On went the interminable flow of vaunting, egoistic boasting. Michael judged the man to be about fifty. He was carelessly dressed, and his hands were not too well kept.

Finally Michael managed to, as he said later, "get a word in edgeways". He asked Stephen to introduce him to the newcomer.

The man stared at him, "Don't you know me? Good God, I know you!"

Michael said very quietly, "That is quite possible—that you know me—by sight."

"By sight! That's amusing. My name is Fisher, John Fisher. I am a violinist of whom you may have heard! Most of the civilized world has heard of me. I've come to Vienna to give a series of concerts and—without conceit—I think I can predict that they will be the best attended Vienna has ever seen. Yes, my playing is something completely out of the ordinary. I have visited all the

capitals of Europe, and have been acclaimed everywhere."
He turned to Stephen, "And how is the pretty sister?
She's an attractive piece!" He laughed, "Someone told
me that this singing fellow—what's his name?—
Occheley—queer name—is running after her. Is it true?"

Stephen froze, "It is not usual, Mr. Fisher, to bandy
ladies' names in a public café."

"Pooh! Everyone discusses the love affairs of actresses
in public! The actresses themselves expect it. She is a
pretty creature, and a good artist; too good to throw
herself away on a comedian, a girl like that wants——"

Michael held a pair of very elegant lemon coloured
kid gloves in his hand, for some moments he had been
drawing them through his fingers, almost reflectively.
Now he leaned across the little table, and struck Fisher
over the cheek with them.

"What—a girl like that wants," he said quietly but
savagely, "is to know that her brother and his friend do
not permit graceless people to express opinions about her
in public. There! Mind your manners, Mr. John Fisher,
or here is someone quite ready to constitute himself your
teacher."

He took the gloves, looked at them attentively, then
with some elaboration threw them under the table. He
turned and smiled at Stephen, "I couldn't possibly wear
them again! Shall we go?"

Fisher's name was not mentioned by either of them,
they walked home in silence. Stephen was very pale,
Michael still flushed and yet beaming with satisfaction.

It was some days later that Nancy told them she was
going to attend the first concert given by John Fisher.
She had, it appeared, met him at a dinner party, given in
his honour.

She looked sharply at Michael, "What did you say?"

He shrugged his shoulders, "I didn't speak, *cara*."

He had been most kind and attentive, and she heard that he was the greatest violinist in Europe.

Stephen said, "In the world—surely?"

Nancy laughed, the charming sound which always made Michael's heart miss a beat, it was like—he thought —a blackbird singing for sheer joy of living.

"The world!" she laughed, "The world is a big place, Stephen."

Two days later, when they sat in the lodgings of La Storace, she talked to the two men of the concert. She considered Fisher quite wonderful, his attack, his mastery of the violin, his tone were all superb.

"Imagine it, he was playing a *morceau* of his own composition, and his E string broke. You could hear the 'twang' of it all through the concert hall. He continued to play, and played so well that the absence of the string was scarcely noticed!"

Michael and Stephen exchanged glances, Stephen was seated at the table, his elbows resting on it, his chin cupped in his hands; Michael sat opposite to Nancy—who was sewing—his immaculate silk stockinged legs outstretched, the light from the fire caught the buckles of his shoes and they sent out little sparkles of light. The scene was one of friendliness, intimacy and comfort. Michael moved restlessly in his chair. For some reason—for which he could not account—he felt suddenly uneasy, almost frightened.

Nancy said, "Wasn't that wonderful?"

Stephen, his voice very crisp and his words coming distinct and rather clipped, answered.

"He wrote that piece—it's poor music by the way—

and in it allowed for the breaking of the E string. To continue to play without it is a proof of his—virtuosity, my dear."

Nancy dropped her sewing, she spoke indignantly. "Stephen, if you were a woman I should say, 'What a catty remark!' Where did you get that information, if information it is?"

"I got it," he spoke slowly, "from Herr Mozart. Mozart knows this man Fisher, and thinks poorly of him—as a musician and as a violinist—I may add, also as an individual."

Indignantly Nancy retorted, "How do you know that Mozart speaks the truth?"

"Because he is incapable of anything but the truth—in his music or in his life," her brother replied.

Lazily Michael spoke at last, "He dresses so badly, this violinist. His clothes are dusty and—his nails need attention."

Nancy leaned back in her high-backed chair, "It is impossible that everyone should emulate Herr Mozart and Signor Occheley, and become beautiful peacocks!"

"It costs nothing to clean your nails!" Michael said.

"It appears that both you and Stephen have taken an unreasonable dislike to Mr. Fisher. Why—I don't know. I like him, I admire his playing, and he has been courtesy itself to me." She folded up her sewing and put it aside, then rose, "Good-night, both of you. I did not know that you could be so—unfair to anyone. Good-night."

As the door closed Michael sprang to his feet. "My God, I believe that she's fallen in love with this second— no, third rate player. Stephen, what can we do? He is years older than she is——"

"Twenty at least," Stephen said slowly, "twenty years is a big gap to be bridged. Michael, whatever happens be wise. This may be just a passing fancy. I know Nancy, she's impetuous, she takes sudden fancies and they die quickly. I beg you—with all my heart—do nothing that can prejudice you in any way. To do so will only predispose her in his favour. Nancy is ever on the side of whoever she believes to be unjustly treated. Mickie, I am speaking seriously and for your ultimate good."

Michael, his head between his hands, muttered wretchedly, "I'll do my best."

It seemed to him that the days which followed were filled with references to—Fisher. If he had no concert, then he was at the theatre; after the performance he was round in Nancy's dressing room. He dined at the lodgings, when both Stephen and Michael pleaded other engagements. He walked with Nancy in the Prater, Michael saw them together drinking chocolate in the smart cafés. He wandered about lonely and acutely miserable. Mozart had left Vienna for Prague, and Michael had no-one with whom he could talk intimately except Stephen, and he was as miserable as Michael himself. Nancy seemed withdrawn, she spoke to them only of ordinary everyday affairs. Her performances were as brilliant as ever, and in spite of his desperate unhappiness Michael continued to delight his audiences.

He should have been able to forget his unhappiness, he told himself. He was popular, he was held in high esteem, even the Emperor showed him special favour commanding him to the palace to meet visiting Irishmen of distinction. True, he assumed an air of gaiety, never wore his heart on his sleeve "for daws to peck at" but the moment that it was no longer necessary to play the courtier, to appear as the amusing singer, his heart sank and he knew that he faced utter and complete misery.

He had loved her for so long, he had retained all his chivalrous ideas of keeping himself for her; if at long intervals he had given way to what he felt were unworthy impulses, he had always regretted it deeply and sincerely.

He might have travelled far, become sophisticated, but he remained all his life a good son of the Church, so far as it lay in his power. He was very young, women liked him, admired him, and if he felt unable sometimes to ignore their blandishments, it may surely be forgiven him.

Nancy said to him one evening at the side of the stage, "Oh, Mickie, come and have supper with Stephen and me, will you?"

He repeated, "Stephen and you?"

She nodded, a trifle impatiently, "You heard what I said."

"I should like to, thank you."

During supper, which was excellent, she was very gay. The big room was charming, for Nancy was a great *prima donna*, with a salary of £500 a year, and allowances regarding fuel, candles and the like in proportion. Michael's lodgings were admirable, but hers far exceeded his in size and luxury.

As he watched her, her delightful, vivacious face all alight with amusement and friendliness, he thought that the nightmare must be over, that now life would go on in that sweet intimacy which had been so beautiful. This was "his" Nancy again, to-morrow they would take chocolate together, he would buy flowers for her, and they would talk happily, gaily, companionably.

The coffee was served, and she leaned back in her chair.

"Tell me, both of you," she said, "why you dislike Mr. Fisher so much."

Michael started, he felt that someone had dragged back the nightmare which he had believed to be over. Stephen frowned.

Michael said, "I've only met him once——"

"But you formed an opinion?" her voice had sharpened.

"Certainly. I disliked him imposing himself upon Stephen and me, Stephen knew him slightly, I did not know him at all. I disliked his bombastic conversation, I disliked his slovenly dress, and—" he paused, "most of all I disliked the way in which he dragged a woman's name into the conversation in a public café."

"Did he mention one woman or several?" her voice was still very crisp.

"One only," Stephen said, "and Michael here took his gloves and slapped him across the face with them! Nancy, don't look like that for surely the story must be all over Vienna, you must have heard it! He then threw his gloves down on to the floor and we walked out. Fisher did—*nothing*. Imagine it! He is not only all that Michael has said but a coward into the bargain. Can you imagine Michael or me receiving an insult of that kind and remaining—perfectly passive?"

She said very calmly, "You and Michael are fire-eaters. John Fisher dislikes arguments, broils and the like. I married him this morning. He will be here in half an hour."

Stephen, his face white, said in a tone which was almost a whisper, "Dear God! Nancy—it can't be true. He's twenty years older than you are."

"It is true," she said. "We were married this morning."

She turned to Michael and held out her hands, "Michael, we can surely be friends. The fact that I have— yes, fallen in love and married cannot change our friendship."

Michael stood stiffly, for he had risen to his feet, and when he spoke his voice was hoarse and strained. Stephen, watching him intently, thought, "He's grown up suddenly. All the boyish look has gone from his face. Poor Mickie, he looks as if he had received a mortal wound."

"Nancy, dear Nancy," he said, "you know how deeply and how long I have loved you. I fell in love on the first night when I met you and Stephen. You thought that I was a girl dressed in boy's clothes. How long ago it all seems. I shall always love you, your happiness will always be something of supreme importance to me. I am still your devoted Mickie Kelly."

She looked at him, and shook her head, "Mickie, don't make a romance out of me. We've been boy and girl together——"

He raised his eyebrows, "Have we?"

"Yes, now I'm a woman and you're a man. It's all different. You can't order people's affections. I *have* fallen in love, the fact that the two people who are nearest to me in the world dislike my husband—well, it's unfortunate, but it can't make any difference to me. We can surely go on being the dear friends we have always been."

Michael drew himself up and stood stiffly, he was not very tall but he seemed to have gained in stature. He looked pale, but his eyes were very bright, and Stephen admired the dignity which seemed to emanate from him.

"Always friends," he said. "You, Stephen and I. I have

only one thing to say, and don't—for God's sake, Nancy imagine that I am talking boastingly—if ever this man treats you in any way but the way which *any man* ought to treat you, he'll answer for it to me."

He took her hand, raised it to his lips and kissed it. Not passionately but with the respect which he would have given to any woman.

"Mickie—you and Stephen have always kissed me when you left."

He stared at her, blankly as if he heard her speaking from a great distance, then licking his dry lips, he said in a voice as hoarse as a crow, "Stephen can still kiss you, Mickie Kelly—must not."

"Mickie——!"

He picked up his three-cornered hat, a hat which he had ordered because it was a copy of one which Mozart wore. He held it against his chest and bowed.

"Dearest Nancy, good-night."

Then he turned and walked out. Stephen went to his sister, she was crying, the tears rolling down her cheeks, her breast heaving with distress and emotion.

"Nancy—why did you do it? Why not have told us?" his tone was gently reproachful. "Surely we deserved your confidence?"

"John made me swear to say nothing—to anyone."

"Ah! Poor Mickie, he has paid pretty heavily for—what he did! The woman Fisher was discussing, my dear was—Nancy Storace! Fisher did nothing, he waited his time—he paid you his attentions. What a splendid revenge on Mickie Kelly! There, I'm going. No," as she made a gesture of protest, "I shall go with Mickie. He has an extra bedroom. I couldn't stay here with—you and your husband."

She dried her eyes, she had stopped crying and now looked at him with eyes which were hostile.

"So you are determined to dislike my husband?"

Stephen drew her to him, "Nancy we've always been very close, always felt a great love for each other, don't allow this marriage to make any difference—don't, my dear, don't. It would break my heart. I'm so proud of you, I have such hopes for you. And now, my darling, trust me. If you are truly happy, I shall—yes, be happy. If there should be—anything but happiness waiting for you, always remember that you have me—me and little Mickie Kelly. There, I must go. Good-night, darling Nancy, dearest of sisters, and may God bless you and keep you happy."

He went out and ran down the stairs, as he reached the front door a carriage drew up, and John Fisher got out. He stood staring at Stephen, his whole air offensive, his voice when he spoke harsh and overbearing.

"Ah, Storace, my brother-in-law. Well, we've given you a surprise to-day, eh?"

"You have indeed."

"And where is the gallant Occheley? Gone home to lick his wounds?"

"Where he has gone and what he is doing is no business of yours, Fisher. It was a new, a novel way to repay an insult! It might have been wiser—and braver—to have adopted another course."

He turned on his heel and leaving Fisher standing staring after him, walked away rapidly in the direction of Michael's lodgings.

He found Michael seated staring into space, his immaculate silk stockinged legs outstretched, his hands hanging limp at his sides.

"Michael, I've come to ask a favour. Can I take up my abode with you? I think that you have an additional bedroom?"

Without moving Michael said, "By all means, I shall be delighted."

His voice sounded dead, mechanical. Stephen laid his hand on his friend's shoulder and spoke very gently.

"Mickie, don't let this hurt you too much. You're Michael Kelly, you've got everything before you——"

The strange, dull voice said, "Have I? Have I really, Stephen?"

"You know that you have. You know that what Vienna thinks, other places will think too. London, Mickie, London! Your own Dublin. To go back there an established—success. You're not going to let this break you! God's truth, imagine the satisfaction it would give that creature! This is his revenge, as I have just told him —yes, I met him as I left Nancy's lodgings, and he had no reply to make. Not that I gave him time to make one."

His hand gripped Michael's shoulder but gently, "Mickie, you love Nancy—as I do. Nancy is going to need that love of ours. You must be ready to help her. This won't last—how I know that, I cannot tell you, but I *do* know it. I'm a sick man, and you remember what your Shakespeare says—'The words of dying men enforce attention like deep harmony'. I'm not actually dying, but —well, there it is Mickie, I want to feel that someone with youth, strength, and possessing real affection for her, is— ready to stand at her side. You'll not fail her, I know that."

Michael sprang to his feet, "Stephen, tell me— honestly—how ill are you? I must know."

That particularly sweet smile of Storace's softened his lips.

"Dear generous Mickie!" he said. "You forget your own troubles in thinking of mine. Oh, I shan't die to-morrow, or the day after, but I shan't make—old bones. I've got work to do first, and I'll do it, but, well, I want to feel that if anything unexpected happened to me, Nancy would have a second brother to watch over her and, if necessary, defend her."

"Stephen, you must take greater care of yourself. You work too hard, you demand too much of yourself. For the rest, dear, dear Stephen I shall always be ready to do anything and everything I can do for Nancy. God grant she may not need a defender, but if ever she did——"

Stephen caught his hand and held it tightly, "If ever she did—he's here—little Mickie Kelly. God bless you, dear friend."

CHAPTER ELEVEN

LIFE during the next few weeks seemed to Michael to be a queer, unreal business. He felt that he lived it in two halves, the one filled with his work, his rehearsing and his study, the other half when he sat in his lodgings and brooded about Nancy and speculated as to her happiness. She was singing beautifully, she looked well, though he fancied—and mentally rebuked himself for allowing the idea to enter his mind—that there were times when her eyes had lost some of their sparkle, when in moments of repose her face looked older, graver.

He repeated to himself again and again, "I want her to be happy—she must be happy. She was made for happiness. Yes, even with Fisher."

Vienna was growing a little tired of John Fisher, his concerts were no longer crowded, and the effect of the broken violin string had lost its value. He was anxious to leave Austria and try his fortune elsewhere.

"Vienna!" he exclaimed to Nancy one evening, "They're a fickle lot. At first they were breaking their necks to get to my concerts. Now, I'm no longer a novelty. They prefer the operas of Mozart. Pah, Mozart! A posturing clown."

She laughed, "You must not speak so about Herr Mozart. To me—to my brother Stephen and to Michael Kelly he is, yes, almost a god."

Fisher shrugged his heavy shoulders, "I have my own opinion, and that of your brother and the peacock Irishman don't affect it. I should have imagined that you would have had more common sense, better musical taste. What is his music? A lot of tinkling tunes! Trifles! Mozart will never write anything that will live, never."

Nancy was a loyal soul, she had always argued with Michael and her brother, together they had debated the claims to fame of various composers, arguing hotly and illustrating their claims by playing snatches of music on the pianoforte. She enjoyed an argument, and began to defend Mozart to her husband. She spoke temperately and with authority, for her knowledge of music was very considerable.

"But John, just consider what he has written—apart from everything else you cannot dismiss 'Figaro'—more than that he is a brilliant pianist, and one of the most generous, kindly men I know."

John Fisher stared at her, then walked heavily over to where she sat and raising his hand struck her across the mouth.

"Hold your tongue!" he shouted. "Who is the master here? Do you, a mere singer, pretend to know more of music than John Fisher? I've stood enough—more than enough of your self-sufficiency. How often have you come back after a performance at your damned opera, smiling and rubbing your hands, assuring me that there was not a vacant seat in the house! What was that for? To humiliate me! Yes, because you had heard from your sour faced brother or that bumptious Occheley that I had only a thin audience."

Nancy, her hand pressed to her mouth, where she felt a trickle of blood running down her chin, gasped, "Have you gone mad? What is this silly talk?"

"Gone mad!" he had turned and was walking up and down the long room, his hands clenched, his voice loud and angry. "The only time I went mad was when I married a cheap singer. Married someone unworthy to be the wife of a great violinist. Your name mustn't be even mentioned in a café! When I did so this Occheley, no doubt your particular bully, struck me over the face with his damned gloves, and then flung them under the table. He said to your superior brother," and here he attempted to imitate Michael's slight Irish inflexion, " 'Oi couldn't wear thim again!' You dare to argue with me, you trollop!"

Again he approached her, again he swung his hand and struck her so that she fell, striking her head against the heavily carved arm of the chair. She lay there, trembling, terrified. In all her short life she had never experienced violence, and it seemed incredible and fantastic that any man—and this was the man she had married, with whom she had believed herself in love—should treat her brutally.

That night was the first of many nights. Again and again Fisher would lash himself into some insane fury, accusing Nancy of things which were utterly untrue.

"All Vienna knows that this Occheley is your lover" or "And this mealy mouthed Mozart, how did you get into his good graces?" "Your brother, writing operas! God help us! Such stuff, such rubbish." "The papers praise you, Pah! Why? Because the three of you have managed—Heaven only knows by what means—to ingratiate yourself with the Emperor. Do you imagine that he might take you for his mistress?"

There were times when she tried to reason with him; tried to beg him to moderate his language, and above all to remember that he was tearing her nerves to shreds.

"I earn my living," she told him, "how can I do my

work when my nerves are in tatters, when I am fearful that someone may see the bruise on my arms, my shoulders—and guess how they came there?"

He glanced at her, "So! Now you fling it in my teeth that you work to get money which helps to keep me! You'll tell me next that these lodgings are yours, and that I am here only on sufferance. You strumpet, you loathsome whore!"

One evening when she had been invited to some great supper party, when Fisher was not included in the invitation which was issued only to the members of the Imperial Opera Company, Nancy returned home escorted by Michael and Stephen. She was in great spirits, the supper party had been very gay, she had realized that she was liked, admired and appreciated. Now as they walked home, for it was a beautiful night, she held an arm of each—Stephen and Michael.

Michael felt that they had all been suddenly transported into the past, when they laughed together and found life filled with amusement. She stood at the door calling gaily after them as they walked away.

"Good-night, my dears—sleep well."

Fisher was waiting for her, he had been leaning out of the open window and must have both seen and heard them laughing and talking. He came towards her, his none too comely face disfigured by a scowl.

"Why didn't you bring your pimp brother and your Irish paramour in with you? You could have continued to laugh and be merry. I heard you all along the street. The great *prima donna,* the favourite of Vienna escorted home by her bodyguard!"

Nancy tried to answer soothingly, lightly. He had been drinking and brooding over his imagined wrongs, nursing grievances, growing almost maudlin with sympathy—for himself.

"Oh, John, don't be so silly. What if we were laughing? It has been an amusing evening——"

"To which your husband was not invited!" he snarled.

"It was given only for members of the Opera," Nancy protested.

"You brother isn't a member of the opera!"

"Stephen is one of the composers for the opera. It was announced to-night that the next production is to be his new work." She was growing angry, she knew that she had come to hate his heavy, sullen face, the smell of stale wine or schnapps which tinged his breath. Instinctively her voice sharpened a little.

"And I presume that the great *prima donna* and her—paramour will be singing the leading rôles! With the admirable brother conducting. It will be almost a family party, eh?"

She picked up her cloak and turned to the door. Fisher suddenly flinging aside all restraint, yelled, "Stay here and listen to me, trollop!"

"No," she said, "I'm going to my room."

He caught her by the arm and dragged her back, striking her with his other hand. It felt like a heavy flail, and to Nancy, the beating seemed to go on for hours. She fell and he kicked her, still shouting—"Get up, damnation take you, get up!" The horrible scene played itself out at last, Fisher exhausted by his own fury, flung her away from him, and sat down intent on pouring out wine.

Nancy gathered together all the energy she still possessed, caught her cloak and dashed through the door down the stairs and into the street. She heard the window flung open, saw Fisher lean out shouting, "Come back, strumpet. D'you hear me?"

She ran, only checking her speed once to kick off her brocade shoes because their high heels made running difficult. She fled on in the direction of Michael's lodging. She reached the door, feeling that the last of her strength had left her. She seized the heavy brass knocker and heard the dull sound as it struck the door, sounding hollow as the noise reverberated in the silent street.

Michael was preparing some mulled wine. He was something of an adept at preparing it, taking tremendous care, and smiling with pleasure as he poured the steaming liquid into glasses for himself and Stephen.

"Mozart loves his punch, I prefer my mulled wine. Well, Stephen this is good news—your new work to go on immediately. I'm not surprised—I found it entrancing when you played it over."

Stephen nodded, "It's wonderful luck. I don't think that it is bad, and I'm rarely satisfied with what I've written. It seems all right when I compose it, and each time I play it over it seems to me to grow less and less vital, more and more colourless."

"Your innate modesty, my friend, and also the high standard which you set yourself. Everyone agrees that your work— Heavens, who can this be at this time of night?"

"Morning," Stephen said, "it's two o'clock."

Again the sound of the heavy knocker. Michael sprang to his feet. "The servant will be sleeping like the dead. I'll go. No, don't move, Stephen, you're tired."

He ran down the stairs, Stephen heard the door open, heard a sudden violent exclamation, and stood peering down, candle in hand into the darkness. He saw the dim shape of Michael, heard the door close and the bolt shoot home.

"Who is it with you?" Stephen called, for he could see that Michael was supporting someone who leaned against him heavily. "If it's one of your drunken singer friends send him packing!" he laughed, for too often Michael's friends arrived at unheard of hours and expected to sit and talk until the dawn came and the candles were burnt low in their sockets.

Michael called back, "It's Nancy."

They were mounting the stairs now, Stephen candlestick in hand ran down to meet them. Nancy was leaning heavily against Michael, her head lying on his shoulder. At the sight of her deadly white face, of the blood which trickled from the corner of her mouth, while her breath came in painful gasps, Stephen staggered back with the sudden shock.

"Nancy, darling, Nancy—what is it?"

Michael said, "She can't talk yet. See that some of the wine is still hot. There, Nancy—we're there! Sit here, lean back, Stephen will give you some mulled wine, and I'll get some water to bathe your face."

He ran from the room, and Stephen held the wine to her lips. She sipped a little, then gently pushed the glass away. "Ah!" the sound seemed to Stephen to be a wail, "Ah, it's been so horrible!"

"Fisher?" he asked.

"Yes—who else."

"Has this—this kind of thing ever happened before?"

She uttered a sound which had it not been so filled with bitterness might have been a laugh, "Dozens of times, but never so dreadful as to-night. Oh, Stephen—it went on for—what seemed to be—hours."

Michael returned, holding a basin which contained warm water, and fine, soft linen handkerchiefs. He knelt on a footstool at her side and very gently and tenderly bathed her face. She had never seen him look as he did now. There seemed to be nothing left of the young, careless, laughing Michael Kelly. He looked so stern, so gentle and yet so resolute.

"Your shoes, Nancy!" Stephen exclaimed.

"I kicked them off so that I could run faster."

"My dear, your feet must be bruised."

"If they're not," Nancy said with a flash of her old vivacity, "they're almost the only part of me that—isn't bruised!"

Michael set down the basin, and said, "Now finish your wine."

"You're a kind boy, Mickie," she said. "I'm grateful to you both. You see, Stephen," and this time her smile was unforced, "how we Storaces run to Mickie Kelly when we're in trouble. First you, now—me. I shall expect to find mama arriving any day!"

Together they questioned her, she answered their questions, they heard the whole dreadful story, heard of the many times when he had beaten her, insulted her, reviled her. They both listened to all she said, merely asking questions and making no comments. When they were in possession of the facts, Stephen said firmly:

"You've got to stay here, Nancy. There is room, isn't there, Mickie?"

"Indeed there is, and if there wasn't—we'd make room somehow. Stephen's right, you must stay here—until you can go back to your own lodging."

She started back as if threatened by a blow, "I can't

go back to John, don't try to make me. He'd kill me. I thought to-night that he was going to kill me."

"No-one would allow you to go back until—" Kelly spoke very slowly, "Fisher has left Vienna—for good and all."

"He won't go, unless I go with him," Nancy said.

"He *will* go," he returned, "long ago, my dear, Stephen and I had someone—removed who was causing you annoyance. What a long time ago it seems, doesn't it? Well, what we accomplished once, we can accomplish again. Now, Nancy asthore, away to your bed, my dear, Stephen will show you where it is—he'll lend you one of his night-shirts!"

Early next morning, Michael—who had talked with Stephen for hours as to what was best to be done, left the house, and made his way to the Imperial Palace. He was well known there for the Emperor Joseph the Second was very fond of the Irishman, he always called him "O'Kelly", and found him amusing and excellently mannered. It was comparatively easy to get an interview with the Lord Chamberlain.

He greeted Kelly warmly, "You're up and about early! I thought that all you singers laid abed waiting for the day to get thoroughly warmed."

"I have come to ask you a great favour; if you will and can grant it, I shall be in your debt for the rest of my life."

"You sound serious, O'Kelly. I usually look for a joke from you. Tell me what is this favour, be certain I shall grant it if it is possible. It is not, I hope, some hitch concerning Storace's new opera? The Emperor particularly wishes that the first performance shall be given on the visit of the Duke of York—he's set his heart on it."

Michael nodded, "I heard this. Storace is to conduct,

and Signora Storace and I are to sing the two leading
rôles, her part is delightful. Now, my Lord Chamberlain,
unless I can put this case before the Emperor, Signora
Storace most certainly will not sing, and if such a thing
should happen, I believe that her brother would decline
to have the opera produced."

The Chamberlain stared, "But what has happened?
I heard that Signora Storace liked the part—now—I don't
understand this at all! Pray speak plainly, I want to help
you, but I must be in full possession of the facts."

"The facts, my lord, are these. Signora Storace came
to my lodgings last night—or rather this morning—her
brother is staying with me. She collapsed on the doorstep. Together we assisted her to the salon, bathed her
face—she was bleeding—and revived her as best we
could. We——"

"What!" the word came like a pistol shot. "Footpads,
robbers—have you any idea where this abominable thing
took place? My dear O'Kelly, there is no need to ask
for an audience with the Emperor, I shall send for the
Chief of Police at once. Be certain that we shall catch these
vile creatures. To attack La Storace! Of whom everyone
thinks so highly, why—she is esteemed by all Vienna.
Had she any idea how many of these criminals attacked
her?"

Kelly said, quietly, "Yes, my lord—one. Signora
Storace was attacked in her own lodging, by—her husband. This has happened many times before."

"Fisher—the violinist! Attacked La Storace! It is
unthinkable! I have never liked the fellow, never knew
why La Storace married him. Many times you say? And
for what reason?"

"I believe," Michael said, "that he is furiously jealous

G

of her success and popularity being so much greater than his own."

"Tut, tut—it's inexplicable. You say that he actually *beats* her! What brutes some of these men are. O'Kelly, wait there, I shall see the Emperor. Believe me, I have not the slightest doubt that he will take very drastic measures."

Michael waited, he felt terribly sad. To him it was dreadful to imagine what Nancy must have been through. He felt that last night when he had seen her huddled on the doorstep, his heart had stopped beating. He felt that the woman he had loved with all the devotion of which he was capable had returned to him smirched and degraded. That the fault was not hers, he realized, nevertheless he was filled with a sick disgust that she could have shared a bed with this man, have lived with him as his wife, allowed her body to be pawed by his coarse hands.

Now, something had died. The old, passionate young love was over. Why he could not have said, but he knew that it was so. He loved her, he would always love her, as he would always love Stephen, but that had been a great romance in his life; he had allowed himself to dream that one day she would marry him, that together they would share their passionate happiness. He had imagined how he would hold her in his arms, very tenderly and yet—demanding. He had dreamed that she would be glad and content to yield to him, and that he would have been her adoring lover as well as her husband.

It was over. He no longer desired her, he simply loved her as Stephen loved her. It was not that he had given his heart elsewhere, there was no woman for whom he felt the slightest tenderness—for whom he knew the faintest flicker of desire.

He thought, "I have my complete freedom, and I

would rather have still been held by invisible chains to her. Why has this happened? She has committed no fault, she is the same brave, generous soul she has always been. Perhaps love such as I have given her wears itself out, burns out, leaving only a warm glow of affection. Ah, what a puzzle life is! It used to seem so simple, so clear, and now—" he moved impatiently in his chair, "everything is complicated, difficult."

The Lord Chamberlain entered, "His Majesty has graciously granted you an audience. Come immediately."

Michael was duly announced and walked down the long room to the desk where the Emperor sat. He was too disturbed to notice the grandeur of the room, the shelves filled with magnificently bound books, and the wonderful pictures. He saw only Joseph the Second, Emperor of Austria. An elderly, plain man with a large nose, and small eyes which were yet very kindly.

He said, speaking abruptly as he always did, "Ah, O'Kelly, now what is all this? La Storace is a member of my opera company, she is indispensable to it—as you are. Who is this Fisher? Yes, yes, I've heard him and thought very little of him. I won't permit this kind of thing for a moment. My *prime donne* going in fear of their lives! Pah! The man must go and go at once." He drummed with the tips of his fingers on the desk top. "Banishment from Vienna, and to take effect at once." He turned to the Chamberlain, "See that the order of banishment is drawn up at once, remember—at once. I will sign it. I want this man—he doesn't deserve the name—to leave Vienna before nightfall. I don't care what engagements he has, they will not, cannot be fulfilled. Is that clear?"

"Perfectly clear, sire."

"Prepare the document then immediately."

"At once, sire."

The Emperor turned to Michael. "Well, O'Kelly, now this opera can go into rehearsal at once, eh? I want it to be a gala performance for the Duke of York. I want to see that he goes back to London and tells them that in Vienna we know how to present opera. Tell La Storace that she will be able to return to her lodging this evening. Fisher will be escorted over the frontier by some of my own guards. The dastardly fellow. She—La Storace—has a mother, hasn't she? Send for her to live with her daughter. She's too young and too attractive to live alone. There, O'Kelly, I've untangled your web for you!"

"Sire, I cannot express my gratitude."

The Emperor rose, and tapped Michael on the shoulder, "Yes, you can, make the Duke of York envious at what Vienna can do."

"I shall do my poor best, sire."

He returned to Nancy, she looked shaken and her face showed signs of bruises, but her spirits rose when he gave her his news. He wondered if she had ever actually loved Fisher, for his leaving Vienna did not appear to affect her in the least except to give her satisfaction. She agreed that it was a good thing for her mother to come out to her, and promised to write to her at once.

"Had that awful life continued for much longer, Mickie," she said, "my voice would have suffered. My nerves are in shreds, and every performance is an effort. I—who used to look forward to each appearance with pleasure and excitement. Never mind, it will pass, and you and I will make this charming opera of dear Stephen's a huge success."

So John Fisher went out of her life, and official notice was sent to Nancy that she could return to her own lodging with complete safety. Fisher was over the frontier, and had been warned that the Emperor would not permit him to return.

Rehearsals began, and Michael flung himself into the work in his usual whole-hearted fashion. His voice was in splendid condition, and he felt that success was certain. He longed for Stephen to have a real and great success, his music was masterly, his melodies charming. He was ready to listen to suggestions, gravely courteous to all the artistes—important or unimportant.

Michael still felt that he was living in a new and strange world, a world from which his passionate love for Nancy Storace had vanished. He was always happy to be with her, together they laughed, and she seemed—since the departure of Fisher—to have become younger, and to have recovered her gaiety. Lord Barnard, the son of the Earl of Darlington was visiting Vienna. He was a young man of twenty, with a long, pale and not unhandsome face. He had conceived a violent admiration for Nancy, and her rooms were always filled with his presents—flowers, chocolates, and trinkets.

Nancy said to Michael one day, "Ah, more flowers from Barnard. He supped with me last night—oh, mama was there. Do you like him, Mickie?"

Michael shrugged his shoulders, he found Barnard something of a nincompoop with his self-conscious drawl and his predilection for speaking French on every possible opportunity.

"I like him well enough, my dear."

She laughed, "Not jealous, Mickie?"

"Jealous! Glory be to God, no!" he replied, and when he realized how promptly and decisively he had spoken, felt startled. He knew that provided she did not get entangled with some brute like Fisher it did not materially matter to him with whom she supped and dined. The days when he would have fretted and fumed, when he would have suffered agonies of jealousy, have indulged in fears and allowed apprehension to overmaster him—were over.

Nancy stared at him, an odd expression in her bright eyes.

"You don't care any more, eh, Mickie?" she asked.

"Of course I care, asthore. Your welfare and happiness matter supremely to me—they always will. But I'm not a raw Irish lad anymore, Nancy. I'm growing up—and so are you. You've got your life to live—and you must live it as you think fit and in the way which gives you happiness. I used to live in dreams, now I've got to live with reality."

She sighed, "I know. But they were wonderful days, weren't they? Venice, the gondolas, Florian's. Our first successes. Ah, well, I suppose that life can still be a rather splendid affair."

The opera was ready, the opera house was prepared for a gala performance. Stephen smiled on his company and told them that he had no misgivings. Michael on whom a new production always acted as a tonic was excited. The house was packed, Nancy's dressing room was filled with flowers, but she seemed nervous, and told Michael as they stood at the side of the stage that she wished the opera were over.

He laughed, "Why? So that you can revel in the storms of applause the audience will give you?"

"I hope so, Mickie—I hope so."

The Emperor entered his box, followed by the young

Duke of York, handsome but already showing promise of developing the Hanoverian heaviness of jowl and figure. The eldest son of the Emperor followed. The audience cheered and applauded, the Emperor bowed, the Duke of York bowed and smiled his slightly vacuous smile, the tumult died and the overture began. Michael, conscious that he was in excellent voice, feeling happy and confident, delighted everyone, Nancy had her usual meed of acclamation when she made her first entrance.

She looked charming, she sent her smile over the footlights to her listeners, her eyes sparkled and she acted beautifully. Michael listening intently, felt a sudden sense of apprehension. She was singing well, but he detected a slight roughness, a hint of forcing the voice which was foreign to her. She was—he felt—making an effort. Her voice had always been so—effortless. It had flowed like a clean stream of sound. There had always been a remarkable flexibility in it, now he thought it was as if "the joints needed oiling".

In the second act they had an important duet together. It was one of the high-lights of the opera. It began brilliantly, only still Michael detected that slight roughness. Suddenly, when she was about to take a high note, no sound came. She stood there, white under her make-up, dumb. A slight murmur of surprise rippled through the audience, Michael holding her hand tightly in his continued to sing, using every ounce of artistry he possessed to attempt to cover what had happened. Fortunately the opera was nearing its end, and Michael and the rest of the company were able to carry the work to its conclusion. The curtain fell, the applause was excellent, but Michael felt that much of it was expressing the wish to show their sympathy with their much loved Nancy Storace.

He went round to her dressing room, Lord Barnard was there before him, saying, "Nanthy, what happened! Weally how dwedful for you. I am so sowwy."

With tears running down her cheeks, she cried, "Oh, go away, I only want Stephen and Mickie."

CHAPTER TWELVE

NANCY was heartbroken, crying, "Stephen, I've ruined your lovely opera!" and "Mickie, how terrible for you to have to sing the duet—and such a beautiful one—alone!"

Never once by word or even inflexion did Stephen show the slightest disappointment, all he was concerned for was Nancy's voice. The Emperor, he told her, had been most distressed. He was sending his own physician in the morning to see her. She was not to worry, for worry would only aggravate the trouble.

"The Emperor said, 'As soon as the voice of La Storace is fully recovered, the opera must be put on again. We will have another gala performance to celebrate her return to us.' He could not have been kinder, more sympathetic. He added that until you were better, your lodgings were at your disposal, and your salary would be paid as usual."

Michael said, "Horace Walpole may refer to him as 'His Royal Rapacity', but I've always found him generous."

The royal physician came next morning. He was a tall, portly man with an admirable manner, and very soft, firm hands. Apparently he knew all about Nancy's unfortunate affair with Fisher.

"Signora Storace you have suffered considerable shock. The voice is a delicate instrument, very liable to be affected by a nervous system which is not in perfect condition. You must rest, for at least a fortnight do not attempt to sing a note. Rest, rest, rest! Eat food which is light but nourishing. Leave heavy dishes and highly spiced foods alone. You are very young—what is it?—only twenty, and young people are resilient. I shall tell the Emperor—who is most distressed for you—that he shall have his *prima donna* singing again very soon—if," he smiled urbanely, "if she obeys the orders of her physician."

It was almost four months before Nancy regained her voice, and was able to use it with all its old ease and clarity. During that time Stephen had an offer from London, for Nancy to sing there, and for him to compose the music for an opera. About the same time Michael heard from Dublin that his mother was gravely ill, his father in failing health and demanding that he should return home and settle many business matters. One of his brothers had been killed in the service of the East India Company, Mark—the father of Fanny Kelly, the actress, was a "ne'er do weel" and quite incapable of managing any business affairs.

Michael again sought an audience with the Emperor. He asked for three months leave. The Emperor stroked his long nose reflectively.

"Three months is not sufficient, O'Kelly. Take six. For six months your salary will continue to be paid. If by that time you have found success in your native country —remain there. If not, your position is waiting for you here. I wish you all good fortune, O'Kelly."

At the end of February, 1787, Michael left Vienna. Nancy, her mother, Stephen—and Nancy's little dog travelled in a coach with four horses. Michael stared out of the window at the familiar streets through which they passed. He felt sad and regretful. Last night he had visited Mozart for the last time. The little musician had held his hand and wished him well.

"We shall meet again, Michael," he said. "I shall write more operas and you will make them a success. I have loved our association, together we have worked very well. We are both young, there are triumphs waiting for us— one day you may even beat me at billiards! There go and God be with you."

That was the last time that Michael saw his friend. Mozart, worn out with disappointments, heartbroken at promises which were made and never kept, watching other musicians—who lacked his genius—succeed and attain high positions while he remained almost un-recognized, broke his gallant heart.

Even the most advantageous offers from England could not stir him. He was disillusioned, it may be that he was too tired to make the necessary effort. He died in 1791, and Michael Kelly mourned him as one of the best friends, and probably the greatest genius he had ever known—or would ever know.

At Munich they found Lord Barnard waiting for them. Michael was conscious that Stephen watched him curiously, indeed he felt some curiosity concerning him-self. He had wondered if the sight of Barnard, with his long, pale face and lisping voice might not rouse in him that sense of jealous resentment which he had always felt previously when any personable young man paid attention to Nancy.

He felt nothing except a slight irritation at the man's lisping voice and his foppish clothes.

"It is a surpwise seeing me again so soon," Barnard said, "but I wanted to show Miss Stowace and her mama—" Michael thought how hastily he had included Mrs. Storace, and how relieved he would have been if she had not arrived with her daughter— "Stwasburg.

It's a charming place and p'waps we can all meet in Pawis?"

Later Stephen spoke to Michael about Barnard, "What's he hanging round Nancy for? D'you think that he imagines he's in love with her? Because if so he can't possibly offer her marriage, can he?"

Michael shrugged his shoulders, "I can't see why not, if he had the courage to brave his father's displeasure—which I'm certain he hasn't got. Shall you interfere?"

"Not I! Much as I love my sister—and I do love her dearly—she's not a child any longer, she must make her own bed and——"

"Lie on it with who she wishes, eh?" Michael said. "Oh, I know, you're right, you can't go about trying to run Nancy's life for her but—" he sighed, "it does seem a pity."

"You've changed, Mickie," Stephen told him, watching his friend with troubled eyes, "a year ago you'd have been ready to kill anyone who spoke as you have just done—about Nancy."

"I know—sometimes it makes my unhappy that I cannot feel so now. I think, perhaps, that really I'm not a very amatory fellow. Perhaps this love of mine for Nancy was never a—physical thing, it was something which was romantic, beautiful." He smiled, "I'm romantic believe me. Most players are, I fancy. They get used to playing romantic parts, in romantic settings, singing romantic words, but—well, there it is, Stephen. Perhaps one day I shall understand myself better."

"You don't want to marry?"

Michael considered the question gravely, then answered, "I don't know, somehow I don't think that I shall ever marry. I should like to have someone near me who loved me, and who I loved very tenderly."

"Yet you wanted to marry Nancy—immediately, out of hand."

Michael laughed softly, "Wasn't that all part of the romance, my boy? I think so. Two gifted young singers —for we were gifted—possessing more than the average amount of good looks—which we certainly do—would have appeared romantic not only to themselves but to the world." He shrugged his shoulders, "It's over! Not the friendship, the affection—they are both there. Always will be, but if—and forgive me being blunt—if I found myself in bed with Nancy, and I think she would tell you the same—we should probably discuss the proper tempo for some duet we had in the next opera. Nothing is so dead as physical love—when it dies! Come let us have supper, I am assured that the cooking here is excellent and the hock superb!"

"Nancy and mama are supping with Barnard," Stephen said.

Michael chucked, "He'll write it down in his damned diary before he goes to bed—in French! Now why the devil write it in French? What a posturing fellow he is— come, Stephen, my bold boy, it's as if a fox were gnawing at my vitals, I'm hungry."

They reached London, the city which Michael at twenty-four had never seen. He thought it less gay than Vienna, less lovely than Venice, slightly cleaner than Naples, and yet he knew that he loved it.

"It's more respectable than my dear Dublin, but— there's a big heart beating here in London."

Together the two young men went to see Thomas Linley who lived in Norfolk Street off the crowded, bustling Strand. He was, as Mozart had told Michael, a charming man, and engaged them both to appear for him at Drury Lane. Michael was overjoyed, to be engaged immediately on his arrival in London to appear at the finest theatre in the town. At Linley's house they met his two daughters, the elder who was married to Richard Brinsley Sheridan. She was a handsome woman, older than Michael and Stephen but very gay and charming; in addition she was an astute business woman and as her father and her husband had brought a considerable part of the shares in Drury Lane, she had every opportunity to prove her ability in management.

So began for Michael a long, successful career which was to gain for him admiration, and even adulation. Linley was very kind to him, giving him additional coaching in his words, for Michael having lived for eight years in Italy, had acquired an accent which, at first, made him appear to be an Italian who spoke English very well.

He and Stephen worked happily together, Stephen as usual working furiously at his composing, and even appearing on the stage at Drury Lane to sing with Michael. He was not well; it seemed to Michael watching him anxiously, that the flame of his genius flared up too brightly as a flickering candle does when it is almost consumed.

They seldom saw Nancy, she had made a considerable success, and taken the fancy of the public immediately. She was seen frequently with Lord Barnard, but her brother and Michael saw her rarely outside the theatre. Michael, in his usual impetuous way giving generous praise where he felt that it was merited—though there were times when he allowed his affection to sway his judgement—managed to make an enemy of one Madame Mara, a celebrated singer in oratorio. Handel's Messiah was to be given in Westminster Abbey, and Madame Mara had come over from Germany to take part.

Michael returned to Stephen one evening and flinging himself down in his usual big chair, threw back his head and laughed.

"Poof! I've seen an angry woman to-night, my boy, if I never see another. Madame Mara, if it please you, asked me, 'What do you think of Anna Storace? Is she as good as they say?'

"I answered, 'In my opinion, Madame, Anna Storace is the finest vocalist in Europe—probably in the world—to-day. More than that, she acts beautifully, possesses immense charm and great distinction.' Stephen, I wish that you had seen her face, if I had said, 'the greatest *operatic* vocalist', she might have forgiven me, for she does not sing opera, oratorio is her forte. She stared at me like an angry tiger, then turned on her heel and left me. I was told later that she fulminated against me shockingly. 'That Kelly, impertinent coxcomb! I refuse to sing with him. His airs and graces! Because it is said that when in Vienna the Emperor showed him some favour. I imagine that the funny little undersized popinjay amused him!' This and more!"

Again he laughed, and Stephen said, "Who told you all this?"

"Sherry, he was there, and caught the full impact of her fury."

"What did Sherry say?"

"Ah, he's a kindly soul is Sherry. His nose may be like the 'red red rose', but his heart's in the right place. He said that I was a good singer, a creditable actor, and added, 'as for his size, Madame, gold and jewels are never done up in large parcels'. That closed the conversation!"

He had some good friends, Michael knew that, and for some reason which he himself could not have accounted, his hero was—George, Prince of Wales. He saw him often at the theatre, and more than once Michael was sent for and stood respectfully before the stout man with the slightly turned-up nose which gave him a delusive expression of good-natured, innocent ingenuousness.

Comparing him with the Emperor Joseph of Austria he was an Adonis, but he had not the ability to do grand things in the grand manner which Joseph possessed. He was inordinately conceited, and once said to Michael after a performance of "Lionel and Clarissa"—that evergreen production—when he sent for Kelly—"Ah, Mr. Kelly," the fat, rather swollen white hand was stretched out graciously, "I have enjoyed the performance. Admirable, quite ad-mirable! One day, when I am in Brighton and you find yourself there, we must make music together. I am not—completely—a tiro where music is concerned, eh, Sherry?" he asked Sheridan who was in the Royal box.

Sheridan answered, "No, emphatically, sir. It might be better for the nerves of some of my artistes if you were."

"How's that, Sherry?" the Prince demanded.

"You make them nervous, sir."

"Egad! 'Pon my soul, one night I'll make an appearance. Yes, you shall announce me as—what?—oh, I shall think of some suitable name when the time comes, I don't doubt. Say . . . Mr. Windsor making his first appearance as—'Lionel' eh?"

Sheridan sent a quick glance flying to where Michael stood, twenty-four, slim, small with a figure which was neatly and gracefully proportioned returning to the heavy form of the Prince of Wales.

"Sir, it's one of our most popular productions. I should never be able to present it again after you had sung it."

"And why, Sherry?"

"Surely, sir, the reason is obvious."

To Michael the Prince was always gracious, simple and kindly. Michael often thought that he boasted and bragged before such men as Sheridan, Fox and the rest in order to assert himself. True, he had a taste for music, and had at various times made small suggestions which had value, but he never—as Stephen Storace—who disliked him—said, had the slightest real dignity.

"Damn it," Stephen said, "he may have a certain taste for music, and for handsome women—but he treats both of them badly."

Michael said stubbornly, "He's a fine figure of a man."

"So was Falstaff," Stephen replied drily.

"He's the first Gentleman of Europe!"

"Warned off the turf because he didn't run his horses straight, in debt to the eyes! No, Mickie, he's a paper and tinsel Prince."

"Ah, well, I *like* him."

Life moved on smoothly and easily, despite the interior troubles, alarms and disasters which were forever besetting Drury Lane, somehow the splendid theatre always managed to survive. Michael and Stephen were, as Michael said, "part of the building". Not only was Michael singing, but he had turned again to composing. His operas were, perhaps, machine-made and hence mechanical, he wrote them quickly, but here and there some melody would catch the ear of the audience and they would acclaim it as something to be encored and encored. His voice was at its best, and his acting—particularly his acting and mimicry—roused them to great heights of enthusiasm. He was known by the people who passed him in the street, along the busy Strand, to the more exclusive parts of London; in the narrower streets round Old Drury, his neat, trim figure always immaculately dressed was recognized.

"There goes Michael Kelly of Drury Lane" or "Look, Kelly, there he is! What a voice, and what charm—the ladies almost swoon when he walks on to the stage." Then again, "There's the Irish lad from Dublin! He can make the birds stop singing with envy."

Yes, life was a good business, filled with work— which he loved—filled with new experiences, with meetings with famous men, with men who were notable for their exploits. He dined with Lady Hamilton, he met Jem Belcher—champion of England, and was surprised to find him a quiet gentlemanly fellow. Sheridan he came to know well, to respect and like greatly. His wit might be sharp and even bitter at times, but Michael admitted "after all it is *wit*, not the vapid rubbish some of them would have you accept as wit."

He loved London, loved the bustle and the noise of the heavy wheels of coaches trundling over the paved streets. He liked the cheery smiles of the women selling fruit in Covent Garden, the sight of the fops picking their way delicately among the cabbage stalks, pomanders held to their delicate noses.

Barnard once said to Michael, "Gad, Mickie, don't you use a pomander? The stink of dead vegetables is tewwible!"

Michael laughed, "Faith, I was reared in Dublin. I thrive on it."

Although he had returned to England for the primary reason of visiting his father and his beloved mother, he had not been able to do so. He had been engaged by Linley immediately on his arrival, and afterwards was always either rehearsing for a new production or appearing in one. He thought constantly of his mother, that kindly, gentle soul who he had not seen for over eight years. He frequently sent her presents and affectionate letters, he was alternately elated or depressed by the reports of her health.

"I can tell what the news is in your letter from Ireland without your having to tell me," Stephen said. "If you are gloomy and cast down—or if you are elated and gay. That shows how matters are with your mother."

The news came that she had died and for the first time in his life—that life of which he had enjoyed, even vicariously, every moment—he knew what a great personal loss meant. For days the thought of her; her gentle ways, her kindness and self sacrifice would sweep over him and almost un-man him.

Each evening they sat together, which they enjoyed doing after their work was over, talking of the day's doings, of their ambitions, their hopes and fears—so far as Michael was concerned, these were few—Stephen jumping up at intervals to play over some part of a score which he had written, asking for criticism, for praise or blame. Wonderful, warm, friendly evenings, in a big comfortable room, a trifle shabby perhaps, but when it was cold a great fire burned and the mulled wine was prepared.

They talked of the latest scandal concerning the Prince

of Wales—"His Gorgeousness" Stephen called him—of
Sherry's latest play, "The Critic" which convulsed them
both when he read it to them one evening at the Linley's
house, of Belcher, or this new man, Pearce, the Bristol
Chicken who was reputed to be the finest boxer which
that "fine town" had yet produced. They talked of
Fox and his eccentricities, of the great Corinthians with
their strange affectations, and their splendid manners and
intolerance.

Michael would sigh, "If I'd not been given a voice, I'd
have liked to have been born in the position to be a
Corinthian."

Stephen shrugging would answer, "Gad, Mickie—
half of them are nobodies. Look at Brummel! What
have any of them contributed to the world's happiness?
Nothing. Selfish men, swimming into the Carlton House
set by reason of some *foible* which is their only claim to
fame. Worthless people! Decorative, admittedly, but
what use are they, except to their tailors, bootmakers and
the like and usually—they're in debt to them." He stopped
abruptly, "Mickie, I've heard that Barnard is to be
married."

Michael looked up sharply, "I wondered how long it
would be."

Stephen continued, "He was at Nancy's benefit on
the 24th of April but though he sent her magnificent
flowers and some trinket or other—I forget what—he
didn't sup with her as he always used to in Vienna."

"Poor Nancy. D'you think she'll take it to heart?"

"I think that she's probably seen it coming, as I have
done. I never liked Barnard as you know——"

"Did I?" Michael spoke with a note of derision in his
voice.

"He's an aristocratic snob! Nancy in Vienna was the pet of the whole place, it flattered him to be seen dancing attendance upon her. Now, he's in with the Prince's set, and—well, he's going to fly higher than Nancy Storace."

On the 9th of June, Michael and Stephen received a message from Nancy asking them to sup with her. She wrote, "I shall be quite alone as mama is staying for a few days with the Linleys."

She was in great spirits, looking her usual vivacious self, her eyes very bright and her cheeks warm with colour. She looked not only exceedingly pretty but brimming over with vitality.

She greeted them both warmly, "How nice for we three to be together again. You neither of you come to see me often enough."

Stephen said, "Why Nancy, you've always got a throng of people here. When we've been working all day and half the night, Mickie and I like to sit and smoke and drink mulled wine."

"Two old bachelors," Michael said, "growing misanthropic and retiring."

"You'll never be retiring, Mickie Kelly, until you retire under six feet of earth! As for working all day— rubbish. I hear of you going everywhere, the man about town. I hear about your new clothes, the perfect fop! I hear of ladies who sigh their hearts out for you, the complete lady killer!" She laughed and teased him all through supper—which was excellent, for Nancy Storace lived well, and her cook was admirable.

Later they sat at the open window, for the night was very hot, and drank the iced wine which Nancy offered them.

She said, "Last time it was very cold, and we drank mulled wine."

"Last time—?" Stephen queried.

"In Vienna—ah, dear Vienna. How I wish that we could all go to sleep and wake to find ourselves there! Yes, have you forgotten the night I visited you both— without any shoes? Then I came because I had run away from a man—if you could call that beast—a man—now you've come to me so that I can tell you about another man—only he has run away from me! Yes, Barnard is going to be married—the daughter of a Duke, no less! Lady Katherine Powlett."

"I'd heard of it," Stephen said.

"You don't mind terribly, m'dear, do you?" Michael asked gently.

She turned to him, her eyes dancing, "Mind! Mickie he was a dreadfully dull dog! Still—I did rather hope that one day I might be a Countess—his father is the Earl of Darlington."

"I've never heard of the place, where is it?"

Nancy said, "I'll be damned if I know! Honestly, I don't somehow think that I should have fitted in with— the Prince's set—Cumberland House, Carlton House and the rest. I'm not popular with the Prince, I was once sitting next to him at supper—no, not here, of course. I kept hearing a most peculiar sound, a kind of squeaking. I asked him if he heard it too. He looked very sulky, like an over-fed, bad-tempered school boy, and said, 'I hear nothing!' He never spoke to me for the rest of the supper, but devoted himself to the woman on his right. Sherry— he was on my other hand—was constricted with laughter that he was trying to overcome.

"I said, 'Did you hear that squeaking, Sherry?'

"He answered, 'Not to-night, but I have heard it.
It's His Highness's stays! They must be a new pair!'
Since then, his manner has always been most chilly
towards me. He's a *silly* man!'"

"Mickie likes him, almost makes a hero of him,"
Stephen said.

"Poof, Mickie probably wants to go to the same tailor,
and if Mickie ever allows his figure to grow like the
P.O.W., he'll look like a bundle of fat—whatever tailor
he goes to."

So Nancy's intimacy with Barnard came to an end,
and it seemed to Michael that she was not deeply affected
by it. No woman, he reflected can enjoy being discarded,
but knowing Nancy's dislike of being bored, her intolerance of people who were pretentious and affected,
he believed that—in her heart—Barnard's departure was
something of a relief. She continued to be a great success,
she was as popular as her brother. As for Michael, it
seemed that he was always busy and yet had time for
everything. He was writing music, and as he wrote his
mind would go back to the advice which Mozart had
given him.

"You have chosen singing as your profession,
Occheley. Stick to that, leave the writing of music to
other people on whom God did not bestow a voice."

He would play over what he had written, and smile a
little wryly. Michael was too good a musician not to be
able to put a true valuation on his work. He wrote easily
—perhaps too easily—the music was pleasant, tuneful and
—uninspired.

He thought, "Dear Mozart, right as always. But, if
you were here I should assure you that I make no pretence
at ever coming within a hundred miles of such music as

you—a genius—give to the world. All I can say in extenuation is that—I do my best, at least my harmonies are correctly written and—" he chuckled quietly, "I enjoy writing my bits of music—no, not music as you, Mozart know it, but—at least allow me to call what I write—my small melodies."

Stephen wrote more slowly, his music was definitely good, and a great future was predicted for him. He was so courageous, he never allowed his failing health to affect his work, he never spoke of it, when people told him that he was growing too thin, he would say:

"I am always thin in the summer," or if it were winter, his reply would be, "I know, for only in the summer time can I persuade a little flesh to remain on my wretched bones."

Nancy told Michael that Stephen ought to come and live with her and her mother, he needed cosseting and coddling. Michael answered a trifle indignantly that he was devoted to Stephen, that he did everything he could to tempt him to eat, adding, "And our landlady cooks very well, I assure you."

Nancy tossed her head, "Rubbish, Mickie, no landlady ever cooks well. Her ideal lodgers are those who go and eat—out of her house. I can imagine so well the uneatable stuff she gives you, and because you can eat so little of the dreadful stuff, you must sit up half the night drinking far too much wine!"

"Come, come, Nancy," Kelly protested, "Wine's good for one. It's a food—the juice of the grapes."

"Every fool in Christendom who drinks too much talks like that!" she retorted, and when he expostulated, she checked him. "Now, Mickie, don't give me arguments and protestations—both you and Stephen drink far too much. Very well, let's admit that wine *is* a food, but there's no call to stuff yourself with food—until you're sick. Until you make yourself ill."

Again indignantly Michael protested, "You have never seen either Stephen or me the worse for drink, never known the time when we were not perfectly capable of doing our work, and doing it well. Stephen has always been delicate, your mama has told me, I am as strong as a horse!"

She shrugged her shoulders, "As you wish! Yes, you're strong now, what is this vaunted juice of the grape going to do to you when you're older? You're twenty-four now, by the time you're fifty-two you'll be gouty and bad tempered."

He smiled, "Gouty I might be, Nancy dear, but bad tempered—I don't think so, and certainly never with you m'dear."

CHAPTER THIRTEEN

THE quarrel with Madame Mara was over. Michael, attending a party where she was a guest, heard her speaking to Ponté, the great French horn player. He was engaged to play that instrument, and speaking to Madame Mara in German said that he didn't know how he would be able to do so.

"At this moment," he said, "I would give the world for water or a glass of beer to moisten my lips."

She answered, "Poor Ponté! If I knew where to get it, I would willingly go myself. There seems to be no-one here to take orders."

Michael, dressed exquisitely as always, immaculate in heavy silk and embroidered waistcoat, heard what she said, and speaking to her in German said, "Madame, I shall immediately concern myself, and at the same time offer my apologies that I did not notice that Monsieur Ponté was lacking something to drink."

He rushed away and returned with a jug of cool beer and glasses. Madame accepted them on behalf of Ponté, who had only time to drink a glass when he was asked to play his concerto. She talked to Kelly, and told him how she had disliked him at their first meeting.

Michael smiled, bowed and took all the blame on himself for having answered her question regarding Nancy in so clumsy a fashion.

"Signor Kelly, will you kindly call on me at two o'clock to-morrow?" Madame said, "I have a proposal to make to you. When I came to England I never intended to appear on the stage, but I believe that shortly you have a benefit—if you care to accept my offer, I shall be delighted to appear. I should wish to sing Dr. Arne's short opera, 'Artaxerxes'."

Michael naturally accepted her offer, and she begged that he would sing the part of "Artabarnes"; the other artists—with his permission—she would chose.

"They shall not disgrace your benefit, Signor Kelly."

That night Michael said to Stephen, "See how it pays —pays dividends, a little civility, and a jug of beer—the result—Madame Mara sings at my benefit!"

He went down to Drury Lane for the first rehearsal. Linley and Sheridan were both delighted, even the dignified Kemble smiled on him and stated that he was "more than gratified". Madame Mara was gracious, and greeted Michael with great and warm courtesy, she assured him that he could not fail in the part.

"And the other artists?" he asked.

"They are good—very good. I promised that we should not disgrace you. There is Dignum, Mrs. Foster —she is very good—and playing 'Arbaces'—one of the most lovely creatures I have ever seen."

"Her name, Madame?"

"She is a Mrs. Crouch, and a singer of great merit."

"Crouch," Michael repeated, "why did she not choose a prettier name. It has an ugly sound to my ears."

"Surely you have heard of her!"

"I believe that I have, Madame, but I have never met her."

"That will be remedied in a few seconds, for here she comes. Anna my dear, I want to present Mr. Kelly to you."

That night Michael told Stephen of the encounter. "She came on to that great stage, and to me it seemed that she brought with her all the sunlight in the world. Never have I seen such beauty, it is not of this world. She is gracious, and modest. Her voice is beautiful. Ah, Stephen—have you seen her?"

Stephen frowned, "Wait a moment," he said, "I'm trying to remember—ah, I have it. She was—it is said— for a time living under the protection of your hero—the Prince of Wales. When he wearied of her, he promised her a substantial sum of money, and had signed a deed to that effect. Later he repudiated it, and declined to pay. She sued him—Michael, surely you have heard the story?"

"On my honour, no! Go on I beg you. I am interested."

"She sued him. The case was tried by a Committee of Inquiry. They treated her very harshly, and finally she asked—in a very quiet voice—to be allowed to see the document again. It was handed to her. She tore it into shreds, and threw them out among the wig-pated lawyers, saying, 'As His Highness does not know how to honour his obligations, I must attempt to show him what value I set upon them'; with that, she left the court with great dignity. That's the story, Mickie—how true it is I cannot say."

Michael nodded gravely, "I can imagine whatever she said or did would be filled with dignity. Yet she is timid and retiring, when we were all laughing and joking she remained apart, just watching us with her glorious eyes."

Stephen listened to the deeper tones in Michael's voice, tones which he never heard unless his friend was deeply moved. Had Mickie, he wondered, fallen in love with the beautiful Crouch? Or was this another of his romantic attachments?

He said, "She's married, you know, to this man Crouch who was in the Navy. I imagine that he has retired, and that she—supports him. I've seen him, a flashy looking fellow, with indifferent manners. I've heard that the relations between them are not too satisfactory."

"In other words," Michael said, "this fellow does not appreciate the gem which is in his possession. Stephen, I'll swear that she is as good as she is beautiful, and—that being so, she must be a saint walking the earth."

"I believe, Mickie," Stephen said gravely, "that you've fallen in love."

Kelly moved restlessly in his big chair, he drummed with his fingers on the leather covered arm, and waited for some moments before he spoke.

"I've told you before, my dear Stephen, I'm a strange fellow. I don't either know or understand myself. I wish that I did. I don't know that I am capable of great physical love—I have no great desire to experience it. That I am capable of intense love and devotion, I *do* know. When I was younger, when I fell in love with Nancy, I imagined that physical love was the ultimate goal of all lovers, true lovers. We grow old quickly in our profession, it may be that all artists do—painters, singers, actors—all of them. I was certain then, during those days in Venice, that to hold Nancy in my arms, to make love to her would be the crown of my earthly happiness. Now —I don't know. I saw this lady to-day, and felt—yes, laugh and call me an incurable romantic if you will—that I longed passionately to devote my life to her, to do everything in my power to make her happy, to advance her in her profession. It's probably fantastic, Stephen, to speak in this way of a woman I only met this morning!"

"You're a fantastic person, Mickie," Stephen said, "your whole life has been a fantasy, your success, your attainments, your popularity—you and Nancy are fantastic people. It's not the least use my saying—be wise, be prudent, perhaps the best thing I can say is—wait a little. If, as I hear, relations between her and Crouch are not too good, well—who knows what may happen!"

"How old is she, d'you know that?" Michael asked.

"I believe about the same age as yourself, possibly a year older or younger."

Michael rose and went to the piano, he sat down and played, his beautiful voice filling the room, a song he had not sung for many years.

"Believe me if all those endearing young charms——"

When the song ended, he came over to Stephen, and laying his hand on his friend's shoulder, said in a voice, full of emotion:

"And that's exactly how I feel, Stephen."

The opera was a great success, the great theatre was packed, and Michael was accorded tremendous applause, Mrs. Crouch—playing a male part, which Michael felt was unsuitable to her delicate beauty and her innate modesty —and Madame Mara were acclaimed with great enthusiasm. The successful season ended, and Michael, travelling by coach, was accompanied by not only Mrs. Crouch but her husband.

Michael disliked him intensely, not only from a sense of jealousy, but because he regarded him as "a pestilent fellow". He was continually becoming enamoured of some woman or other, and while his wife never referred to his infidelities, it was obvious that she suffered from the knowledge that they existed.

They travelled to Dublin, where Michael realized afresh the desolation caused in his life by the death of his mother. The house seemed different, it was well kept, and his father was delighted to see him, but something essential had gone. He stayed at home, the Crouches had lodgings in the town. He saw her constantly, for they gave several concerts together, and at each meeting he knew that she attracted him more and more.

She had a delicate beauty, and lovely colouring. Her eyes were not only magnificent but kind in their expression. She was very quiet, retiring and modest. She might receive acclamations from her audiences, but Michael always felt that she accepted them with slight surprise, her manner being almost depreciating. To him, she was sweetness itself, yet never for one moment assuming that there might be any closer association between them.

For himself, he knew that he was deeply in love. Then almost impatiently he discarded the expression—"in love". He loved her, loved her tenderly, completely, and —so he told himself—for ever. He wrote to Stephen, who, when Michael left London and their lodgings were given up, had gone back to live with his mother and Nancy—"I am puzzled. My dear friend, how often have you heard me say this? How tired you must have grown at my indecisions and uncertainties. Only you would tolerate anyone as a friend, who was so unsure of himself.

"Yet, I am not completely unsure. I know that I am experiencing love as I have never known it before. I fell in love with our dear Nancy when I was still very young. I may not be much older—in years—but I am in experience. This lady is, I am certain, not happy with her pestilent husband. The stews see more of him than his wife does! Had I it in my heart to believe that she was entirely happy, I should retire from the lists—if indeed I have really entered them—and live for the rest of my life on the memories of a gentle voice, a warm handclasp, and tender smiles.

"If he left her, which believe me, should some charmer arrive on the scene, he might very well do, I doubt if I, even if she divorced him, wish to embrace marriage; always supposing that she would consider me as a husband. That I could and would give her devotion, affection, and every consideration, that we have much in common, I do not doubt for one moment. That I am capable of offering her more, those physical tributes which surely are only natural, I do not know.

"That is a confession, Stephen, and one which no man could make to anyone he did not love and trust. Most men would regard it as a deep humiliation, I do not even regret it! I make out a balance sheet—debit and credit. To my credit there are items stating that I am fairly presentable, that I have ability in my profession, I am kindly dispositioned, I have sufficient in my make-up to have the tenderness of a woman, not that I am in any way an effeminate man—except maybe in my love of fine clothes—but I have never been endowed with the wish to build any relationship with a woman on a foundation which was chiefly physical.

"So, we shall see. I am in love, and so in love that if it shall turn out that it is possible for me to live the remainder of my life with this lady, I shall devote my life to her service——"

Crouch, a handsome fellow in a flashy fashion, left his wife. He ran away with a Miss Ryder—or Rider—she was young and impressionable, and his obvious good looks attracted her as they had once attracted Anna Maria Phillips. Her father was distracted when the two of them fled to France, and begged his daughter—both by letter and in personal interviews—to return. She vowed that she loved Crouch to distraction, and that to leave him would kill her.

Many years later, Michael speaking to Anna Crouch mentioned Miss Rider. She smiled at him, that lovely smile which never failed to stir his heart.

"I have no hard feelings regarding Miss Rider. I only hope that Crouch makes her happier than he ever contrived to make me. It was a miserable time, Mickie, and had it not been for my work—and you, I think that I should have sunk beneath the weight of unhappiness. I shall never do anything which might for a single moment disturb their happiness."

Together Michael and Mrs. Crouch began a tour of the provinces. It was wildly successful, her beauty, both of voice and person attracted everyone, while Michael's good looks and his happy manner with all with whom he came in contact made him friends everywhere.

Very carefully they observed the proprieties, never staying in the same lodgings, and indeed, it was not until nearly the end of the tour that Michael, supping with Mrs. Crouch, opened his heart. They sat in the rather ordinary room provided by provincial landladies, where the furniture smelt slightly of dust, where the heavy sideboard was sadly in need of a polish, and where there were over many ornaments and foolish mementoes which added nothing to the comfort and certainly not to the beauty of the room. The food was reasonably good, and Michael had brought some wine which he knew was excellent.

H

Supper was over and he begged to be allowed to smoke. Anna rose and smiling, said, "I expected that, I have provided those long pipes which you enjoy—and tobacco. I only hope that it is a kind which you like."

"You are far too kind," he said and his voice sounded harsh and constrained. "Far too kind, Anna."

He prounced her name as the Italians do, dividing it sharply, making it sound like, "An-nah!" It was the first time he had ever used it, and she glanced at him quickly. He was busily engaged in filling his pipe, but when it was filled to his satisfaction, he laid it down and with his hands clasped on the edge of the table, began to speak.

"The tour will soon be over," he said, "What am I going to do?"

"Go back to Drury Lane," she said gently, "there is this opera of your friend Stephen Storace waiting for our arrival. You, Nancy Storace and myself. We shall make a great success of it."

Michael nodded, "Indeed, for dear Stephen's sake I want this very sincerely. 'The Haunted Tower'—it's very excellent. In addition, we have Bannister and Baddeley— they're good! Oh, it will be a success. Not a doubt of it. I was thinking—selfishly no doubt—of myself."

"Explain to me, please," she asked.

"Anna, I am in love with you, more, I love you devotedly and sincerely, with all my heart and soul. At this juncture, I feel that if I do not see you every day my heart will break. My dear, my most beautiful and wonderful, you are free, your husband has proved completely faithless. May I come and lodge in your house?" He laughed, "How blatant that sounds! But I mean it."

She rested her elbow on the table and her chin on her hand.

"You know," she said slowly, "what people will say?"

He laughed, "The same as they are all probably saying now, at this moment. I shall no doubt hear presently, that Crouch only ran away with Miss Rider because I had alienated your affections."

"He did that himself long ago," she said.

"No-one will entirely believe that."

"Mickie, tell me one thing," he saw the colour rise in her cheeks, heard the sudden catch in her breathing, "are you asking me to be your mistress?"

He rose and coming to the side of her chair, took her hand in his. Her's was cold, and he laid it against his elaborately embroidered waistcoat to try to instill a little warmth into it.

"My heart's delight," he said, "that is for you to decide—one day. For myself all I ask is to be able to be with you, to have the privilege of your kindness and tenderness and to be your most loyal and devoted servant for the remainder of my life. People will talk, it has been said that I have been the lover of Nancy Storace, they have said unpleasant things concerning Stephen and me, they have said—oh, they have said so much. Well, let them say. Incidentally, let me say that neither of those statements is true. I was in love with Nancy, I shall always love her, Stephen is my dearest friend, one of the greatest men I have ever known. Stephen Storace and Mozart! The imputations are lies, that I swear. I swear it on everything that I hold sacred, Anna."

"And you know, don't you, that for a time I lived under the protection of the Prince of Wales?" she asked.

His charming, kindly smile softened his lips, "Here's the conceited Irishman!" he said, "That was before you met Mickie Kelly from Dublin!"

"And if some day, I was unfaithful——?" she asked.

The smile faded, "I should know that I had failed in proving my complete devotion to you."

He lifted her hand to his lips and kissed it, very gently, and with great respect. "I have sworn my allegiance," he said, "now I shall wait, with as much patience as I can muster, for your decision. Everything shall be as you wish, for you are the mainspring of my whole existence. There, I must leave you, or your landlady will have some pretty stories to tell to her cronies. I bid you a good-night, and remember that you have—my whole heart."

They returned to London, and Kelly went back to his old lodgings very lonely without Stephen. He was waiting, he told himself, and he must wait patiently for Anna's decision. He was young, but already he had developed a certain philosophy. He assured himself that Anna must not be persuaded, influenced, she must make up her mind and do what she wished. It was not that his love was not strong and unwavering, but there were times when the thought of the happiness which might come to him, induced in him what amounted to a sense of fear.

Meanwhile rehearsals were in progress, Stephen, looking thinner than ever, directed them. The music was beautiful, and Michael knew that his friend had dealt generously with him. He had two songs one, "Spirit of my Sainted Sire" exceedingly difficult, but Kelly's voice was at its best and he rendered them so exquisitely that even at rehearsals, the company would applaud him.

"You've reached untold heights," Michael told Stephen, "this is your masterpiece. I am proud to be allowed to sing in it."

"My masterpiece? I don't know, Mickie. I have written so much, and the music is pouring out from me all the time, I feel that I am driven, that I must not waste time. And what will happen to the music I have written, Mickie? I wonder——"

"It will be played after you and I are here no longer. It will delight audiences a hundred years hence." Michael assured him.

During rehearsals, Michael was disturbed by the news which came to him of Mozart. He was in bad health, he was tired and disillusioned, more he wrote to Michael of a "grey stranger, who follows me. He demands constantly that I finished my Requiem. I have no idea who he is, he only begs me to finish it, then turns away and—is gone."

It was during rehearsals that Nancy Storace visited him at his lodgings. Michael was tired and depressed, it seemed to him that both Stephen and his beloved Mozart were desperately ill. Anna was kind and charming to him, they met at rehearsals, and very rarely at other times. Were matters going to develope as he hoped, or would she one day tell him that he had been nursing hopes which could never be realized? It was lonely living without Stephen to talk to, and both Nancy and her mother were determined that the life of two young bachelors was not the best for Stephen.

Michael rarely felt incilned to go into the town in these days, the thought of clubs, chatter, endless discussions, and speculations regarding the inner politics of Drury Lane held no attraction.

Invitations reached him, cards for routs, balls, concerts—with pleasant meetings to follow—and he refused them all. Instead, he sat alone, working at his part in the coming opera, or else allowing himself to dream of Anna Crouch. It was on one of these solitary evenings that Nancy Storace arrived to see him.

He rose, smiling, "Why Nancy, this is delightful."

"Mama would be angry if she knew that I had come alone, she is growing very rigid not to say straight-laced. I wanted to see you alone, Mickie."

"You *do* see me alone!" He moved to bring her wine, and set it beside her, pouring out a glass for himself.

She twirled the glass round by the stem, watching the light from the candles catch it and make it shine as if rubies were lying there. Michael saw that there was a frown between her well marked eyebrows.

He said, "Yes——?"

"I've heard that you are enamoured of Anna Crouch. Is it true?"

"I see no reason why it should not be. She is beautiful —and good."

"She lived under the protection of the Prince of Wales!"

Michael raised his eyebrows, for an actress or opera singer to live under the protection of one of the Royal Family or some member of the aristocracy was not considered as anything approaching a mortal sin. Rather it was a matter for congratulation—while the association lasted. It surprised him that Nancy, who had lived so long in the theatre, who knew what went on there, should adopt this attitude.

He wondered if Nancy's friendship with Barnard had been completely innocent. Not that he attempted to criticize her, Nancy must live her own life, and provided she came to no harm—as she had done with the abominable Fisher—it was no business of Michael's.

He said, as lightly as he could, "Nancy, might that not be the pot calling the kettle black?"

She pouted, "Oh, I've never made a public show of myself. When the prince went bankrupt she entered her name in the list of creditors! It appeared that he had promised to pay her some huge sum or other."

Very gently Michael laid his hand on hers, "Nancy dear, do you remember once in Vienna when I had played at the *ridotto* and lost more money than I could pay immediately?"

"Yes—I remember." Already her voice had softened a little.

"You came to me in a great taking—demanded that I told you the exact amount of my indebtedness. You insisted that I took the money from you, and added, 'In England gentlemen pay their debts!'"

She flashed back at him, "So they do. I have never thought of the Prince or his 'hangers-on' as gentlemen! But imagine suing a man for—giving your favours! You don't suppose that he promised her money for the pleasure of merely gazing into her eyes, do you?"

"I don't know," his voice was reflective, "God knows, they're lovely enough."

Nancy rose, pushed back her chair and walked to the fireplace, she stood staring down at the leaping flames, then turned.

"I'm told that she flies to strong waters when the least thing upsets her!"

Michael laughed, "My dear, you're an actress, a singer, haven't you learnt that 'they say'—these people who know everything—that of us all. I've heard it said about you! I know they say it about me. I'll admit that there's some truth in what they say of me—only not strong waters, *wine*! I don't care for spirits."

For the first time Nancy Storace laughed, "Mickie, you are incorrigible, you laugh at everything! There, I've said my say. I only came because I'm so fond of you, because I don't want to see you do anything which you might regret."

"And had it not been that I am so fond of you, m'dear, I'd have done what the Prince did a few nights ago, to some young lady who thought it clever to be impertinent to him. He put her across his knees and—smacked her!"

"Vulgar coarse creature! Who did he have to assist him, pray? Unless the girl weighed as light as a feather, Grampus George could never have managed to do it alone! He'd have caused a seizure."

"Tut, tut, you're speaking of your future king! There, let's forget it all, only continue to be my dear friend. I even forgive you for what you have said about Mrs. Crouch, because I believe that your words were caused by real consideration for me. Another glass of wine, and then allow me to escort you home."

Their little discussion was over, and together they walked back to the house which Nancy shared with her mother and Stephen. She held his arm, and he carefully picked their way through the dirty, muddy streets. At long distances a lamp shed a faint, quavering light on the damp roads, and here and there *flambeaux* flared outside great houses where some entertainment was being given. In dark doorways beggars crouched, and held out grimy hands as they passed whining for charity.

Arriving at the Storace house, Nancy insisted that Michael should come in; remembering the prospect of a lonely evening he consented very willingly.

Stephen rose to meet them, "Ah, you truants! Where have you been? Wandering about the streets at this time of night. Now, listen, a new song for the 'Haunted Tower' —'Hearts of Oak', it is called. A really stirring ballad. Or I believe that it is."

He played the song, and turning to Michael said, "Come along, Mickie, give us a stave!"

They sat and discussed the coming production, Stephen and Nancy went on to speak of the affairs of Drury Lane. Michael had never been interested in them. He loved the theatre, was proud to walk the same stage as those great figures of the past; but as for the quarrels and squabbles of the management—he cared little who ran the theatre so long as Michael Kelly was included in the cast lists. His voice was in splendid condition, his popularity was almost unbounded, and—although he squandered most of his salary—he was always able to pay his debts.

He loved London, and until the melancholy which overcame him during the time of uncertainty as to Anna Crouch's decision, enjoyed ruffling it with the best of them. His ready wit made him welcome everywhere, his manners were admirable, and his smile warmed the hearts of many beautiful women.

London was a constant delight to him, he loved the fine houses, the broad river with its busy traffic, he liked to see the great coaches roll past, to see the face of some grandee he knew at the window, recognizing him and waving a hand in greeting. True there were times when the mercurial temperament of the Irishman asserted itself—when he thought of his mother, of his beloved friend Mozart, even when he allowed himself he could grow sentimentally reminiscent over the sweet and beautiful Ortabella.

But these descents into melancholy were frequently more enjoyable than otherwise.

The night of Stephen's "Haunted Tower" presentation came, the opera was acclaimed everywhere—Michael, Nancy and Anna Crouch shared the chief honours. Stephen, a patch of scarlet on each pale cheek, was delighted. When they took a call, and Michael waved to Stephen to join them, he came, shy and diffident, as always, to share their triumph.

The Prince was in his box, Nancy whispered to Michael, "Your hero surely cannot grow much fatter, can he?"

Michael replied, his eyes twinkling, "Surely 'by the Grace of God' anything is possible!"

He sent for the artists, and in his slightly grandiloquent manner thanked them all. Michael watched when Anna Crouch made her elaborate curtsey before him. The heavy, painted face merely showed its customary affable smile.

"You were—as always—admirable, Mrs. Crouch."

"I am obliged, sir."

That was all.

To Nancy he was courteous but cold. "You always delight us, Miss Storace."

"I trust that I always shall do so, sir."

When Michael stood before him, his smile widened, "Ah, this Irishman! What a fellow you are, Kelly! I declare that your voice, like good wine, improves with years. How d'you get along with Sherry here, eh? Difficult fellow, don't you think?"

"Mr. Sheridan and I," Michael said, "I believe get along very well, sir."

The Prince in high good humour cried, "Sherry, see that you never quarrel with Michael Kelly. He's as fiery as gunpowder, and if he walks out of Drury Lane—God, I'll never walk into it again."

Sheridan replied, "I shall remember the injunction, sir."

That night a note was brought to his dressing room. it was written in Anna Crouch's delicate, pointed hand, it ran:

"I hear that your lodgings are not very comfortable. Miss Storace told me. I have two rooms which are at your disposal whenever you care to occupy them. I remain, yours faithfully, Anna Maria Crouch."

So Nancy had relented, and his dear Anna had come to a decision.

CHAPTER FOURTEEN

MICHAEL was happier than he had ever been in his life, he loved Anna devotedly, and for the rest of her life and his that devotion never wavered. She was gentle, even timid, but her kindness was wonderful. They observed conventions—outwardly at least, and when they toured, which they did every year, they always occupied different lodgings.

Nancy Storace meeting Michael one morning, his eyes shining with happiness and good health, his step unusually jaunty, and his whole air exuding joyousness, said, "Mickie, you're a sight for sore eyes, you look radiant!"

"And why not, darling?" he asked, "I've everything in the world to make me happy. To me, it seems that Covent Garden shines like—well, like Saint Mark's in our beloved Venice."

He turned and walked with her, and she laid her hand on his arm, "Is she all that you hoped?"

"All that and more. She is wise—without being a blue stocking, she speaks ill of no-one——"

Nancy, always irrepressible, said, "Except Mrs. Jordan!"

"You're wrong," he answered, "she never speaks of Mrs. Jordan at all! She certainly, if they met wouldn't pull her skirts aside as does Mrs. Siddons."

"Poof, 'Our Sally' affects a lot of that overdone modesty. As for Jordan, I have a certain admiration for her——"

Michael pursed his lips and whistled, "Whew! And why?"

"She must be a wonderful woman to tolerate that gawping half witted Clarence. They say that his idea of an evening's entertainment is to read aloud to Jordan—of all things—'The Lives of the Admirals'! And her vitality—how many times has Mrs. Jordan 'been indisposed' and unable to appear—I have lost count."

"This is all scandalous," Michael said with mock gravity, "but it's a fine morning and the sunshine is making us indiscreet. I heard this only last evening. You know that Clarence sends down to the Theatre and collects Jordan's salary regularly?"

"We all know that! He's a pimp and she's a fool."

"Pindar's latest effort is this:

'As Jordan's high and mighty squire
Her play-house profit deigns to skim,
Some folks audaciously inquire
If he keeps her or she keeps him.' "

"I could never bother to inquire," Nancy said, "it's common knowledge. But why does Anna dislike her so much?"

"She detests her vulgarity for one thing—you heard what happened at York when she turned her back on the audience——"

"Yes, yes, and a mighty poor audience it was I'm told. Mickie, I must leave you, I have to buy some ribbons. Give my love to Anna."

So Nancy had forgiven him, and Stephen had always been loud in his praise of Anna Crouch. Admittedly her voice had lost a little of its clarity, Michael admitted that, for as he always said, "I'll lie about most things—to save my skin or a friend's—but I'm damned if I can lie about music or voices." Even so, Mrs. Crouch used her voice with such artistry that the lack of complete clarity went unnoticed, and was atoned for by the excellence of her acting.

She had been travelling by coach, and stood up to push a heavy bag on the rack above her into a position of greater safety, when the coach lurched suddenly, and the bag slipped forward and fell on her throat. She suffered terribly, and even when the bruises disappeared, the blow had undoubtedly damaged some of the vocal cords. Then too, she suffered from some mysterious attacks which caused spasms and incredible pain. The first time Michael saw her in the grip of one of these attacks, he was almost demented. They were driving to Oxford where they were engaged to sing on the following day.

They stopped at Henley for a meal, when he noticed that she was dreadfully pale, and shivering violently.

"Anna, darling, what is it? You're ill!"

He saw the sweat break out on her forehead, her voice was shaking when she spoke. "It's—just one of my usual attacks. Oh, the pain is dreadful. It will pass, I swear that it will pass. Don't distress yourself, Mickie."

Michael like many men, invariably appeared to grow bad-tempered when he was anxious or concerned about someone he loved.

"Not distress myself! Gad, what should I do—go on eating boiled mutton!" He rushed to the door, flung it open and shouted for the landlord, "Here, bring a doctor, get some of your women to assist Mrs. Crouch to bed. Get hot bricks wrapped in flannel. Where the devil is that doctor? She's dying, I tell you!"

The red-faced landlord, his eyes almost starting out of his head, stuttered, "He's here—he—he is having his dinner."

Michael almost frantic with anxiety stormed, "He must leave his dinner! I'll pay for twenty dinners for him. Bring him, you blockhead, and send your women, find Mrs. Crouch's maid."

He rushed back into the room, to find her with her head on the table groaning, he fell on his knees, and put his arm round her. "My darling, the doctor is here—we'll get you to bed. Tell me is it very hard? My poor sweetheart—Ah, here is the doctor. Thank God you're here."

She was undoubtedly very ill and in great pain. Leeches were sent for, and she let them bleed her. The doctor gave her a sleeping pill.

"It will induce sleep and dull the pain," he told Michael.

"Opium, eh?" Michael said. He had seen Kemble take them at the theatre when he was in pain. "When will she be able to continue her journey?"

"My dear sir, you mustn't dream of moving her! It would endanger her life. No, she must remain here. You say that you're singing at Oxford, then I am afraid, my dear sir, that you must sing there without my patient."

Michael promised, and sat by Anna's bed until the last possible moment. She opened her beautiful eyes, heavy with the opium she had taken, and weary through the pain which she had suffered.

He said eagerly, "You're better? Tell me you're better."

Her voice was very weak, but she smiled at him, "Yes, the pain is gone. But—Oxford?"

He said, "I go to Oxford alone."

"You'll come back to me?"

"My dear—I couldn't live without you."

He went to Oxford and there found a very well-known doctor, he begged him to return to Henley with him and to attend Mrs. Crouch. The great specialist consented to come and they found her better but still very weak.

He considered, "It is difficult to give an exact name to this disturbance, but for the sake of the heart, I recommend small doses of brandy." Turning to Mrs. Crouch, he asked, "Have you ever tried that?"

"Sometimes, but I dislike it," she said.

"Pooh, dislike! You take it as medicine. Mr. Kelly, please see that brandy is always provided for my patient. Not, you understand, as a regular thing but in moments of pain."

Michael reflected, "And that disposes of the story that Anna flies to strong waters!"

They returned to London, and it was on the 7th of December, that Michael, late in the evening, almost staggered into their house. His face was ghastly, and he was shaking like a reed. Tears were running down his cheeks. Anna rushed to him, distressed.

"Mickie, you are ill!"

He stared at her, blankly, vaguely. Then shook his head.

"No, Anna, but one of the great lights of the world has been extinguished. Mozart is dead. The dark stranger has called at last and taken him by the hand. His Requiem was finished. He was tired. He left this world—please God to find a world which will treat him more kindly—the day before yesterday at midnight."

Later, he gathered the whole story of the man he had

not only admired but loved. He had been ill, but to his wife—who was away—he wrote cheerful and hopeful letters. No-one was very much interested in Mozart, he was written down as something of a failure. His last injunction to his devoted wife was not to allow the announcement of his death to be made, until his friend Albrechtsberger should have time to apply for the post of Kapellmeister at Saint Stephen's, which Mozart held.

His sister-in-law visited him, and he said, "Stay with me until the end, the taste of death is already on my tongue."

No-one had bothered to give him a good funeral, his very modest coffin was hurried to the graveyard, where it was buried among paupers.

Michael Kelly lashing himself into such a fury of indignation as Anna Crouch had never believed possible, instituted inquiries, wrote to authorities, made representations. They were of no avail. Papers had been lost, forms mislaid and—it was impossible to trace the place where the body of the great little musician had been laid. Mozart was lost among the—paupers.

His death made an indelible impression on Michael, who until the end of his life could never speak of Mozart without admiration, could not speak of the manner of his burial without a flaming anger.

"Ah, had he sent for me!" he cried, "I would have attended to it that he was buried in a manner which befitted his genius. Anna, listen, in future years, his name will shine gloriously. People will acclaim him, the greatest singers will be proud to sing his music. Oh, my wonderful Mozart—to listen to him, to laugh with him, even to weep with him—that is his music."

Meanwhile Stephen Storace was wearing himself out.

Music poured from him, and if the "Haunted Tower" had been greeted as a masterpiece, the opera which followed was sufficient to send the whole town wild with delight. "No song, no supper" with the lyrics by Prince Hoare, sent London wild. Then followed "Dido" which charmed everyone.

Stephen, thinner and paler than ever, took his call as "Author" and then staggered back to his chair set in the prompter's corner.

Michael begged, "Stephen—stop! Let us go to Italy, somewhere where the sun shines and you can regain your health. You, Nancy, Anna and I! Let's leave the audiences wanting, your health is worth all the applause in the world. Stephen, be wise—more than that—be kind to the people who love you so devotedly."

"No, dear fellow," Stephen shook his head, "I must write. In Italy I should get sunshine, but I should still have to—write. I am wretched every hour when I'm away from my desk or my piano. It's a kind of fever, I think. Music twisting and turning in one's head, begging to be let loose on the world."

It was not the slightest use attempting to dissuade him, he joked about his illness, saying, "My illness? Why? It is that I am a musician!" and continued his work. He finished another opera, "The Pirates" and swore that he would not write another note for a year. Michael and Nancy were delighted, they began to make plans to get Stephen away from London, somewhere—Nancy insisted—where there was not a pianoforte within at least ten miles.

"And no pens or ruled paper shall be allowed in the house!"

Two days later Michael calling to see Stephen, found

him, his face flushed with excitement, jotting down music and humming softly as he did so.

"What about your promise!" Michael cried indignantly. "A year, you said, now in two days you're at it again. What's happened to the other—363 days? Stephen, you're worse than a dram drinker. No more to be trusted near a piano, than they are with a bottle."

Stephen laughed, "Listen to this, Mickie," and swinging himself before the keyboard he began to play, saying at intervals. "How do you like that?" or "This is still rough, but it will be all right when I've polished it."

Michael perched on the edge of the table, swinging his legs to the music exclaimed, "Charming!" "You've excelled yourself!" "Ah, that's divine!" completely forgetting his rôle of attempting to deter Storace from working.

The door was flung open, and Nancy rushed in. She turned on them both in a fury, and Nancy in a fury was something to remember. Her eyes flashed, her cheeks flamed, and she looked like some avenging goddess.

"How dare you! Stephen, I'm ashamed of you, can't you keep your promises? Why make them at all if they are of such piecrust material? Here am I, out to get something for your dinner which will really tempt you to eat, and the moment my back is turned, you're at your damned pianoforte. You, too, Michael Kelly, you pretend to be his friend, and you allow him to do this, while you sit like some silly school-boy, on the table, swinging your legs and crying, 'Bravo!' Imagining, no doubt, how well the voice of the celebrated Mr. Kelly will sound singing the music composed by a dead man! Oh, yes, it's no use saying—'Nancy!' in that tone. By the time this music is played at the New Drury Lane Theatre, the man who wrote it——"

She burst into tears, and Stephen left the piano and put his arm round her, Michael seeing her fumbling for a handkerchief pushed his own immaculately ironed one into her hand, saying, "Nancy, I'm so sorry. The music just carried me away."

"I don't believe it's so good as all that," she sniffed, like a sulky child.

"It's some of the loveliest music he's ever written," Michael declared stoutly.

"Oh, you always say that. I never knew two men who were such mutual back patters as you and Stephen. If Stephen played the scale of C major and said he'd composed it, you'd swear that it was heavenly music."

Michael smiled, Nancy's temper was evaporating, "I shouldn't, oh, no, I shouldn't. I should ask him to transpose it to A minor."

"And I should do it," Stephen added, "I'm quite ready to leave C majors to 'Papa' Haydn."

She picked up a sheet of the scored paper on which Stephen had been jotting his notes and studied it.

"You write so badly, Stephen," she grumbled, "How can I tell if it's good or bad?"

Her brother took the sheet from her, and sat down at the pianoforte, Michael stood on one side of him, Nancy the other. All the anger had gone from her charming face, she was grave and intent. Once or twice she whispered, "Ah, Stephen, it's good!"

He finished playing, and she was as excited as the two men had been, what was it to be called, how much had he written, was there a good part for her?

"How can I finish it?" Stephen asked, his eyebrows raised in comic dismay, "if you forbid me to work?

It must simply remain—an unfinished masterpiece by the famous composer, Stephen Storace."

"Oh, well, if you work in *reason*, not every hour God sends, it might not do you much harm—what do you think, Mickie?"

"It might be better for him than fretting and—champing at the bit," Michael admitted. "Only, Stephen, as Nancy says, not to work every hour of the day and most of the night."

"No, no, I'll be reasonable," Stephen promised. "But it is rather a pleasant bit of work, don't you think?"

They talked, as they had always done, excitedly about Stephen's work, their plans and prospects—they agreed that Fate had treated them very kindly—Michael thirty-one, Stephen one year his junior and Nancy the youngest of them all, with their names already established, their careers filled with past successes, and it seemed reasonable to believe, future triumphs.

Suddenly Nancy cried, "Mickie, what is the time? Heavens above," when he told her, "and I must prepare the chicken for our dinner. It's a beautiful bird, it will be a dish fit for a king when it's stuffed and roasted. Mickie, go home and bring Anna here and dine with us. Mama's away. You shall make the bread sauce, Mickie."

Their quarrel had ended, as all their quarrels did, with laughter and much talk, with admirably roasted chicken, Mickie's own special bread sauce, and the consuming of two bottles of hock which he and Anna Crouch brought with them to amplify the meal.

The New Drury Lane Theatre was opened in March, 1794, when flaunting all superstition "Macbeth" was given, magnificent with Mrs. Siddons, Kemble and his brother Charles, while Michael composed the incidental music. In a following production, when he was playing with Mrs. Crouch, he had to rescue her from a burning tower. One night as he rushed up the bridge to effect the rescue, a carpenter stupidly removed one of the supports and Michael fell heavily a considerable distance on to the stage.

He was not greatly hurt, but he was furious with the carpenter, and when Sheridan came round and attempted to placate the angry Kelly, he told it later, that Michael turned to him and demanded:

"Ah, now, Sherry, it's all very well to make light of it, but supposing I'd been killed—who would have maintained me for the rest of my life?"

On the 12th of March, Stephen's opera "The Iron Chest" was produced, it was not a success—Kemble was ill, Colman also, and it was obvious to everyone that the young composer himself was in a dying condition. He attended rehearsals, being wrapped in blankets and carried to Drury Lane in a sedan-chair. There he sat at the side of the stage, shivering, in spite of the blankets in which he sat huddled. He was taken home and went to bed, the following day when Michael called to see how he fared, he found him, propped up with pillows, attempting to write the final passages of one of the songs which Michael was to sing in "The Iron Chest".

Stephen shook his head, and laid down his pencil, saying, "I must be ill when I can't finish a song for you, Mickie. I've tried, but I can't manage it. Here are twelve bars, take them and finish the song yourself. Don't let anyone persuade you to let other than yourself do it, remember that. You've always dealt so kindly with my music, added such lustre to it—go on doing so."

Michael held his hand, and tried to master his emotion.

"Stephen, you'll write many more songs for me, and I shall always be proud to sing them."

"No, Mick—it's been a good time—we've made a wonderful trio—lately it's been a quartette. And just as harmonious. Your Anna Crouch is a good woman. There, I must sleep——"

Michael watched him close his eyes, he lay there breathing rapidly, looking so tired that Michael almost longed for that quick, shallow breathing to come to an end so that Stephen might have rest. His friend did not speak again, and with tears running down his cheeks, Michael stumbled down the stairs.

He died four days later without recovering consciousness. He was buried in the old parish church of St. Marylebone, close to the entrance of the Marylebone Gardens where his father had acted as manager many years before, and where his aunt and his mother had made those famous fruit tarts "using only the finest Epping butter".

For Michael, his passing meant something terrible. It may be that he had conceived something amounting to a superstition, that he, Stephen and Nancy would always move forward and upward together. Stephen had been his close man friend. Michael had many friends, indeed his popularity was unlimited and ranged from the highest to more humble persons, but only to Stephen had he really opened his heart, confessed his failings and confided his hopes and ambitions.

He said to Anna Crouch, "I feel as if I had lost a limb—an arm or a leg with Stephen going. Ann-ah, dear as you are to me, his death is the end of my youth. Men love women, not all love them as I love you, which is to distraction, but each man needs one other man to be near to him, and without sentimentalism, dear to him."

Some of the gold and the glory went with Stephen, Michael was happy with his dear Anna, he was successful and by 1799—when he was still a young man—was in complete musical control of Drury Lane.

He should have been happy, money was plentiful, his provincial tours with Anna were always successes, she was adorable, no woman could have been more kind, sympathetic and yet—he told himself—"my mouth tastes sour". When he was alone with Anna he could be the old gay and sparkling Mick Kelly—when friends dined with them, Charles Lamb and his sister, Michael's niece— Frances Maria Kelly, the daughter of his wastrel brother Mark—with what Lamb called her "adorable plain face" —Sheridan whose wit kept the table in a roar of amusement, even Kemble—though Mickie had to admit that he brought such dignity with him that the conversation had to be kept on a very high level—at those times he was the delightful host, attending to the wants of his guests, charming to everyone, but often he would fling his arms round Anna and cry, "Never leave me, without you— God knows what would happen to me."

She would hold him close and whisper, "Michael, only one thing shall ever part us, and that is something stronger than us both."

Everything was changing, he told himself. Even the clothes which he had loved were becoming out-moded. Men were wearing darker materials, they were discarding the elegant knee breeches for pantaloons which came down to the ankle; his much admired Prince of Wales had grown so stout as to be ungainly, his brothers were despised and hated—"Silly Billy" who had left Mrs. Jordan and married into respectability, the sinister Ernest and all the rest of them in bad odour. The Corinthians still cut a fine figure, still kept alive the splendour of the Prize Ring, though even there rumours went around that everything was not completely "on the square".

Two figures remained untouched by the dislike of the people—Horatio Nelson and the Duke of Wellington, then Lord Arthur Wellesley. True Nelson might indulge in a romantic *liaison* with lovely Emma Hamilton, but he was still "England's darling", and Wellesley was a hero— the public hostility towards him lay in the distant future.

Then, too, Michael was concerned with Nancy Storace. She was still young, her voice was beautiful, her acting admirable, but she had conceived an affection for a singer, John Braham.

When she told him, Michael said, "He's younger than you are."

She tossed her head, "What of it?"

"His real name is Abrahams."

"Does that matter?"

Michael shrugged his shoulders, "Are you going to marry him?"

"Are you going to marry Anna Crouch?"

"God knows that I would, if I could. She is still married to Crouch."

She held out her hands to him, "Mick, don't let us be cold to each other, I can't bear it. I've not had so much happiness in my life that I can afford to let any slip. You'll admit that he is a good artist?"

"Most excellent." Michael's smile broke out, "Almost as good as you are, Nancy asthore. Does he love you?"

"He says that he does. We are planning a Continental tour—why not come with us, you and Anna?"

Michael hesitated, how he longed to go back to Italy.

How he longed to revel in the beauty, the warmth, even the smells which had been part of his life. He thought with a sense of nostalgia of the places he had known—of Sicily with its beauty, the oranges hanging there so plentiful that no-one bothered to attempt to steal them, or if they did—what mattered? Genoa, Leghorn—ah, that meeting at Leghorn! His beloved Venice, and Vienna—no, he didn't want to see Vienna again, without the chance of meeting that small, agile figure, wearing a three-cornered hat and a red paletot. The Emperor was dead—no, Vienna held too many memories for him.

He shook his head, "Nancy dear, I'm the musical director at the Lane. I am writing music for various operas—how Stephen would laugh—never unkindly, but my efforts are completely lacking in the least spark of—what he had—genius. I wonder what Mozart would say? He'd give me the same advice that he gave me years ago—but I can't leave Drury Lane, Nancy dear.

"I'm still young, but my voice won't last for ever, and I must make money while I can. No, Continental tours are not for me."

She looked at him curiously and closely, "Mick you're not actually unhappy?"

"My dear, no. With Anna I am the happiest man alive. Only," his voice grew a little wistful, "perhaps we all flowered too soon. You were a *prima donna* at sixteen—I was a leading tenor before I was twenty. Stephen, dear Stephen, wrote too much, and the bright light of his genius burned away the candle too soon.

"We've had all the triumphs while we were young, we're old, Nancy, old. We've crammed experiences into a few years. What is there left for us? I'm only turned thirty. . . ."

"Thirty-six or seven——" she reminded him.

"I know, but I am already suffering from gout."

"Your own fault!" Nancy retorted, "I wonder that Anna does not prohibit so much wine. It will kill you, Mickie."

"Ah, m'dear, I must live my own life in the way that suits me. There, arrange your tour with Braham, and please God that you may find happiness with him. If there is any service that I can do you, call on me. Introductions, arrangements—let me know. You know," he spoke very earnestly, "that I always have your interests at heart, don't you?"

So Nancy departed on her tour, and was acclaimed everywhere. There was no doubt that Braham was a fine singer, with a commanding presence, and she—although she was allowing herself to grow too stout—still possessed great vivacity and attraction.

Michael said to Anna Crouch, after Nancy had left for the continent, "The quartette has dwindled to a duet once more."

"Nancy will come back, Michael," she told him.

"Somehow, I don't feel that the same Nancy will ever come back."

"Then we must make our duet all the more melodious," she said.

He met her beautiful eyes and smiled back at her, "My darling, so long as you sing in this duet, it will always be quite, quite perfect. Ah, I may grow depressed, but at heart I'm a happy man, and God knows, a fortunate one. Kiss me, Ann-ah."

CHAPTER FIFTEEN

MICHAEL continued at Drury Lane. He loved the place, true the theatre might be new, but there still existed the old tradition. He was respected—less, he thought wryly, for the quality of his music than for the ability to produce something tuneful when the occasion demanded, and for his unfailing good humour. It was rarely that he allowed his quick Irish temper to get the upper hand, and even when it did, he was ready to crack a quip and send everyone into roars of laughter.

"Mickie's tempers" they were called, and often at long and rather tedious rehearsals, he knew that one of his temperaments brought fresh life to the work. At such moments he allowed himself to lapse into his Irish brogue, and even though through disuse of many years it had become distinctly "stage Irish", it delighted his hearers.

"Now, glory be to God, sind to Bow Street for somewan to arrest these people for they're murdering the music —and it's suffering a painful death." Or, "Shure, elephants would be filled wid envy for they could never tread a measure so heavily!" But immediately he realized that new life had been imbued into his artistes, his smile would break out, and he would beam at them from his blue, kindly eyes and scatter praise everywhere.

In the provinces he was always acclaimed and fêted, his Macheath in the Beggar's Opera, with Mrs. Crouch, was an unfailing draw, houses were packed, and encores were the inevitable rule.

Michael hated encores, he deemed them inartistic

and bad for the action of the play, but the audience refused to be satisfied, and always with a little gesture of deprecation, he was forced to give them.

His life with Anna Crouch was completely happy, by her very tranquillity she soothed that spirit of his which either soared to the heights of gaiety or sank to the depths of melancholy. True there were many times when like the majority of the wits of his day, Michael enjoyed jokes in company with his friends, particularly with Sheridan to whom he was growing more and more closely allied. They sat smoking, drinking, one vying with the other as to who could turn the most apt phrase, or crack the neatest quip.

They all drank heavily, though it was Michael's boast that no-one had ever seen him "the worse for liquor", in consequence the majority of these wits were already beginning to feel the twinges of gout which rendered life unpleasant and which made their tempers difficult to restrain. After stormy rehearsals or discussions at The Lane, it was a relief to get back to Anna Crouch and let her kindness and gentleness soothe away his frayed temper. Michael missed her terribly when she had to leave town to fulfil engagements, though he discovered that there were many of these which she refused, offering various excuses as her reason for doing so. He was sufficiently quick witted to understand that the real reason was that she did not want to leave her home—and Mickie Kelly.

He taxed her, very gently, with it one day when they were sitting over a dish of tea, which Michael—like most Irishmen—enjoyed tremendously.

He said, "I saw Bannerman this morning, he's in town engaging artistes for his coming season."

"Really?" Her tone was only mildly interested.

"I asked him why on earth he never offered you an engagement? I said, 'The finest singer you could find and undeniably the best looking of the whole lot o' them.' He stared at me, then said that he'd approached you every time he'd been in town, and that you were never sufficiently well or had previous engagements. Has he communicated with you this time, m'dear?"

"Yes, I heard from him several days ago. He wrote very civilly."

"And you refused? Now, Glory be to God, what made you do that?"

She shrugged her fine shoulders, "I was afraid of having one of those horrid attacks—or that my throat might give trouble, I thought that after all—in London— I have my own doctor close at hand, whereas in the provinces——"

He leaned forward in his chair, and wagged his finger at her in comic reproof, "Anna Maria Crouch, you are simply sitting there making excuses—come on now, be honest—you didn't *want* to go now did you?"

"That may be," she admitted laughing, "perhaps I'm growing lazy and—after all—home is so comfortable. You make it so comfortable, Mickie."

Michael threw back his elaborately dressed head, for he still wore it curled in the manner of the Prince of Wales, and laughed. She thought how his laughter seemed to bubble out of him, like clear water from a spring; it was such essentially young laughter.

"Oh, bless you," he cried, "what an adorable creature you are, my wonderful Anna, and what a fortunate fellow I am."

She was so proud of him, of his gaiety, his popularity and his ability for making friends. She loved to hear other artistes say in the green room, "Have you heard Mick Kelly's latest?" or "Did you hear what Mick and Sherry got up to the other day?"

He might be nearly forty, but unless his enemy gout attacked him, he was like a boy, and his movements were as active as ever. He walked so lightly that someone nick-named him "Spring heeled Jack", after a famous highwayman, whose widow had married Sir John Lade, the well known sportsman, whose great pride was his accomplishment of being able to whistle through his teeth like a hackney coachman.

Nancy Storace was on the Continent, and from time to time Michael heard of the successes which she and Braham were making everywhere. They returned together to Drury Lane in 1805, they were still in close association, but Michael fancied that Braham was less attentive than he had been at first, and that Nancy lacked some of her old gaiety. Michael had a profound admiration for both of them as artists, Braham's voice was excellent, and he was a favourite with his public. He was inclined to be boastful concerning his successes on the Continent, and Michael listening to him recounting them was conscious of a growing irritation.

Sheridan, who was listening said dryly, "And the Storace?"

"A great success, of course," Braham answered in a tone which to Michael seemed to hold a certain amount of patronage, "Oh, yes, a distinct success."

"Possibly," Sheridan's crisp voice was unusually gentle, "Almost as great as your own, eh, Mr. Braham?"

"Oh, I should say that she ran me a very close second—very close indeed."

Michael's face was scarlet with fury, he clenched his

fists, and his eyes blazed like blue fires, "Shall I tell you what I think, Mr. Braham? That you were very markedly successful in being introduced to Continental audiences under the auspices of the Storace. In other words, she carried you along on her reputation until you became established. Remember that the Storace was a *prima donna* when she was—fifteen."

The younger man stared at him, so this was the famous Kelly temper. He'd known that Kelly was devoted to the Storace, as he had been to her brother, but—really—to take offence like this was too much.

"When she was fifteen? When I was still a very small boy at school! I should be seven years old when the audiences were offering her their applause. Imagine it!"

"What I can't imagine," Michael retorted, "is that you ever were at school!"

Sheridan said smoothly, "Well, Mr. Braham, you must repeat your Continental successes for London audiences at the Lane. Good morning."

Michael told Anna that he was worried about Nancy.

"She's not the same somehow. She's let herself grow too stout, and she's acutely conscious that she is eight years older than Braham. So is he! It's my belief that he's tired of her, that he wants to marry and—settle down."

Anna Crouch, her lovely face clouded, her voice filled with anxiety shook her beautiful head.

"How sad, Mick—for Nancy loves him, I'm certain of that. I've spoken to her of him and watched her face light up when I have praised his voice. He's an admirable artist——"

"That's the devil of it, we need him at the Lane, otherwise, I'll be damned if I wouldn't get the fellow the sack!"

"You can't do that, my dear. You know as well as I do that personal matters must not affect the running of a theatre. 'The play's the thing—'. Do nothing, Mick, I beg you."

"There's a son, you know——"

She nodded, "Nancy told me. She wants him to be brought up to be a priest. She said—oh, the tragedy of it!— 'Better put an end to this unhappy family of Storace. Stephen dying so young, and now—my life ruined.' I reminded her that she still held her place in the hearts of the public, and she laughed—such a bitter laugh, so unlike our Nancy—and said, 'Yes, that maybe, but I've lost that place in the heart of a man who promised to adore me as long as life lasted.' "

The association dragged on, and in 1808 Nancy came to see Michael in his room at the Lane. She had grown very stout, some said coarse, though to Michael her bright eyes and lovely skin made her still be—if a somewhat blurred picture—the Nancy he had known when they were both young.

She greeted him as always, asking how his gout was, and when he growled that it was giving him hell, laughed—but a kindly laugh—saying, "Faith, didn't I tell you years ago that it would catch you and lay you by the heels?"

"I'm not laid by the heels—yet," he retorted.

"It's affecting the delightful Kelly temper!"

"Who says so? Not Anna? No, only one thing affects my temper, when females invade my office when I'm busy and have nothing to say except to tell me to leave wine alone. Then—yes, I grow irritable."

"In other words, tell me to mind my own business, eh?"

I

He stared at her, his blue eyes sombre, "Dear Saints, I wish that you'd ever learn to do that successfully, m'dear."

"Well, I'm doing it now. I'm going to retire. Yes," at his gesture of protest, "yes, Mickie, it's time——"

"Time! Damned nonsense! You're young, your public adores you. What is this idea of retirement, tell me?"

"Not so very young, Mickie," she said sadly, "I've grown fat—coarse is the word that is always being flung at me. I can face most things, but not unhappiness.

"I loved the days when we hadn't much money, when to have coffee at Florian's was—an event. I loved success, our life in Vienna, those long talks which you and I and Stephen used to have—how we used to talk! There was nothing about either music or singing that we didn't know! Do you remember the last time—when I railed at you and Stephen for working when he ought to have been resting? How it ended in us all at the pianoforte, listening to his music, making suggestions, offering small criticisms? He used to call us—The Triumvirate! Happy times, Mickie, happy times.

"No, I want to go out in a blaze of glory. A benefit! Colman must write a farewell speech for me—I'll make them cry! I've bought a small—well, smallish—house in Herne Hill—don't look like that, Herne Hill isn't the North Pole or even Liverpool! I've saved money, you'd never think that now would you? Addle-pated Nancy saving money, but I have done."

"Have you left Braham?" Michael asked, he knew that his lips were shaking, his eyes filled with tears. Stephen gone, Nancy preparing to take her farewell of the stage—only Michael Kelly left. He felt desolate.

She shrugged her too ample shoulders, "Not actually,

but it's wearing so thin, that I can't hold it together much longer. Like an old coat, there are more patches than the original material. He's not unkind to me, he's just—indifferent. There's someone else. Well, he's young, younger than I am, and who's to blame him?"

"You're still in love with him?" Michael asked abruptly.

"In love, no. I'm in love with the remnants of my youth, I still want to be admired, yes, and desired. I'm neither. Just fat, old Nancy——"

Michael sprang to his feet, "Nancy, don't! I can't bear it! Go home and think this over again, talk it over with Sherry——"

She laughed, "Sherry doesn't really like me a great deal——"

"With—oh, with anyone who has a little sense. This is a mood. It will pass. If you're unhappy with Braham, leave him. Damnation, to talk of retiring at your age! It's nonsense, I tell you."

She laid her hand on his shoulder, "My dear, I've made up my mind, I'd rather leave my public before my public leaves me."

"To bury yourself at Herne Hill—wherever the place is—I shall never set eyes on you, you'll turn into a cabbage," he grumbled.

"I swear—on anything you like—on the foundation stone of Drury Lane—that I shall come and dine with you and Anna—if you'll have me, once every week. Never set eyes on me indeed! You can't get rid of me so easily, Mickie Kelly."

So in May Nancy had her benefit and farewell performance. She sang "Love Laughs at Locksmiths" and "The Cabinet", and also the farewell ode which Colman had written for her, sang it so charmingly and touchingly that there were few dry eyes among the huge audience. They had loved her for her artistry, for her gaiety and for her versatility, true she had grown too stout for her years —she was only about forty-two—but her face was as attractive as ever, her voice as clear—or almost—as it had always been.

Michael watched her from the wings, his heart very full. Nancy was so much part of his life, they had shared the same successes, the same griefs, they had laughed and been gay together and now she was leaving London to bury herself in what was practically the country, and all because of this wretched man Braham.

He sighed heavily, and Colman who was standing near him, said sadly, "Aye, it's a thousand pities, there'll never be anyone to touch her—not that she's ever been as beautiful as Mrs. Crouch, but she's a far better actress."

Michael nodded, "Nancy's always been—unique—always."

She kept her word and every week—except at such times as Michael and Anna Crouch were touring the provinces, came to dine with them. Anna liked her, and their dinner parties were very gay, but to Michael it was never the same spontaneous gaiety they had enjoyed before.

Anna asked her one evening when they were alone, if Braham lived at Herne Hill. Nancy grinned, her expression that of a cheeky school-boy, "Lives there? Not he. Oh, he comes out sometimes, usually when he wants to offer his friends a good dinner—I'm still a good cook, you know—and show them the delights of rural life, but even those visits are growing few and far between."

"It's abominable! Why not finish for good and all—why not marry again?"

"Because—well, for two reasons—no woman likes to know that a man she loved doesn't love her any longer, women are dreadful 'pretenders', Anna. They can live in a world of pretence for years. And also—the second reason, I'm still married to Fisher."

"Fisher!" Anna exclaimed, "You've not seen him for years."

"And hope never to see him again," Nancy assured her, "but I never troubled to divorce him—so presumably I'm still married. Besides—oh, it would all be too much fuss and bother."

The final separation with Braham came in 1816, when Nancy told Anna Crouch and Michael that "it's all finished! He told me last night that he is going to marry—mark this!—a very charming and respectable young lady." She added reflectively, "It's all Lombard Street to a china orange that she's as plain as a pikestaff!"

Anna cried, "Oh, Nancy—what a shame!"

Nancy laughed, "What's a shame—that this prospective bride is as plain as a pikestaff? She may have money to gild her looks."

"You know that I didn't mean that."

Michael growled, "Bad cess to him, the damned Sheenie!"

"I've known some damned pleasant folks who were—as you call them—Sheenies, Mickie. You can't lump them all together."

"I'd not wish to lump that fellow with anyone else, it would be damned unpleasant for the—other people."

"Oh, let's forget it, let's enjoy ourselves," Nancy

begged. "I'm sick of talking with, talking at, talking of my—late *protector*!"

But she was desperately hurt, some of the things which Braham had said to her at their last meeting hurt desperately—her age, her weight, the amount she drank had all been used as taunts, and they had wounded her. The pain remained, and Michael noticed that she was looking ill when she came to see him.

He begged her to let him send for her doctor, Hooper, but she refused almost irritably, saying that she had never felt better. Anna Crouch was away when Nancy came to dine on 24th of August, 1817, the other guests were an Italian singer, and Savory the chemist. Nancy knew them both very well, and liked them.

Michael, watching her, felt a sense of apprehension, and as the evening passed he noticed that she seemed to be drawing her breath with increasing difficulty. By the time her carriage came to take her back to Herne Hill she was scarcely able to walk. Savory begged her to allow him to bleed her, but she laughed—admittedly rather shakily—and assured him that she would be all right.

Michael wished to drive back with her, he could return home in the morning, she said, "What come back and sleep at my house! With Anna away! Fie, Mickie— don't let us have any more scandals for Drury Lane to enjoy! You can send Dr. Hooper in the morning, I'll give you permission to do that. Good-night, Mickie— *Buona motte* Signor, Mr. Savory, can I give you a lift to Bond Street? No? Then—Good-night."

Michael lay awake until the small hours, he was worried, and wished that Anna had been at home, she would have insisted upon his going back with Nancy.

As soon as it was possible he sent to Dr. Hooper, begging him to go immediately to Herne Hill.

When he arrived there, Hooper found Nancy terribly ill, he told her that he intended to bleed her at once, adding, "Believe me, there is no time to be lost."

She looked at him, her heavy eyes twinkling, "What—to-day? It's Friday——"

"Yes, what of it?"

"Bleed me on a Friday—most unlucky! No, the first moment after mid-night if you wish, but on a Friday! You forget I'm full of stage superstitions."

He protested, begged, implored but she was adamant, her theatrical superstition was too strong. Michael arrived about mid-day, and Hooper met him.

He had driven over, and came rushing up the garden path like a madman.

"Curse it, they kept me at the Lane—how people talk! I had it in my heart to curse the lot of them. How is she? Is she better?"

Hooper slipped his arm through Michael's and drew him into the house. "I'm sorry, Mick—terribly sorry——"

"She's worse? My God, let's get the Court physician, he must be used to such cases—I'll send back for him."

"Mick, it's too late. The Storace died an hour ago."

He felt Michael stagger, and lowered him gently into a chair. His face was ghastly, drained of every vestige of colour.

Suddenly he covered his face with his hands and sobbed as if his heart were broken.

When Anna Crouch returned to their home in Great Russell Street that evening, she found Michael huddled in an arm-chair beside the fire, although the evening was warm. He rose to greet her, and at the sight of his ashen face she cried out, "Mickie, you're ill, my dear one, what is it?"

"No, I'm not ill," his voice seemed robbed of all expression as his face was drained of colour, "No, I'm not ill. I had the fire lit because I felt so cold—so terribly cold. Anna, Nancy's dead."

"Nancy, Nancy Storace! Mickie, when?"

"This morning, Hooper was with her. I got there too late."

She made him go back to his chair, and kneeling beside him, put her arms round him and held him close, whispering, "My poor Mickie, oh, my dear, I am so grieved for you. Darling, don't cry so—it hurts me to hear you sob like this," for he had burst into tears when she put her arms round him. "I'm sure that Hooper did everything that was possible——"

"He wasn't allowed to do anything," Michael told her. "He wanted to bleed her and she wouldn't let him."

"But why—she's been bled often!"

"Because," and in spite of his grief, she heard him catch his breath in what was the travesty of a laugh, "because it was Friday. She'd never do anything important on a Friday, never sign a contract or even begin to study a new part. Hooper told me that he did all he could to persuade her—begged, threatened, coaxed—all no use. He said that he believes that bleeding might have saved her."

Anna shook her head, "I don't know, dear, when one's time has come I don't think anything can—save you."

He sighed, "You may be right. Dear Nancy, she was always wilful, all her life—and not such a long life either. Anna, there's only you left now. Nancy and Stephen both gone."

She kissed him tenderly, "I shall never leave you—we shall grow old together, be pointed out by people as the oldest members of Drury Lane—the famous Michael Kelly and Anna Crouch who was once quite an attractive woman."

"Ah, God bless you, you'll always be lovely."

She was adorable to him, she sympathized with his fits of acute depression, went with him to make all arrangements for Nancy's funeral—she was buried in Saint Mary's Church, Lambeth, and her coffin was followed by all the most distinguished singers of the day.

Nancy had saved money, with all her careless ways she had never squandered what she earned, and her cousin, a Miss Trusler, benefited to the extent of nearly £50,000.

After the will was settled, Anna said to Michael, "I imagined that she'd have left some of that money to you, Mickie."

He answered quickly, "No, no. She wished to, but I begged her not to do so. I have sufficient, I could retire to-morrow if I wished to do so. You see, my dear, in the past so many people have accused Nancy of having been my mistress. So many people spread the story that I was her lover. All lies, B'God, as you know. Had she left me money, can't you imagine the wagging of heads, the whisperings, the 'What did I always say' and 'Didn't I tell you?' that would have gone on. Braham is providing for the boy, I don't think that our Nancy was capable of much motherly feeling—a true friend, a loyal friend, a friend who never wavered, but—a mother, no."

Life went on, without the gay weekly dinners, and Nancy's chatter—a theatrical gossip which might—and often was—scandalous, but never bitter or spiteful. Anna always said that she could say unconscionable

I*

things which never carried a sting. Now, Anna arranged small dinner parties at Great Russell Street on the nights when neither she nor Michael were working, and tried to invite people who would not only interest Michael but amuse him.

The first time she saw him really whole-heartedly amused after Nancy's death was one evening when Sheridan dined with them and she told how Cumberland the playwright had brought his children to see Sheridan's "School for Scandal".

Sherry observed, "How he dislikes me, that fellow— as much as I dislike his plays! Yes, go on Anna, tell us what happened."

"The children laughed immoderately," she told them, "and each time they laughed Cumberland's brow grew darker, and he hissed at them, 'Be quiet, you silly little fools, what is there to laugh at?' Finally the poor little things were so cowed that they sat stuffing their handkerchiefs into their mouths to stifle their laughter."

Sheridan shrugged his narrow shoulders, "How unfair of Cumberland, imagine him not allowing his poor children to laugh at my comedy. Now I went to hear his tragedy a few nights ago, and I laughed heartily all through the play!"

Possibly only with Sheridan did Kelly recover his boyish love of joking, and he would return home and regale Anna with stories of how the two of them had done this or that. He invariably dropped into his native Irish brogue when he recounted these stories, as for example when he told of the lawyer and the horse.

"Sherry and I were walking from King Street to Henrietta Street, when up rides Holloway, the solicitor. Himself in a flaming temper. He complained that whenever he called on Sherry, Sherry's French valet always refused him admission. I might tell you, m' darling, that Sherry owed Holloway money——"

"Tut, Sherry owes everyone money—go on."

"So here's Holloway talking twenty to the dozen, and Sherry just standing with his eyes on the horse. Sherry knows about as much about horses as a babe unborn. When Holloway waits for a minute—to draw breath, Sherry points to the horse, and says in the voice of one who has seen a vision, 'I never in all my life saw such a lovely creature.' I, of course, added my praise to his. Says Sherry, 'Now, Mister Holloway, d'you remember a short time ago I was speaking about a horse I wanted to buy for Mrs. Sheridan?' He'd never had any idea of buying a horse for Mrs. Sheridan! He goes on, 'What a beautiful horse for a lady.' Holloway says, 'I'm willing to sell him, Mr. Sheridan.' 'You are!' Sherry almost shouts, 'Now surely my luck's in to-day. What are his paces like? Can he canter prettily?' Holloway says that there's nothing this horse don't do to perfection. Sherry says, "Now to oblige me, would you just canter him round the market, so I can form an opinion.' Holloway sets the nag into a smart canter, the moment he's turned the corner, Sherry says, 'Good-bye, Mick, I'll see you sometime soon,' and with that walked off through the churchyard, where no horse could follow him and away to Bedford Street. Be sure that I slipped away too."

He added, "People round about were all laughing— I'll lay any money the only person who did not find it amusing was—Holloway."

Perhaps Anna Crouch who was a seriously-minded woman, found some of their escapades slightly foolish, and felt that it might have been better had Sheridan devoted more time to his share of the management of Drury Lane, instead of leaving most of the business to Kemble, Colman and Michael Kelly. She said nothing, for it was wonderful to her to see her beloved Mickie in good spirits, and to hear him laugh was a joy to her loving heart.

They were wonderfully happy together, and even when Drury Lane was passing through one of its many periods of depression, when money in the treasury was woefully lacking, and difficulties besetting the management on every side, Michael would return to her—possibly tired out—and taking her in his arms say, "Darling, it's wonderful to come home."

CHAPTER SIXTEEN

ANNA CROUCH appeared at Drury Lane for the last time as "Celia" in "As You Like It", and never had she received warmer or more tumultuous applause. Kelly watched the performance, beaming with pride and pleasure. What a woman she was—admirable as a singer, excellent as an actress, and what a cook and what a good companion! He let his mind wander from the play, and allowed his thoughts to take full possession of him. Was it possible that the theatre—and how he loved everything connected with it!—had attained its greatest possible height? Would ever again such a galaxy of artists exist, such names, such tremendous figures? Many of these names would go down in history as the names of the planets of the stage—Kemble, Siddons, Storace—dear Nancy—Kean, Jordan, Billington—unpleasant woman though she was—his own niece, Fanny who was forging ahead and hailed as a fine actress, even perhaps one day people might talk of little Mickie Kelly.

Ah, it was a fine time, a rich time, not always in actual profits, he reflected, for Drury Lane was continually facing some crisis, some disaster—the fire for instance, in which all Stephen Storace's music had been destroyed, along with much of his own.

"Not that my stuff matters," he thought, "Mozart was right, he was always right—still, I've always written as well as I could, and if it's not great music—which it certainly isn't, and who'd know that better than Mick Kelly—it's honest stuff. I've never lifted a phrase from this one or a melody from another in the hope that no-one would recognize what I'd done."

That night he told Anna what a brilliant performance she had given, adding, "If you ask me, m'dear, you're at the very peak of your career."

"That's one of the reasons, Mickie, that I'm going to retire—yes, don't expostulate, my mind is made up. As Nancy once said, I'd rather leave my public before they leave me."

"But my dear Ann-ah," Kelly protested, "why leave the stage when you are at your very best? The idea is foolish. You're young——"

She smiled, "Not, possibly tottering into the grave, but not even you with your notable ability to flatter, can call thirty-eight—exactly one's first youth."

"Plenty of them are older than that! Only they don't admit to it. Oh, my dear one, don't retire yet! Not for years, and years. We can't afford to lose you at the Lane."

She came and sat nearer to him, laying her hand on his, she spoke gently but with that firmness which he had come to realize meant determination. Anna was always gentle, but once her mind was made up on any matter, she never deviated, never wavered.

"I'll try to make you see reason, my wild Irish boy," she said, "to begin with, I think that I'm losing my pleasure in acting, it may be that I'm tired. Then too, ever since that stupid accident you remember, when the bag fell on to my throat——"

"Now would I be likely to forget it!" he exclaimed indignantly.

"My throat has given trouble. Surely, Mick, you're too good a musician not to know that some of the notes are—well, not what they were? They're growing rough, the ease has gone, it's an effort to put them over. The critics have often praised my singing as being—effortless. They won't say that much longer, you know what they are, make one slip, sing one night when your voice isn't quite at its best, and they're after you like a pack of wolves."

Michael frowned, "Aye, damn them! Very well then, leave singing alone, though I've noticed nothing wrong with your voice, you can out-sing the lot of them! You've more art in that pretty little finger than Billington has in her whole body."

"Yes, I could do that, I suppose, but I am not primarily an actress. Oh, I can act, on occasions I can act very well indeed—I've no illusions about my work—but I am a singer. There, let me give you another glass of wine, and stop looking as if the world were coming to an end."

So Anna Crouch left the stage of which she had been so bright an ornament, and devoted her time to Michael and his wants. She had made light of her retirement, but in her heart she knew that she was a sick woman. There were those mysterious pains which attacked her from time to time which nothing seemed to relieve. At first a little brandy had eased them, then the small doses ceased to have any effect, and she was forced to take more, and also to rely on opium pills. She never confided to Michael anything of her physical troubles, she knew him so well, knew that he would panic, send for relays of doctors, listen to every suggestion that might be made to him at the Lane regarding aches and pains and their cures. She could imagine so well, how he would come home with one "infallible cure" after another and insist on her trying them. Nothing would be too fantastic if some artiste told him that he, or she, knew of "someone" who had benefited by these noisome concoctions.

Finally a day came when Michael found her in the agonies of an attack; ill as she was she tried to soothe him, to give him assurances that it would pass and leave her all right again. The attack passed, and unknown to Michael, who once she was out of pain firmly believed that she would never have a recurrence of the trouble, she visited Sir Matthew Tierney, a friend of Kelly's and physician to the Prince of Wales.

She made him swear to keep her visit a secret, and told him of her sufferings. He examined her, and then, his face very grave, begged her to dress and allow him to talk to her.

She listened to his careful, measured phrases, and realized that he was trying to tell her that the case was hopeless.

"How long shall I have?" she asked.

"Dear Mrs. Crouch, that is a question which no physician can answer."

"Will it be—very unpleasant?"

"We shall do our best to spare you all the discomfort possible."

She sighed, "Ah, my poor Mickie! You swear, Sir Matthew, not to breathe a word of this to him—to anyone! If I find that a hint of this has reached Michael Kelly, I shall—" she laughed and he thought what a lovely creature she was—"simply denounce you as a liar."

"I give you my word, my word of honour. You're a gallant woman, Madam. Would that all my patients were so brave in the face of adversity."

"Never!" she still smiled, "I'm a veritable poltroon, I almost faint at the sight of a cockroach."

Later when Michael returned from the Lane, he was full of some new infallible cure which the stage carpenter had given him.

"It doesn't sound too pleasant, but he assured me that his mother who lived to be ninety-six suffered from pains in the stomach and derived great benefit from it. I wrote it all down," he pulled a paper out of his pocket and prepared to read the prescription to her.

She took it from him and put it in her reticule, saying, "I'm going to copy your hero—the Prince—and try a new doctor."

"A new doctor? Who?"

"Doctor Brighton. If it suits him, why should it not suit me? It's not too far for you to be able to come and see me very often. You will come often, won't you, my dear one?"

Michael seized her hands and kissed them, "You've only got to say the word and I'll leave the Lane and come and live at Brighton until such a time—please God—in the near future—when you're well enough to come back to London. Just say the word, sweetheart."

She leaned forward and kissed his cheek. "You'll stay in London and do your work. Mick, you're at the top of your profession, you're relied on—mark that—at the Lane, and there are precious few people that poor theatre can rely on. No, come down to Brighton whenever you are able, and watch me getting better and stronger each time."

Anna went to Brighton, and took a house on West Cliff. Michael rushed to Brighton whenever he could leave his work and his devotion to her was never more evident. She hid the gravity of her illness from him as long as possible, and on his visits protested that she was growing stronger every day.

"This air! It's wonderful. One day—when you too retire—we'll live here and grow younger every year."

Michael laughed, "Then, completely rejuvenated, we'll go back and burst on the Lane as two young and completely new artists!"

Only Anna's sister, who had come to Brighton in order to be with her, Mrs. Horrebow—who brought with her her small son, Harry, of whom Mrs. Crouch was very fond, knew how often when Michael left for London, her sister would burst into tears.

"What will happen to him, my dear devoted Mickie! God help him, he'll be so terribly lonely." Anna cried.

When it became apparent that Anna's condition could no longer be hidden from Michael, she begged that she should break the news to him herself. He never told anyone what passed between them, they only knew—those who were in close attendance upon Mrs. Crouch—that he came out of her room, his eyes red with weeping, looking as if he had been sorely stricken.

"The best doctors in England," he told Mrs. Horrebow, "she must have everything, my poor darling."

He sent for Sir Charles Blicke—Governor of the Royal College of Surgeons, Dr. Bankhead and his friend Sir Matthew Tierney. Together they consulted and finally admitted to the distracted Michael that the case was completely hopeless.

Michael moistening his dry lips, asked hoarsely, "How long?"

They temporized, it might be a month, even two—longer than that they doubted.

"And to operate?" Michael asked.

"Impossible. She would never live through the operation."

He clutched at Tierney's hand, "Make it easy for her, Matthew, for God's sake make it easy."

"Everything shall be done that is possible."

Michael never left the house, there were long intervals when she was conscious, and at those times he sat at her bedside, holding her wasted hand and trying to give her comfort. She had periods of delirium, but when they passed she was perfectly calm and talked with him of the plans for her funeral.

"I'll be buried here, Mickie—somewhere overlooking the sea. Don't allow them to make a show of my funeral, my dear, I want it simple—in every way. And oh, my dearest, kindest friend, don't be too unhappy. Your life must go on, don't let me think of you as heart-broken, remember all the splendid times we've had together. When we've laughed—yes, and cried together. Dear, dearest Mickie, God bless and keep you."

"Anna," he cried, "Anna, don't leave me, don't leave me."

She smiled, very gently and serenely, "My dear, do you think that I *want* to leave you. Only if my time here is finished—if I am called, I must go."

Slowly she sank into a coma, and on the 2nd of October, 1805, Anna Crouch left this world in the forty-second year of her age. She was buried in the old parish church of Brighthelmstone, overlooking the town and the sea. Her funeral was as she had wished, simple and dignified. Poor Kelly, broken with grief followed as chief mourner, tears streaming down his cheeks, scarcely able to stagger along under the weight of the grief which—literally—bowed him down.

He wrote the inscription which was to be engraved on her tombstone, it is flowery, as were all such inscriptions at that time, but through the flowing periods comes something which is real and deeply sincere.

Anna Maria Crouch
During many years a Performer at Drury Lane Theatre. She combined with the purest Taste as a Singer the most elegant simplicity as an Actress; beautiful almost beyond parallel in her Person, she was equally distinguished by the Powers of her Mind.
They enabled her, when she quitted the Stage, to gladden Life by the Charms of her Conversation and refine it by her Manners.
She was born 20th April, 1763
and died
2nd October, 1805
This Stone
is Inscribed to her beloved Memory by him whom she esteemed the most faithful of her Friends

Michael left Brighton, having written to Drury Lane that he begged for leave of absence for some considerable time. The management replied, he said. "Most kindlly and begged me to absent myself as long as I deemed it necessary. They added some sympathetic words regarding my loss."

He stayed away from London for two months, trying to overcome in some measure his overwhelming sense of loss and desolation. He visited friends who were congenial and kind, who did their best to rouse him and force him to take up the threads of his life again. Then he returned to Drury Lane and flung himself into his work, a little older, a little more of a sufferer from his old enemy—the gout. He even played "Henry" in "The Deserter", but he had determined to leave the stage. He had shared too many triumphs with Anna Crouch, and he told Sheridan, "I see her everywhere—on the stage, in the corridors— not as I saw her last, my poor Anna, but as she was when she played here at the very height of her beauty."

Sheridan nodded, "Work, Mick, that's the best—nay, the only palliative. Immerse yourself in work."

Michael did work, he composed, he produced, but he had no real wish to sing or act again. He wrote the music for a pantomime, "The Forty Thieves", and "Adrian and Orrila", which due to the intemperate habits of Cooke who was to play the Prince, almost ended in disaster. Cooke arrived at the theatre drunk.

Kemble insisted on the play being done, no matter if Cooke were drunk or not, Harris, Kemble's co-manager, declared that it should not be done. Kelly was sent for to make a decision. Harris was furious and excitable, Kemble very calm—outwardly at least—and dignified. Cooke was raving with drink, shouting abuse at Kemble who completely ignored him. Finally James Brandon, the box office keeper, persuaded Cooke to come to his house, where he put him to bed, applied cold compresses to his head, and when he woke after a profound sleep, plied him with very strong black coffee.

Michael was slowly emerging from what seemed to him to have been a terrible nightmare. He even consented to sing again, with the celebrated Italian, Angelica Catalini, and together—in the company of Catalini's husband, a diplomat, they left for Ireland. Their visit was a tremendous success, but nothing could tempt Michael back to the stage for long. He was tired of it, he had too many memories, the contrast between the past and the present was too great. He appeared as a favour to his friend the Earl of Guilford, in some very aristocratic amateur theatricals when both Mr. and Mrs. Kemble were in the cast, but his heart was not in the theatre any longer and he longed to get away.

He still attended Drury Lane, still wrote occasional music, but the savour was gone, although he still gave dinner parties where the wine and the food—often cooked by Michael himself—were delicious, and when he would whip himself into a semblance of his old gaiety. Mrs. Horrebow and her son Harry were very good to him, and Michael had a great affection for the young man, who went with him on a visit to France; when they returned Michael appeared refreshed and filled with energy. He composed the music for Kean's appearance in "Macbeth", his last work being "The Lady and the Devil" which brought his total of compositions up to sixty-one in the space of twenty-four years.

Then tired of London, and almost unable to walk because of his gout, he retired definitely to Brighton. It may be that in spite of the unhappy memories which the town held for him, it still held recollections of his beloved Anna which belonged to the days before she was attacked by disease.

He had an excellent housekeeper, Mrs. Walters, who it was rumoured—in the usual scandalous fashion, was his mistress, some people even credited or discredited Michael with being the father of her small daughter, Julia. He was sixty-three, so crippled that he had to be wheeled about in a wicker bath chair, for to walk was practically impossible; it seems definitely unlikely that he began a family at that time of his life.

He was no longer affluent, for he had mismanaged his

affairs, and had lived expensively. He admitted as much to
Theodore Hook, who engaged to write his memoirs.

"Good food, good wine and lovely women," he said,
"these surely are what makes life worth living, so long as
you abuse none of them. I have loved two women in my
life, loved them both devotedly—Nancy Storace was one
—when we were both young, making our way together—
the other, as you know was my beloved Anna Crouch."

The Prince, who had just completed his famous
Pavilion, was most gracious to Michael, and several times
invited him to concerts, always treating him with the
utmost courtesy. George, Prince of Wales, had many
failings, to Kelly he always remained a hero. As a young
man Michael had longed to have his clothes made at the
same tailors, he had wished that he might attain the
Prince's *panache* and charm of manner. Now, growing old,
lonely and not too well blessed with the world's goods,
George instructed that Michael Kelly should receive
£100 a year from his privy purse. It was said that George
never paid his debts, but he contrived to be generous on
many occasions.

Michael tired of the loneliness of Brighton came back
to London, to his house in Tavistock Row. It was
sufficiently near the Lane for him to be wheeled there and
contrive to occupy a box.

"It's painful," he told Kemble, "but the thing—this
theatre business gets into your blood, and it's like an itch.
When I know that the time is almost due for the curtain
to rise, damn me, if I don't get fidgety and restless,
feeling that—I ought to be there. Not that anyone cares
now, whether I'm there or not!"

"My dear Kelly," replied Kemble so urbane and
dignified, "to know that you are watching our poor

efforts is always to be conscious of an honour paid to the players."

Sometimes his niece, Frances Maria Kelly, would visit him, she had first acted with him when she was a very small girl, and he was still fond of her. She had made a great place for herself, though Michael felt that she was over-ambitious. Charles Lamb had wished to marry her, but she refused him.

Michael had never cared a great deal for Lamb, he said, "Yes, charming, I don't doubt, but too fanciful and whimsyfied for me. Still he has a great appreciation of the theatre. Just—he's not the kind of fellow I make any headway with."

Frances—Fanny—as she was called, would come and spend an hour or two with him, and Kelly leaning back in his big chair, his foot on a gout stool would talk to her of—the old days.

Kelly delighted to find someone with whom he could talk, his whole face lighting up with pleasure at recalling those days which—no doubt in retrospect acquired an added glamour and brightness; Fanny Kelly with her "adorable plain face", her large eyes shining with interest, her whole expression showing that she was absorbed and entranced with her uncle's recollections.

No doubt she incited him to talk, not that Michael had ever needed much encouragement, and no doubt the witticisms of Sherry and his companions had gathered point and brilliance through constant repetition.

"They must have been wonderful days, Uncle Mickie."

"Indeed and they were, m'dear. I often think that the present time can't hold a candle to the old days. Life was an adventure, there was romance—yes, even in the clothes we wore. Now, people go about looking inconspicuous—they want to be unremarkable. We used to glory in being conscious that passers-by turned to look after us. Imagine me to-day walking down Bond Street— if this cursed gout didn't prevent me from walking anywhere—wearing a suit of pale blue silk embroidered with silver lace, cocked hat, silk stockings, and shoes with scarlet heels. Yes, indeed, I had such a suit—and a damn fine fellow I thought myself in it, b' Gad.

"I've told you of Mozart in his scarlet pelisse, and scarlet hat trimmed with gold lace. God bless the man, he was as vain of his appearance as I was—and that's saying something, Fanny."

"You've met so many wonderful people, haven't you?" Fanny knew exactly when to gently urge him on to talk.

"I've lived history, m' girl. Talked with Casanova, and an unpleasant feller he was too, you felt there was something—well, made you want to cross yourself, to ward off the evil eye when he was talking to you. Yet women liked him! Ah, well, bless them, they take to funny things, don't they? I've sung to, drunk with, and listened to Charles Edward Stuart, the Young Pretender, though he was no more a 'pretender' than I was. He was a horse of a very different colour to Casanova. Ah, I don't doubt that he'd had his fling, he'd lived his life pretty hard, but you felt that though he might be a rake—there was no evil in him. I saw that poor unhappy queen Marie Antoinette return to Paris with her husband, Louis the Sixteenth—poor lady, my heart bled for her."

"Napoleon, did you see Napoleon?"

"The little Corsican, indeed I did. Nothing to look at, a big head, and a manner lacking in courtesy." He chuckled, "And I knew the man who beat him, Fanny,

Horatio Nelson. No two men could have been more completely different. Napoleon—never would I call him 'Emperor'!—full of his own importance, strutting like a paycock, and Nelson, bearing the marks of what he'd suffered doing his duty to his country, the patch over one eye, one sleeve pinned to his coat—empty, quiet and modest. He moved with short, very light steps, and saw more with his one eye than other men see with two. I knew Lady Hamilton also—yes, beautiful, rather like a rose which is just a little overblown, but charming. For strict beauty she couldn't come within a mile of my beloved Mrs. Crouch, nor of Mrs. Billington, if it came to that." He chuckled, "Dear Ann-ah, how she disliked Billington, the only person I ever heard her speak of harshly."

"And Storace, Uncle Mickie?"

"Now, there was a rare girl. I wonder if she was really as pretty as I used to believe, or was it just that she seemed to carry a light inside her? I wish that I'd a picture of her —though no artist could have really caught Nancy's expression—there were too many of them, they flickered across her face as you've seen the cloud shadows pass on a sunny day, when they move over the green fields. Ah," he sighed, " 'We are such stuff as dreams are made on', like dreams we pass and after a while no-one remembers us."

"Uncle, you and Storace and her brother and Mrs. Crouch will always be remembered—you've all been part of the English theatre. How could people forget!"

He wagged his head, "You'd be surprised, Fanny dear, how short memories can be. How right Shakespeare was, 'The evil that men do—' you know the rest. So villains are remembered and decent men and women, faithful

artists, honest folk are forgotten. There, m' dear, my old
tongue has wagged long enough, melancholy is descend-
ing upon me. I'm going down to Margate, they tell me
that the air is good and—" he paused, "Brighton,
perhaps brings back too many painful things to my mind."
He sighed, "Ah, my dear friend, what a sweet creature
she was! So I shall try Margate and get someone to push
this old ruin about in my green wicker chair. Come and
see me there, Fanny, if you can make time. Not many folks
come now—and Gad!—I haven't got it in my heart to
blame them!"

"I will, Uncle Mickie, I will indeed."

Michael went to Margate, and there he died suddenly
on Monday, 9th October, 1826. He was alone, his man-
servant found him dead when he entered to call him in the
morning. He was only sixty-four, but he had lived all
those years with his life crammed with incident. He had
warmed his hands at the fire of life, his heart had never
grown cold, and it was said of him that scarcely one of his
friends and intimates could remember hearing him speak
with ill will against anyone.

His body was taken to London by water, and the
greatest secrecy was observed, though why this should
have been so it is hard to imagine. The correspondent of
The Times wrote that he saw a long wooden packing
case, marked "Glass—keep this side upward" put on to
the steamer. It was not until he noticed on deck Michael's
wicker chair, that he realized that the case contained all
that was left of Michael Kelly.

His body was taken to his house in Tavistock Row,
and thence to Saint Paul's Covent Garden, "The actors'
church".

So ended the career which had begun when a tiny

boy stood on a table and sang to a party of men, all smoking long churchwarden pipes, while his mother fretted and fumed that it was long past his bedtime. The little boy who, watching St. Georgio enter a fruit shop, selecting such fruit as took his fancy and calmly eating peaches and nectarines, made a mental vow, "One day I'll walk into a shop and eat fruit like he does."

He had been lucky, he told Stephen Storace, "My luck's astonishing, never do I find that my pocket is thinly lined, lined so thinly that there might be no lining at all, for all the good it was, but something comes along. I sing for a duchess and am handed a heavy purse, to say nothing of having lived in the palace with her musicians, eating like a fighting cock for three days; or along comes some impresario who has heard of me—and mind you, Stephen, there were precious few people who *had* heard of me in those days—from this one or that one, and hey presto! I've an engagement." He had laid his hand on Stephen's arm and his voice had softened, "The greatest piece of luck I ever had—was when a girl called Nancy Storace mistook me for one of her own sex dressed in boy's clothes, and—we began to talk. That and the moment when my dear friend, Mrs. Crouch consented to share her life with me. I ought to go down to posterity as 'Lucky Mickie Kelly', eh, Stephen?"

Stephen answered, "Lucky, eh? I don't know, perhaps the word—worthy might fit you better, for you deserve every bit of good fortune that has come—or ever will come—your way."

"It's you that should have been the Irishman," Michael returned, "for you're as full of blarney as an egg's full of meat. But, you're a grand feller."

Sometimes, perhaps, in the early dusk, a trim, very

elegant figure walks briskly to Drury Lane, his step is light, he still has applied to him the nickname "Spring Heeled Jack". "Though," as Lady Lade once said to him, "The devil only knows why, for Jack was a far finer man than you'll ever be, Michael Kelly."

The figure enters, and stands inside the entrance of the grand old theatre as if for a moment he needed to get his bearings—he'd seen so many changes at the Lane. Others join him, the tall, stately figure of Sarah Siddons gives them a majestic greeting as she passes. Sheridan says, "Why the devil does Sally wear shoes with square toes and no heels!" Colman is there, and Kemble stays for a moment to discuss some new incidental music which Michael Kelly composed and rehearsed that morning. "Admirable, my dear Kelly, admirable." Sheridan shrugs as the great man moves away, "Kemble speaks as if he were God preparing to create the world, and having created it, be certain that he would 'find that it was good'."

A boy rushes up, "Mr. Kelly, sir, Mr. Kelly, they're waiting for you."

"Ah, now, my boy, don't get yourself flustered. Michael Kelly's always there when he's wanted," and stepping lightly, the little man follows in the wake of the boy's hurrying footsteps.

A moment later the orchestra is heard, playing Kelly's music, Sheridan cocks his head to listen more intently, then murmurs, "Aye, he's good that little Irishman," and slowly the figures fade away.

EPILOGUE

WE sat talking, when Peter rushed in. He was entranced because he had found a copy of the original Michael Kelly memoirs. I pointed out that they were not actually written by Kelly, but by Theodore Hook.

"And," I added, "Kelly was remarkably annoyed because Hook had left out some of his best stories."

"Is his music ever played now?" Peter asked.

"I don't think so. Whether it was worth preserving—I don't know. Kelly himself never had any great opinion of it, he only insisted that it was—honest."

"And Stephen Storace?"

"A different pair of shoes altogether. Stephen was a musician, highly regarded by Mozart himself, and you can't have greater praise. As you know, every line he wrote was destroyed in the fire, or one of the fires at the Lane. They did produce 'The Haunted Tower', it must be twenty or more years ago. I never heard how successful it was."

Peter, thumbing the pages of Michael Kelly's book, said, a trifle peevishly, "Need we have that radio on all the time? I can't think about Mozart and those people and listen to some rubbish like 'Come and kiss me, baby dear'. It's sacrilege. Where is Kelly buried?"

I said, "In the Actors' Church in Covent Garden, but you won't find his grave. It's disappeared, and with it his epitaph. That was the churchyard through which Sheridan escaped after he played his trick upon the lawyer—you remember? Nancy too, I asked Simmy to go

286

to Saint Mary's Church Lambeth to find it—Nancy's tomb. The curate knew nothing of it——"

Peter interpolated, "Or much about Storace I suppose!" Peter is whole-hearted about opera, and there was indignation in his tone.

I said, "The church was completely rebuilt, except for the belfry, over a hundred years ago. Nancy died in 1817 . . . well, there you are."

Muriel had listened, keeping very quiet, now she spoke and her voice was very gentle.

"Some time ago I went up to Saint Nicholas' Church —it's the old parish church of Brighthelmstone, and looked for Mrs. Crouch's grave. No-one had been buried there for over fifty years, they told me. The headstones— except for those dreadful memorials like coffins and boxes and the like, except of course the family vaults, are placed against the walls.

"I searched everywhere, and found in the north west corner, a stone—the inscription almost obliterated by the action of the sea, on which I managed to decipher—it's quite a plain stone—'. . .nna Maria' then a 'C' and then a space and an 'h'. Lower down is the remains of a date '18 . . .' and one word still can be read—it is 'Beloved'."

I glanced at Peter, he is tender-hearted, and I saw that his eyes were filled with tears; he said, "I think Michael Kelly would have liked that—just her name and that one word."

"And Stephen?" Muriel asked, "I always think that he must have been a very dear person."

"Buried in the old church of Saint Marylebone, in the High Street. I've tried to make inquiries, I believe his memorial stone, erected by Nancy and her mother, is still there under the gallery."

Almost indignantly Peter cried, "You see, they are all—forgotten! Those people who were such figures."

I shook my head, "Not quite, for here are three people talking of them, wondering about them—no, Michael knew this was how it would be, and—well——"

" 'After life's fitful fever they sleep well,' " Muriel said, adding "I am sure that Shakespeare will forgive me for adapting his words. Bless them, what nice people they must have been. I must catch my last train! Peter, you'll get me a taxi?"

"I'll come with you," he said, and tucking his two precious volumes under his arm, they went after bidding me good-night.

Gardone Riviera
November, 1954.